HAUNTING BLUE

R. J. SULLIVAN

DEDICATION

To Linda, who never doubted this would happen.

ORIGINAL 2010 ACKNOWLEDGEMENTS

What a long, strange trip it's been! I have many friends, editors, and peer writers to thank: Debra Holland, Ash Roland, Kelly Mortimer, Charles Cafrelli, Mary Kay Woolsey, Cory Emberson and Mom and Dad. Their suggestions and input all helped to make this story stronger. Anything that still doesn't work at this point is strictly my fault.

2014 NOTES AND ACKNOWLEDGMENTS

This book is a re-release of my first novel, originally published in 2010. I did some tweaking throughout and corrected a mistake in the timeline I'd overlooked the first time. Because I liked it, I added a short poem by Nicole Rinaldi and slipped it into chapter one. In the original release, the main story chapters read "Present Day." Because I have since written *Virtual Blue*, a sequel set in 2013, those chapters now read "2010". This not only locks the story in time, but I won't have to adjust the pop culture, computer technology, and music references. So there.

2014 THANKS

John F. Allen, Rodney Carlstrom, E. Chris Garrison, Monica Kelver-Kellogg, Nicole Rinaldi, Michael West, Amanda DeBord, Bonnie Wasson, and Stephen Zimmer.

2020 THANKS

Bryan Donihue for helping me through the republishing nightmare… er… process.

CHAPTER ONE

These are the longest three hours of my life.

I knew this would happen, and, sure enough, here I was, stuck in the car with Mom giving me the evil eye. Mother and daughter trapped together in our Range Rover for 180 intolerable minutes.

In all fairness, it didn't start out that way. While Mom made her client calls on the cell phone, I created a zone of rock music around myself while scribbling out a poem to vent off steam. Just me, the iPod, the earbuds, and the cooler-than-Aragorn lead singer taking me away, freeing my mind and spirit. I folded my knees against my body, crouching so no one driving past could see me.

At seventeen, already a high school junior, I still waited for the growth and boob fairies to visit me the way they had my classmates years ago.

Most of the time, I hated being so small, but today, I could shrink down into the seat and close my eyes, bobbing and rocking to the rhythm of the tunes.

So I jotted this rant poem about not being ignored by Mom while Mom ignored me. Your daily dose of irony.

> *Mombot*
>
> *An empty space on the couch,*
> *A droning in my ear;*
> *You provide for me,*
> *But you're never here.*
>
> *You don't see me.*
> *You don't hear me.*
> *I can't be me.*
>
> *You want your own robot,*
> *A perfect, genial girlbot.*
>
> *No blue hair,*
> *No need to care,*
> *An empty space on the couch.*

Antsy punk teen pens a mother poem. That's me. What can I say? The cliché exists for a reason. I'm the 2010 model, the latest of an endless string.

Not that all of my poetry is like this. No one's going to read this one; it's just to keep me sane during the drive. I have a professional standard, after all. Better to stab the paper than stab other things, right?

Mom punctured my "zone" with what she considered the height of mother-daughter diplomacy. "What *is* that crap you're listening to?"

I braced myself for the argument but tried to answer the question. "It's Linkin Park, Mom."

"Like Abraham Lincoln?"

I fought back the smirk that threatened to cross my face. "No, Linkin like...um...L-i-n-k-i-n." I spelled the name, trying not to roll my eyes. *God, my mom is so out of touch.*

"Well, they're louder than hell, Fiona. I can hear them right through your headphones."

I wanted to reply that I could hear her right through the earbuds, too, but I had promised myself I'd be on good behavior today.

"Where's the Britney disc I got you for your birthday?"

My birthday? You mean my tenth birthday? Melted into a silver puddle in the trunk if I'm lucky. "It's packed away. I just felt like a change of sound, Mommy Dearest." *Oops, better watch it. That came close to pushing her buttons.*

Too late. I could tell I'd already gotten to her.

She took a deep breath, brushing the dark bangs from her eyes before continuing. Mom had let her normal business-friendly short haircut grow long the last few weeks in favor of attending to the more important chores associated with moving the office.

When she got angry, like now, the wrinkles around her mouth became more pronounced, and her dark blue eyes flashed; a predator-like warning I'd learned to recognize over the years.

She spoke through gritted teeth. "I thought you *liked* Britney Spears."

"Well, yeah, when I was a kid." Of course, Linkin Park also went back a few years, but the difference in quality made it unfair to compare.

"When did you get into this loud crap? What happened to those nice singing bands like Boyz II Men and INXS?"

I stifled a chuckle. She didn't mean INXS. But it wasn't worth correcting her. We had enough to fight about.

But Mom didn't want to argue about music. She'd just set me up to blindside me. "This is Joey's influence, isn't it?"

Actually, over half the tunes I'd ripped into my iPod had come from Joey. U2, Tori Amos, The Doors; a whole world of music I'd never experienced until him. "It's not just Joey. This is what everyone listens to in Broad Ripple." True enough. In Broad Ripple, everyone hung out at the coffeehouses, and most were college students. What did she *think* was gonna happen to my impressionable young mind?

Mom's nostrils flared. At times like this, the stress caused from years of balancing single motherhood with her skyrocketing career would shine right through the caked on makeup. I could almost feel sorry for her, but then she would blow it all by saying something obvious and dumb.

No exception today. "Your friends from the Café Expresso were too mature for you."

"Well, stop the presses and rewrite page one!" I rolled my eyes at the familiar complaint. Next would come a comment about my blue hair. I decided to forestall it. "*You* moved us to Broad Ripple, remember? *You* took me to the biggest college hangout in Indy, and I ended up making friends with the college students. And now you finally stop playing super-lawyer long enough to notice? Here's a clue, when I take up bingo and shuffleboard, you can safely assume I'm hanging out with an even older crowd."

I reached into my pocket where normally I kept my trusty cell, intent on escaping into my own conversation or at least say hi to Joey. My fist clasped on the hollow cloth pocket and I couldn't hide the disappointment from my face.

Mom didn't miss any of it. She saw the look, read my hurt, and attacked. "Oh, no, no cell phone calls. Your cell stays with me until I get every penny back from the overcharges last month. Four hundred dollars! Spent to text a boy just down the road! Don't you have any sense of responsibility?"

I folded my arms, feeling my face burn, and tried to shrink down into the seat. "Well, since I just quit my job, you might have to keep that phone for a while."

"I'm sure they have fast food restaurants in Perionne. You'll figure something out."

We sped along I-69, stewing in an uncomfortable silence. I averted my eyes and looked out the window, watching the endless flat farmland whisk by. The moving van followed.

Mom started again, her forced, even tone revealing the hot temper percolating beneath the surface. "Those hours I put in paid off. As the senior partner of *Shaefer and Gerrold*, I helped build the firm, and I've kept us living pretty damn good while I did it."

Now, the whining started. I'd heard it all before, and I could easily tune it out. She rambled on anyway. "The property opportunities are so much greater in Perionne than in Broad Ripple. More land, larger houses, older families. Clients from there have requested me specifically." She nodded once, convinced she'd made her point.

My mother, the lawyer. Sounds like a bad TV sitcom. She handled acquisitions, bankruptcies, and property distribution. She practiced her courtroom delivery all the time, though I'm sure any conversations she'd had with judges took place over email or a minute or two in their office long enough to get a signature.

"Opportunities like this keep a nice roof over your head. They also keep you in the best schools in town." She stopped defending herself and attacked. Sharpness entered her tone. "Even when you can't keep up the grades."

So much for being on my best behavior. She wants the "Mom of the Year" award? I'll pop this little bubble right now. "Mom, what time did I come home last night?"

Her face flared red beneath her makeup, and the car swerved. The silence that followed spoke volumes. She knew as well as I she couldn't answer. Not last night, not any night, six months back.

I reached for my iPod, thinking we'd finished the conversation. But Mom collected her composure and started in again. "I understand they have an amusement park in Perionne."

Apparently, the question about my comings and goings was too hot for her. She continued on like the previous five minutes had never happened. "You'll probably have an easy time finding kids your own age there. I'll admit I didn't know that much about your 'friend' Joey, but I could see enough. Look at how much you've changed, just in the last month."

"That had nothing to do with Joey." Now, it was my turn to flush. Every time she said the word "Joey," heat would creep into my face.

Mom didn't approve of the denim jacket, the earrings, the bracelets, the half-tees, or anything else I chose for myself. She'd hit the roof when she saw the dye job. I didn't explain the blue hair. Everyone in the Café Expresso wore some form of colored hair, streaks, spikes, highlights, especially the poets and writers I hung out with. They were comfortable expressing their individuality, and that's how I wanted to be.

Instead, I'm sitting here, trapped and squirming. That'll teach me.

I ruffled the pages of my paperback, *To Kill a Mockingbird*, wondering if I would have a chance to read any more of it. The novel sure had me pumped up for small town hospitality, yessirree.

We continued north to a road laughably labeled *Highway 20*. We passed a sign informing us that Perionne lay ten miles east of La Grange. Helpful, I suppose, if you knew where or what La Grange is. We took the exit, and the road deteriorated into large chuckholes, sudden dips, and narrow shoulders, which made the car rock maddeningly for those of us trying to read in the passenger seat. The signs insisted you could still travel fifty-five miles an hour. Through the trees, I could see a billboard advertisement of Perionne Park. The aerial photo looked like a traveling carnival with rickety spin-and-barf fair rides.

"This will be good for you," Mom said. "Maybe you'll realize how ridiculous you look, and you'll dye your hair a more respectable color."

I knew she'd get around to the hair. "Thanks for the support, Mother."

"Oh, you think I'm being mean?" The lawyer façade dropped, and she scowled at me. "I should have made you cut it off. Shave it off and go to school bald."

"That's child abuse, Mother."

"Are you telling me about the law, young lady?"

Whoops. Wrong approach. "My friends liked me this way."

"You mean Joey liked it. Were you going to get a nose ring like his, too? That would look really attractive. Jesus, Fiona, I thought you had more brains than that."

I slipped lower into my seat, wishing I could somehow float up through the roof and out of the car.

"You're better off never seeing him again. One thing I've learned in life is that you have to make your own mistakes, so go to school looking however you want."

I shrugged. Soon, Mom would settle into her new office, and I'd be left alone. I just had to endure another few days. But she'd brought up Joey, the one person I'd been trying desperately to forget. Those thoughts only dredged up the hurt, and I didn't want to face the pain right now. It was too fresh. We'd only said goodbye last night.

Sweet, crazy Joey. I'd let him pick the color of my hair. He had loved to run his fingers through the strands. We'd had a rocky relationship, but my heart hurt when I thought about breaking up with him. Every time I'd tried, I would feel a cold hollowness in my chest. Then, I'd put it off another day and the pain left.

Over time, I realized Joey was no good. The drinking, the smoking, the fits of self-abuse. He said nice things to me, he truly had a talent for poetry, and he was great in bed. *Oh, yes.* The first man I'd been devoted to. My head spun from the previous six months of passion. I wanted to be with him forever. It killed me when I found out I couldn't control the monster side of him.

Especially after the incident last month.

Then, Mom laid the news about the move on me, and the point

was moot. In her own way, Mom had done me a favor. Not that she needed to know. Any of it.

The pain returned. And this time, nothing I did would make it go away.

I grabbed at my abandoned earbuds. My silver bracelets rattled. Between my earrings, the chains, and the buttons strewn across my denim jacket, I served as a walking advertisement for Claire's. I liked the look. Still did. But if I really wanted to, I could've ditched the buttons. Heck, I could've dyed my hair brown and been done with the whole thing. Let Mom think she'd won.

No way.

I'd keep the hair. And if I was going to glow in the dark, I might as well jingle. Better to be damned for who I am. Either that, or shave my head and go dyke.

I looked out across the expanse of highway and over the tops of the trees to a cluster of rust-colored track supported by a wooden framework. The roller coaster of Perionne Park appeared as a series of arcs dropping off and disappearing through a gathering of high-rising branches.

Having nothing better to do, I stared at the towering structure, then had an uneasy feeling the coaster stared back; the arched structure bearing a closer resemblance to a lumpy sea creature than wood and steel. We approached, the highway leading us past the park, and a cold, chilling jolt of fear coursed down my spine.

Panic overcame me, along with an urge to throw open the door, jump for it, and run like hell. My body tensed from the anxiety. Something wasn't right about that place. What, I couldn't tell.

Even though I didn't want to do anything that might get her attention, I risked a quick glance at my mother. She projected her usual stylish confidence, showing no symptoms of the uneasiness overwhelming me.

Uneasiness? More like sheer terror. I swiped a hand across my forehead and stared, dumbfounded, at the cold wetness reflected on it. I craned my neck in the direction we'd come. I could still see the coaster, slipping away over the horizon. I took a deep breath.

With a clear head, the ride looked neither impressive nor scary. Instead, I saw a dilapidated old relic; outdated, rickety, and pathetic. A few hundred yards from the coaster, the top half of a Ferris wheel rotated above the trees, seats sun-bleached in pasty yellow and pink. That was the only other object visible from the highway, completing the depressing picture. Cheap, small fun for cheap, small minds.

Abandon hope all ye who enter here.

Perionne, Indiana, a sign read, *Population: 6500. Soon, 6502.* Up ahead, I saw a small cluster of suburbia surrounding a town hall and school building. *Must be a ninety-minute drive to anything remotely resembling decent shopping.* Even Walmart had passed through without stopping. I swallowed back cold fear, telling myself it could all turn out okay if I stayed on my best behavior.

For all the good it'd done me so far.

CHAPTER TWO

My first day at Perionne High School was a disaster.

The beginning of the end started in American Folklore, taught by a Mr. Haplin. Well, my schedule listed him as "Haplin," but everyone called him "Hap." Fine with me, I'm sure he imagined it endeared him to us and made him cool. He couldn't have been further from the truth.

I wanted to grab a seat in the last row, but a fat guy with dark hair and greasy corkscrew curls already occupied the back. Like Jabba the Hut surrounded by three toadies, he lorded over his domain. The guy wore a sweat-spotted redneck T-shirt and a black denim jacket. He could barely squeeze his oppressive bulk into the chair attached to the desk. His beady dark eyes bugged out of his piggy-face when he saw me. He scratched five-day stubble on his reddened cheek, daring me to invade their space.

Hap entered the classroom, shutting the door behind him. Tall and lean, he towered over us. A huge bald spot circled his head as if he'd been freshly scalped. Perching on the edge of his desk, he looked and acted young, for a teacher, I mean, perhaps in his early thirties, and he spoke with a quiet hesitation, as though still new to the whole public-speaking thing.

"Hi, kids," he announced, sounding like Mr. Rogers. "Today, we're going to continue our discussion on Perionne legends." He glanced at a single sheet of paper before placing it behind him on his desk. "But first, I want to introduce a new student joining us from Indianapolis. You've probably already noticed this colorful girl sitting toward the front. I'm sure you'll want to introduce yourself." He grabbed a loose sheet of paper and searched for my name.

I started talking before he could announce me. My nickname bore little resemblance to my real name, so there wasn't much point in saying it. "My name's...my last name's Shaefer, but my friends back home called me Fi-Fi." I folded my arms and stared at the other students. I could see a couple of guys open their mouths to say something, but I glared at them, and they drifted into silence. I created my own aura of intimidation and shook everyone up, almost.

The large guy sitting in the back row cackled. "Now I know why she looks like a dog."

The entire room laughed, pretty much ruining my forceful first impression.

"Clinty!" the teacher snapped. "Are you looking for another suspension? You know I'll do it."

Clinty shut up, and the rest of the class clamped down on their own laughter.

Mr. Haplin turned to me. "Sorry. Tell us about your look. It's quite different. Is blue hair the thing in Indianapolis?"

"Not quite. Maybe downtown. You see more of this look in Broad Ripple. It's by Butler University, so it's an older Indy suburb, but also a college town. A lot of people dress like this, though nowadays, you see more vampire children than anything else."

Mr. Haplin nodded and smiled, but kept any conclusions to himself.

"Well, class, take the time to welcome...Fi... Ms. Shaefer...on your own time. I'm sure you'll have a lot to learn from each other."

Hap grabbed a large spiral-bound booklet from his desk and held it out to me. "This is our material for local legends. We're reaching the end of it and then going on to worldwide folklore, but I suggest you study it on your own, as the material will be on the first test at the end of September. So you only have a week. I've also attached a schedule. After that, we'll begin on the textbook."

I took the offered papers.

He turned, approached his desk, and sat on the edge of it.

"Now...Fi-Fi...this provides the rest of us with a unique opportunity. Turn to page twenty and tell me what you know about Gunther Stalt."

I flipped through the handout as I replied, "Gunther who?"

"Oh, come on," a student whispered.

I opened the handout to a newspaper clipping. A head-and-shoulders photograph of a middle-aged man stared back at me, his gaze glaring off the page. His hair, which hung down to his broad shoulders, appeared to be graying, though it was hard to tell from the Xerox. The headline to the article read, *PERIONNE LOCAL ROBS BANK*. A second clipping screamed the headline, *STALT STILL AT LARGE*.

"You just handed it to me. How am I supposed to answer the question?"

"Puh-lease." This time, I could tell the comment came from Clinty.

"I see," Mr. Haplin said. "So, living in Indianapolis, you've never heard of Gunther Stalt?"

"No. Not a word. But I guess he robbed a bank."

Disbelieving laughter filled the room.

Hap turned toward the group. "Class! Now, Fi-Fi, what would you say if I told you Gunther Stalt is as famous here in Perionne as, oh, say, Kelly Clarkson or Steve Jobs are around the world?"

"I guess I'd have to take your word for it."

On the next page, another headline caught my eye. Dated November of 1992, it read, ***GHOST OF GUNTHER STALKS FORMER GIRLFRIEND***. A sketch of a scarecrow-like apparition accompanied the article. The apparition extended its left arm, with a hook for a hand, foreshortened and out-of-proportion, as if the character was reaching off the page toward the reader. I couldn't help but smile at the melodrama.

"This proves an important point." Hap strode to the dry-wipe board and started scribbling with a bright green marker. "A lot of folklore is regional." He underlined the word. "In fact, most folklore is known only in a specific area. The Robin Hoods and Johnny Appleseeds are few and far between." He turned toward the class and smiled at me.

I couldn't help squirming. *Oh, shit, I'm starting to become the teacher's pet. This isn't happening.*

"Now. Who can tell Fi-Fi about Gunther?" He looked at the front row. "Steve?"

A clean-cut, average guy in a gray Nike polo shirt answered. He looked at his desk as he spoke. I had a better view of his swoosh on the left pocket than I did of his face. "Gunther robbed the Perionne National Bank in 1990. He disappeared that night, taking the money with him, and has never been seen again," he lowered his voice, "Unless you count the ghost."

The class tittered.

Hap chose to ignore the comment. "Right. Now, does anyone know why this was such a big deal?"

I certainly didn't. Judging from the silence that followed, no one else did, either.

"Ah," the teacher declared, his tone chastising the class as a whole. "You all thought you could fake your way through the discussion without reading the material, didn't you? Thought you knew everything about Gunther? Chuck, why is he such a big deal?"

Chuck shrugged, but offered up, "I guess because people started seeing his ghost afterwards."

"Well, that's true. The Ghost of Gunther."

A quiet murmur buzzed around the room.

Hap waited for the class to settle down. "In general, folklore has a habit of tying back to the supernatural or fantastic, and Perionne folklore is no exception. The facts behind the folklore relate to someone who died under mysterious circumstances. In this case, Gunther Stalt." He waved a hand in the air to dismiss the topic. "We'll get to that in a minute. Why did people start seeing Gunther, though? What created the excitement?"

Nobody answered.

"Think, kids. How many bank robberies have occurred in Perionne?"

Not too damn many, I would guess, but nobody raised their hand.

A hint of frustration leaked into Hap's easygoing façade. "You kids remember Hank Simone last year? They picked him up the next day in Michigan. And remember Fred Lionel? What happened to him?"

One student called out, "His girlfriend found the money crammed in his mattress."

A few people chuckled.

"Correct. What happened to Gunther?"

Steve raised his hand. "Nothing. He never got caught."

"That's right, Steve. An unprecedented situation. It had never happened before, and, in fact, hasn't happened since. Now, here's what you would have found out, had you read your articles."

I had scanned the article while Hap talked and found the answer a few seconds before he asked, but thought it might compound my popularity problem to volunteer a correct answer.

"Gunther's bank heist is the only unsolved robbery in Perionne." Hap paused a moment to let the fact sink in. "Think about where you live. We're a fairly closed community. Everybody knows everybody. What do we know about each other? Clinty smokes marijuana in his dad's tool shed. It's not something I normally bring up in class, but Michelle McKinley and George Lewis were discovered messing around behind the large pine tree near Baptism Lake last month." Haps raised his hands, wiggling his fingers into a pair of quote marks while saying "messing around."

I cringed, wondering if Michelle and George attended the school and would have appreciated being used as scandalous examples. *American Folklore Lesson Number One: Better be careful, or I could wind up as an example in next year's class.*

"Gunther robbed the bank wearing a white mask. There was no clearly identifiable picture taken of him by the security camera, but all the eyewitnesses positively identified him. Why? Because they knew him. They recognized his jacket. They knew he had his hand in his pocket to hide the prosthetic arm and hook. They knew his walk. They knew his voice."

Silence settled into the room. At last, Hap had everyone's attention.

As if he sensed enlightenment dawning upon his class, Hap's voice grew more animated.

"In theory, it's nearly impossible for a local citizen to commit a felony in Perionne. Quite simply, you're going to get found out. From a parent's perspective, it's one of the great attractions of living in a small town. I'm not saying that to scare you, it's just a fact. And yet...the article tells us Gunther escaped authorities. It was many hours before the police found the body of Jeff Crimley, Gunther's accomplice, dead in the hospital parking lot."

Hap scrawled a second phrase on the board, *unresolved mystery*.

"Okay, class. What mystery are we talking about?"

Hands shot up around the room. I listened while scanning an article about a middle-aged lady who'd seen Gunther's Ghost staring at her on numerous occasions. The article featured an accompanying photo of Gunther Stalt and a young woman, petite with dark hair and a wide smile. The year under the photo read, *1983*; the article's dateline read, *1995*. The article identified the woman as Mary Steeber, Gunther's high school sweetheart, and further claimed Gunther's Ghost stalked her almost every night. Apparently, the ghost got its kicks torturing the exes.

The smiling image of Gunther held me for several seconds before I turned the page. Even in the old photograph, his aggressive, mesmerizing personality shone through.

"They never found the money," one student said. "My dad says Gunther still has the money, and it's cursed."

"There was no body," a second, feminine voice called out. "Gunther is still alive and pretending to haunt people. He's living in another town and coming through Perionne every now and again to scare people. That's what *I* think."

Hap paused. "Ah...right. You're all correct, in one way or another. There's no money, no body, and not one policeman found any clues, except the getaway car. Gunther eluded authorities until the trail ran cold, which brings us to our next topic. What happened? Jen has touched upon one of the more colorful ideas going around. Although I admit, it's more plausible than the ghost sightings we're always hearing about."

"Hey," Clinty called out. "My pa told me he saw Gunther. My pa was driving north on Summit Street, and he looked out the window and saw this guy hitchhiking; only the guy was holding out a hook. Pa got so freaked, he skidded his car onto the shoulder of the road and went right through the body."

"Yes, Clinty. Fantastic stories like your father's keep everyone talking about—"

"Are you calling my pa a liar?" Clinty's beefy fist pounded the tabletop.

I cringed, fully expecting foam to spew from Clinty's mouth. A laugh, sharp and purely involuntary, escaped my lips. The rest of the class had kept their responses to a quiet murmur, so my outburst proved loud and cutting, unfortunate for me.

Clinty turned in my direction. His look said it all, *You're dead meat. Great. Just what I need. Clinty as an enemy.*

Hap, oblivious to the drama playing out in the form of exchanged glares, pressed his argument. "I'm not calling your father a liar, Clinty. But the situation has created the proper conditions for people to think they're seeing a ghost because that's what they want to see. Like the Loch Ness monster that is really a floating log."

"Pa didn't drive through a floating log, Hap," Clinty said. "You can't drive through anything but ghosts. Gunther is dead, all right, but he has a score to settle. We just don't know what it is yet. That's what my pa told me." A hint of intelligence lit the blustering bully's eyes. But only for a moment, and then it flickered out.

No one spoke. Nobody else wanted to contradict the volatile redneck. They didn't care to be next on Clinty's shit list, right beneath me.

"Well," Hap said, "this has certainly stimulated passionate conversation. Let me ask you kids, how many of you believe in the Ghost of Gunther?"

Clinty's hand shot up, along with the rest of the back two rows. Certainly not an accurate poll, but five others, over half of the rest of the class, raised their hands as well.

I listened without comment, even as the opening notes to *The Twilight Zone* theme played in my head.

I OPENED my locker and stashed the Xeroxed handout on the shelf. When I reached for my English book, two pairs of hands grabbed me from behind and pinned my wrists against either side of the locker frame.

The old locker ambush. Clinty couldn't wait until lunch or after school. He wanted to get into it right here. Stupid me had expected something clever, or at least subtle, from him. I wouldn't make that mistake again.

Between the two of them, Clinty's eager helpers subdued me with ease, whipping me around to confront him face-to-face. I didn't fight. The pair of large brutes could easily manhandle my tiny frame, even if I *did* struggle.

Panicking wouldn't help me, so why bother? Besides, the anger flaring in Clinty's eyes at my decided *lack* of cowering made it all worthwhile.

The two thugs made quite a show of jerking me from my locker while keeping my arms pinned to my sides, pulling me into the middle of the hall for everyone to see. I cursed my own stupidity and Clinty's lack of forethought at this attack. But I knew my moment would come. I just had to wait him out.

They didn't realize where I'd come from, or what I could do. On my old turf, I had to fend off the drunks and the drug addicts looking for an easy mug-and-grab, looking to steal something they could trade for another fix. Then, there were the college linebackers. After a couple drinks, they all thought they were God's gift. All I needed was a little persuading.

These pricks would be simple in comparison.

The two laughing buffoons, mistaking my submission for defeat, had already loosened their grips on my arms. The thug on my right even released one hand to scratch his head. I restrained a reaction, even when Clinty circled behind me. I could feel his eyes checking me out. I wasn't at all surprised when a large hand prodded against my shirt and groped one of my boobs.

Still, I yelped, and my face flushed.

Clinty sauntered in front of me. "Laugh at me, will ya? Think you're so smart, do ya?"

A crowd gathered to see if they could get their sensibilities assaulted.

The two henchmen pinned my arms around my back then shoved me toward a grinning, drooling Clinty.

"Three against one. Pretty brave, assholes."

Clinty reached out and gripped a handful of hair, pulling 'til my eyes watered. "Wha's this? It's a blue-haired bitch in heat!" He snorted a whistling laugh. "Hey," he said, thrusting his chubby face so close to mine I could smell rancid chewing tobacco on his breath. "Is this all the blue hair you got? I'm curious."

One thing I'd learned in Broad Ripple; when a stranger underestimates you, play the game. But make it count, because surprise only works once.

I made it count.

I kicked out. The toe of my combat boot connected with his shin. It cut through his jeans, and he yelped in pain. His grip slackened on my hair.

Throwing out my elbows, I dropped toward the floor and slid through the hold his cronies had on me.

I thrust my hand into my jacket pocket, where I kept a studded leather strap for situations like this. The looped leather eased over my knuckles. I pulled my fist out of my pocket, drew back, and smacked Clinty in the face with everything I had.

All three hundred pounds of redneck staggered, his head whipping sideways from the impact.

My other assailants turned and bolted.

Clinty shifted his head back into place. A look of stunned stupidity slipped across his features. Blood poured from his nose. It seemed to dawn on him that his friends had disappeared. His panicked gaze darted around the growing crowd, realizing that whatever the outcome, this fight had become public.

People started yelling. Whether they cheered against him or for me made no difference to me.

He screamed and charged, but I had already moved away from the lockers, punching at his chest while I backpedaled down the hall. I waited a few beats, sidestepped his attack, and set my legs. I drew both arms back, hands wrapped around the studded leather. I waited until he charged me, then slammed my fists into his ribcage.

The blow made a popping sound that brought a hush to the crowd.

Clinty teetered and veered toward the wall, losing control of his knees. He went down with a crashing thud right into the row of closed lockers, more closely resembling a falling oak tree than a human being.

Something snapped inside me, and I lost control. "Small town shit! I'll kill you!"

The crowd burst into an enormous cheer, not that I paid much attention.

All the frustrations from the last few days gathered in my dinky, lightweight body, and then erupted. I pounded Clinty's face, chest, and stomach. I kicked and punched and clawed and screamed until two teachers and a group of students managed to pull me away.

The vice principal wasn't amused. Neither was Mom. She pulled up right behind the ambulance.

Both Clinty and I got suspended. The vice principal told me to go home. Clinty would be taken to the hospital. The school nurse said Clinty had a broken nose, needed stitches, and probably had several cracked or broken ribs. I seriously doubted the part about the ribs, but that didn't keep the school nurse from saying it loudly and often to any teacher or faculty member within hearing range.

I walked the gauntlet to Mom's SUV, overhearing the awed whispers of my classmates.

I stood near a small group in various branded shorts, T-shirts, and running shoes. Apparently, gym class had stopped so that everyone could gather to watch the paramedics wheel a moaning Clinty toward his ride.

His gaze found me, and his body jerked like a wild animal. "I'll get you for this, you bitch!"

I grinned back at him and waved, knowing I'd infuriate him even more. Lying on the gurney, beaten and bruised, his threats fell flat.

The crowd turned as one, taking a step back to give me room or make sure they weren't next. I thought I saw stares of respect, or fear.

~

MOM DID NOT TAKE the news of my suspension well. She hadn't said a word the entire trip home.

With a distant feeling of dread, I sat in the living room, sinking into the darkened leather couch. No sense trying to avoid the inevitable. Part of my mind admired how the matching leather chair and glass tables fit so much better in this new house than the old one. After years of wondering about my mother's taste for big, expensive furniture, I realized she'd finally found the big, expensive house to match.

Today, before she left for the new office, Mom had absorbed herself into her Cool Professional character — that's *Miz* Leona Shaefer to you. I knew she planned overseeing the reloading of the Shaefer and Gerrold client database at the new offices. Now she'd had to leave her "important" work early and come to the school, then home to reason with the problem child.

Mom's face was red from the heat of anger. She didn't bother to ask me if I'd been hurt. She went straight for the lecture. "What the hell is this, Fiona? You think I don't have enough troubles? Do you know what it's like to completely remodel an office? Do you have any concept of what I've been going through today?"

The irony triggered my own anger, and the sarcastic reply spit from my mouth before I could contain it. "No, Mom. Do you have any idea what it's like to have a group of boys try to gang-bang you in the hallway? During school hours, I mean."

Her hand jerked to hit me, but she held back. The anger my jibe caused disappeared in a flash, and her face transformed from red-hot anger to a barely contained patience. "Fiona, I know this transition is rough, but try to give it a few weeks. You have to learn to like it." She sighed in resignation. "But you might try wearing a hat for a while until your natural hair color grows back in. Or how about we go ahead and dye it to something less outrageous? I'll spring for the bottle."

"Jesus, Mom! I get jumped in the halls, so it must be my fault. That's your idea of supportive? I happen to be in the right here, just in case you were wondering."

"Fiona, they confiscated a weapon from you."

"And a good thing I had it, too, or else we'd be having this conversation in the hospital."

"Then you'd better adapt to the situation! You don't have a choice. Besides, what were you thinking, getting into a fight? This is all because of that Joey..."

Great. Only two days after the move, and she was already repeating herself. I sighed and waited out the tirade. I knew, from past experience, she had nothing more important to say.

CHAPTER THREE

"WAKE ME UP INSIDE! WAKE ME UP INSIDE!" I snapped my eyes open to the siren vocals of Evanescence's Amy Lee exploding from my iPod alarm clock at a volume set to rattle teeth. "SAVE ME FROM THE NOTHING I'VE BECOME!" I slapped the off button, muttering a quiet "Amen."

I sat up, momentarily shocked I hadn't awakened from the bright sunlight showing through the sheets I'd hung over the windows. Mom said we'd have to shop for "window treatments" as soon as she had time. I knew, unless I'd made a prior appointment, I was out of luck for several months.

The alarm could mean only one thing. School. My uneventful suspension was over. Uneventful? Okay, maybe boring would be the better word describing my last few days. I even broke down and read a science fiction novel, even though sci-fi didn't interest me much. That was more Joey's thing. And *Stranger in a Strange Land* had a rep as something special. According to Wikipedia, it had cultivated some sort of cult following back in the sixties, similar to the very awesome *The Lord of the Rings*. A guy raised on Mars is taken to Earth and is perplexed by what passes for "normal" here. I could *grok* it.

I listened for sounds of Mom. *Total silence. She must have an early meeting.*

I slogged through the morning bathroom ritual, dressed for the day, and then grabbed my backpack off my rumpled *Lord of the Rings* quilt. I almost made it to the door when I thought better of it. I returned to my room, making a beeline for the wooden closet door.

The Box, an old cigar box held closed by rubber bands, lay at the bottom of the closet toward the back, already buried by fallen clothes. I rifled through the contents until I found my switchblade. I reverently picked it up, gripping the cool, heavy handle; the blade still shone from the recent polish I'd given it right before I'd stashed it for moving day. *If Clinty wants a rematch, I'll be ready.*

I stepped out the front door, overcome with a sudden uneasiness.

The previous owners had kept our lawn lush and trimmed. They'd also added a stepping stone path that cut through the grass to the driveway. I stepped off the porch and onto the path, sensing someone watching me.

I looked at the house next door. An old woman, no, an *ancient* woman perched in a rocker on her covered porch. She stared at me. Her gaze took me in. I slowed my steps to a meek walk, and then I stopped. My feet didn't want to move, so I stood where I was.

A faded, off-white cloth-like *something* lay over her knees like a pile of cobwebs, a pair of knitting needles entangled within. Her lips pulled upward into a crinkled smile.

I turned away and walked toward the sidewalk.

"Young woman," the crackling voice called.

Damn. Just a few seconds from a clean getaway. This I *did not* need.

I replied with my most respectful voice. "Yes, ma'am?"

"You're the new neighbor," she proclaimed with deliberate slowness, as if we didn't exist until she'd spoken it. "It's good to have young people around. There aren't enough in this town. Just a bunch of us old ghosts haunting the streets." Her eyes glazed over. She seemed to drift away for a moment.

Who was I to pick a fight with a senile bag? "Yes, ma'am."

The woman squinted at me, staring. An uncomfortable chill ran through my body at the close scrutiny.

"My eyes ain't what they used to be, girlie. Come closer. I swear, your hair looks blue! Come, girlie." She motioned with one gnarled hand. "Closer. I won't bite you."

I stepped across the yard and waited for her to realize my hair color was not a trick of the light.

"My name's Sylvia, and I'm pleased to make your acquaintance." Her eyes widened. "My goodness, girlie, I thought *my* hair looked bad after my last trip to the beauty parlor. I hope they gave you a refund." She attempted a laugh that came out a shrill cackle.

"Actually, I did it myself. On purpose."

Even *I* couldn't help but smile. She broke into a cough and had to catch her breath.

She leaned forward in her chair. "So, you're Fiona Felicity, the Shaefer daughter. Fine mother you got there. Bringing a lot to our community."

I shuffled in the tall grass, crackling the brown leaves, wondering if I should take credit for something I had no control over. I decided to keep it neutral. I focused on the oak tree in her yard, something we didn't have.

This was one of those "mixed" neighborhoods. The older home-owners had cute little houses with wraparound porches. Then, there were the newbies, like us. The previous owners had taken the small lot and built a house covering nearly every inch of land. We still had a front yard, but no back. I wondered how long it would be before all the houses were like ours, large and grand, but missing the charm and warmth of the smaller places. Still, I had to admit, Sylvia hadn't been diligent with the upkeep. Her place could use a coat of paint and a gardener with a troop of helpers.

"Yes, ma'am. Please, call me Fi-Fi, though, ma'am."

"Fi-Fi. I already heard stories about you." She cackled and sputtered like a dying car engine. "Great, wonderful stories."

"Stories?"

"Inquisitive. Destined for trouble. But a great spirit. I'll be watching you. Each spirit offers its own unique shape to the community. Yours could shape the rest of us, if you put in the effort."

I rolled my eyes. "That...trouble...was just a misunderstanding. Someone at school was looking for a fight, so I gave him one. But I don't plan to stay in this town long enough for anyone to have to worry about me being a problem. Soon as I graduate, I'm gone."

The old woman sighed. "Perhaps. But if you're always looking over the next hill, you can never enjoy the valley."

"I didn't ask to be here. And yeah," I shrugged. What did it matter what I admitted? "I don't like it here."

"Well, perhaps we can change your mind if you give us a chance. Then again, perhaps not."

She continued to stare at me, and my legs weakened.

I took a step. "I need to get to school." I struggled for an appropriate exit line. "Nice to meet you, Sylvia."

"Wait just a minute, girlie."

I stopped. *What more does she want from me? Last thing I need is to be late my first day back.*

"You got sumthin' in that pack of yours you need to be leavin' at home." She pursed her lips and raised an eyebrow.

My thoughts went straight to the knife safely nestled among my books and papers. "I don't know what you mean."

"Nothin' but trouble in there, trouble you don't be needin', girlie."

The look of confusion I gave was real. I remained silent. *There is no way she could possibly know...*

"The knife, girlie. Get caught with that, and you'll never be goin' back to that-there school, and young ladies need to learn."

My mouth opened and my jaw dropped about five inches. "How did you—"

"Doesn't matter. You turn right around and put that thing away."

I wanted to leave, but my feet felt like they were encased in cement.

"Go on, git!"

My feet decided to oblige. I turned and took two steps but then chanced a glance over my shoulder.

The old woman was gone. The rocker moved at a steady pace, even though there wasn't a lick of wind. *How did she possibly get up and go into the house in the span of two seconds? I don't want to know.*

I turned and stumbled toward the door of my house, grateful to shut out the old woman and the old rocker. She gave me the creeps.

I returned the switchblade to The Box. She was right about one thing, that sort of mischief had caused me enough problems. I hoped I could stay out of trouble long enough to graduate.

I MADE it to school on time and decided to ignore my classmates, absorbing myself in my classes. Back in Ripple, in spite of what my teachers liked to call my "personality conflicts," I'd made it a point to maintain an "A" average. That is, until last year when Joey made my head spin and my brain work backwards, as well as my grades. If nothing else, I came into town with a clean slate and no distractions.

I'd made it through third period without an incident. Clinty had yet to return to school, and I took some satisfaction in the thought that his injuries had left him in so much pain (but only *bruised* ribs, thank you very much) he might be out another few days. More likely, he'd skipped class to light up with his cronies, but hey, I can dream, can't I?

My new English teacher, Mr. Robbins, a humorless man with thinning dark hair, stood before the class like the executioner waiting for the condemned. To me, however, his assignment offered a ray of hope and an easy "A."

He wanted us to write a free-verse poem on any subject. Most of the students groaned, asking the usual delaying questions, "How many pages?" "What's the minimum number of lines?" "How many words per line?" Et cetera, et cetera, et cetera, as the king of Siam might say. Meanwhile, I penned a rough draft into my notebook before the hour ended.

I scribbled, biting my lip, unable to contain my excitement. A creative assignment, right up my alley, just what I needed to boost my average while I tried to catch up on all the days I'd missed.

I read through the lines of my draft:

> ### *American Idol Finalist*
>
> *The camera eye*
> *the single I*
> *Ole One-Eye*
> *Pans*
> *down her shirt*
> *and up her skirt*
>
> *She'll be singing*
> *something*
> *about teen suicide*
> *I think*

I left class in a terrific mood, letting the current of the crowd carry me to the cafeteria. Most people ignored me, and I ignored them. Fine with me. It would change or it wouldn't. Today, I floated on a cloud of optimism. Even the pizza-shaped grease couldn't wreck my spirits. I methodically chewed my food, holding pizza-stuff in one hand and my copy of *The Bell Jar* close to my nose.

A thumping noise shook the table. I glanced over the book. A small, wiry guy had taken the seat across from me. Most guys I knew were putting on weight, but he hadn't started yet. His short brown hair was rumpled in spite of his severe military cut.

I stared at the source of the impressive thud that had ruined my concentration. A stack of paper filled with some sort of programming code lay between us. I saw enough programming nerds in the halls to know programming code on sight. What that code *meant*, however, was another story.

I couldn't concentrate on the book. The amazing thing was he'd buried his face between two pages, and he hadn't looked up yet. He must have found the table by some sort of sixth sense, which now helped him find the food on his tray while he flipped through the pages.

The nerve of this geek; sitting at my table, taking me out of my novel, and ruining my concentration. And not even bothering to notice me.

I studied his face. He'd been trying to create a goatee, but so far had succeeded in growing dirt-colored peach fuzz under his chin. He wore a jacket of slick brown leather that looked too nice and fit too well, and thus blew his façade.

It was the sort of lame-ass camouflage a computer geek would use to keep punks like me off him, ironically guaranteeing we'd whale on his ass the moment we had a chance.

Still, that was then. I no longer condoned the hassling business. Besides, I thought I noticed Aragorn-blue eyes. If I could get his attention, I could confirm it.

Numbered lines filled the pages he held. Computer-garble. Several years ago, my second-grade teacher taught us some commands in BASIC to help us understand how a computer "thought." I could probably make "Fi-Fi Shaefer is a Beauty Queen" scroll up the screen forever until you stopped the program, but nothing more. If you could find a computer that accepted BASIC. I used spreadsheet and word processing software, and, like everyone else, lived part-time on the Web, though I hadn't found the time to check my Facebook page since we'd moved. But I knew nothing about programming, on account of my allergy to math.

I had to clear my throat about three times before he glanced my way, a startled expression cracking his zombie-bland face.

"Oh, hello." His voice was normal enough, not hesitant or quiet; a little apologetic, perhaps.

And I was right about the piercing blues. Lucky me.

I indicated the stack of papers with the grease-covered dough in my hand. "School project?"

"Oh, no. Just a program I wrote. It's sort of a number randomizer, for a role-playing game. You know, *Dungeons & Dragons?*"

"Oh, yeah," I nodded. D&D, in spite of its reputation for being a geek-fest, permeated several cliques in the college crowds to different extents; though, of course, the Goths in Ripple preferred a live action vampire version. "I know some people who played, back in Ripple. I figured there'd be some sort of law against D&D around here."

He laughed. "Well, there was, but my friends and I erased it from the town's computer files a few months ago." An embarrassing, seal-like laugh erupted from his throat. He cut it off a few seconds later when he realized I hadn't joined him. He moved right into his next thought without skipping a beat. "That hasn't kept a group of us from getting together."

He extended a thin-fingered hand. "I'm Chip. Chip Farren. And you're Fi-Fi Shaefer, the girl who beat the shit out of Clinty Buckner."

I couldn't help it. I giggled and grinned. "My reputation precedes me."

"I know a lot of guys who are glad you did that, including me. He's been tripping me all semester. Real pain in the ass, but I couldn't...." He seemed to internally switch gears and then restarted. "Well, hey, I guess you want to be left alone. I'll just sit somewhere else."

"No. Wait, Chip Farren. You're the first person who's approached me since I've come to this town, even if you didn't see me for the first five minutes."

Chip grinned. "How do you know? Maybe that's just what I *wanted* you to think."

I laughed. "Nice recovery." That's when I noticed the *Starship Troopers* paperback sticking out of his backpack.

I pointed. "I just read a Robert Heinlein."

Chip's eyes followed the direction of my finger. "Yeah? Which one?"

"*Stranger in a Strange Land.*"

Chip grinned, and his eyes lit up. I imagine I looked the same way. "That is a great one, if you can get past the two-by-four messianic symbolism at the end."

I nodded. "I wish they'd make *Stranger* into a movie instead of the one you're reading. *Starship Troopers* the movie was a steaming pile. But my..." I stopped myself short of saying "my boyfriend". "A *friend of mine* owned the DVD. Watched it all the time. I think he just loved the co-ed shower scene."

Chip rolled his eyes and plucked the paperback out of his pack. "Here. If you already thought the movie was bad, you'll really hate it after reading the book."

I gripped the paperback, marveling at the crinkled, ruffled pages, noting the bookmark partway in. "Don't you want to finish it? This looks pretty old."

Chip waved a dismissive hand. "I'm on my third time through it. It's my dad's. We won't miss it for a few days."

I held the book between my fingers for a few moments. Accepting his offer meant committing to something. At the very least, we'd have to talk again.

I decided that would be a good thing, and placed the book in my own pack. "Thanks, Chip." I returned his grin, happy I had made my first friend.

CHAPTER FOUR

"I got laid off today." In the living room of the clean but small house he shared with his mother and pregnant girlfriend, Gunther Stalt broke the bad news.

"What?" Lily Mills didn't give him a chance to say more. Her long dark hair bobbed in emphasis to her screaming tirade. "How in the hell could you lose your job? All you were doing was pushing a broom through an amusement park!"

Gunther dropped onto the worn leather couch, once an attractive tan, years later faded to the color of old paper grocery bags, and hung his head. He let a deep sigh escape. *Just what I need, Lily all pissed off and making me feel more like a failure.*

"What the hell good are you?" Dropping her arms to her sides, Lily paced and yelled. "We're living in your mother's house. We have a baby coming. You promised we'd get our own place. All you had to do was keep your job."

"It wasn't like that." Gunther hated the whine he heard in his own voice, hated being in this position. "I'd already told you once the season was over..."

Lily cut in. "And you're drunk, too! Don't try to deny it."

So he'd had a few beers. His supervisor had lowered the boom right before lunch. He knew better than to come straight home, so he'd spent the rest of the day at the Cat's Cradle, tossing down a few and steeling up his courage.

The boss's poor timing infuriated him. He and Crimley had just locked their plan in place. A couple more days would've made all the difference. Now, he had to take shit from Lily, and he couldn't say anything about the plan. All Lily could see was his failure, and that angered him most of all.

His prosthetic arm hung limp against the side of the couch. By old habit, he turned the hook so the dull curve could beat a rhythm against the leather without puncturing it. "Mama said we could stay. It ain't so bad here. At least she keeps the place clean."

Arms akimbo, Lily looked ready to spit fire at him. Lit from behind, her shadow cast into the room. The darkness caused by her overlarge belly threatened to devour him.

Gunther avoided her gaze. "I'll take care of it. I know this is screwed up. I know. Look, the park is closing for the season. They had to make some cuts."

"The park's not closed yet," Lily huffed. "And of course, you're the first man they got rid of."

Gunther clenched his teeth against his seething anger, trying to respond in a calm voice. "They don't keep the park running in the winter, and it's almost winter. I can try to get back on next spring. It's not my fault."

Lily's dark eyes bulged in self-righteous anger. "It's never your fault, Gunther." She winced and placed a hand against her lower back, while her other arm gripped the back of a chair. "It's not your fault you lost your arm. It's not your fault you lost your job. I suppose it's not your fault that I'm pregnant, either. Well, guess what? You're at least half to blame for that, and you can't weasel out of your responsibility."

Gunther struggled to keep from rolling his eyes at Lily's tirade. He hated to grovel. "I'm not gonna run away. I told you I'm gonna take care of this." He lifted his head and met Lily's gaze. "I promise."

"Shit!" Lily yelled. "How're you going to take care of anything?"

"That's enough. Shut your mouth." Gunther couldn't take much more of this.

Lily stomped closer. "I can't keep waitin' tables. And I'm not gonna support your lazy ass *and* a baby."

Gunther stared ahead at the maple coffee table before him, decorated with an oversized tacky green candle. He hated that candle. Lilly had bought it three months ago to "add a little color to the house." Everything about it screamed "bought by white trash from the clearance shelf." It hurt his head just looking at it.

Tears welled in Lily's eyes.

She shook her head, wiping at the wetness on her face. "Look at you. You think 'cause you lost your arm the world owes you a living? It's been three years. Get over it. Find a real job so we can move out."

"I said that's enough, woman." His good hand reached out and wrapped around the broad base of the candle. His knuckles whitened from the grip he held on it. *I need to get control again. I need control over something in my life.*

"Lord A'mighty, you think your dick been cut off 'stead of your hand, the way you go on, I swear…"

With a growl and a flip of his wrist, Gunther sent the bulky candle sailing across the room, slamming Lily in the chest. She toppled backward against the wall, stunned.

Gunther rose from the couch, storming toward her, holding the hook out like a weapon.

Lily blinked, her eyes staring through him, unfocused.

He towered over her, gloating at her helplessness.

She held one hand up as if to ward him off, the other arm cradled around her protruding belly. "Gunther! Gunther, wait!"

He drew the hook back and swept it forward.

She screamed and rolled away from him. The hook punched a hole in the wall just above Lily's head. *I'll shut her whining mouth and get rid of the brat she's carrying, too!*

"God! Gunther, stop! I'm sorry, baby." She shrank away from him.

"Oh, you're sorry now, huh? Ya little bitch." He grinned down at her. He had control now. For these few seconds, he held her life in his hands, and he liked the way it felt. "I gonna slice ya for what you said."

The front door swung open and an elderly woman stood in the doorway, a scowl smeared across her wrinkled features. "Gunther Luke Stalt, what the hell do you think you're doing?"

"Mama?" As if he'd uncovered a nest of hornets, Gunther jumped back several feet.

The woman stepped forward, standing straight and tall, wedging herself between her son and the frightened girl. Her voice carried the confidence of final authority. "You just shamed me. You've shamed the family, bullying the woman who's carrying your child."

Gunther crossed his arms. "Mama, she said terrible things. She didn't show me any respect." He could hear the pouting tone of his own voice, and his face warmed at the realization.

"You'll get no respect here. Haven't earned any. Go on, Son," the old woman spoke.

Gunther stomped toward the refrigerator and snatched a bottle of beer. The room closed in around him.

His own mama ordering him to leave the house! It might be small, and not too fancy, but his mama had raised him here. "So be it, then. I don't need either of you. I can do fine on my own." He'd show them.

He'd show everyone.

~

A RELENTLESS EARLY November sun beat down on the tiny hotel room. Gunther looked around his pitiful surroundings; a beat-up recliner that looked like it'd been left at the side of the road leaned against the wall. Across from the flea-infested excuse of a bed sat a twelve-inch black and white TV perched on a rusty metal stand. He'd tried to watch it earlier, but could only get one station to come in. In the corner, a small square of linoleum with a stopped-up toilet served as the bathroom.

He grabbed a bottle of beer and tried to get comfortable on the chair, but a spring bulged out right where the center of his back should rest.

Gunther leaned forward. The cool beer sliding down his throat eased the tight knot in his belly. He took a shaky breath, frustrated at his mama for taking Lily's side.

What about *him*? What about *his* pain? *He* was the one who lost his arm.

He closed his eyes at the memory. Every night, he tried to put the memory behind him, and every night it haunted him. In his mind's eye, he still saw the meat plant where he'd made a good living before the grinder accident. He felt the grinder lock onto his hand, and that damned machine pulling him forward as it chewed his bones and muscles. Did Mama and Lily have any idea what kind of torture that was? And now, he couldn't even keep a job as a janitor because the damn broom kept slipping off his hook.

How could he begin to explain his anger? Like a dam ready to burst from the strain, he wanted to scream that what happened to him wasn't fair. That he shouldn't have to spend his life barely able to clean up after other people, to work like a dog for peanuts.

Gunther threw his head back and swallowed the final gulp of beer. On impulse, he hurled the bottle across the room. The satisfying shatter of glass impacting the worthless TV screen calmed his nerves in an instant.

He took a deep breath and thought about the plan then spoke into the still-warm air. "I've got to do something. Might as well get started."

Gunther rose, walking out of the stuffy room and into the dark night.

CHAPTER FIVE

I got my poem back with a screaming red *F* slashed in thin lines across the top half of the page.

I stared down at the paper in disbelief. The bell rang for dismissal, but I stuck around, furious and shaking, while the rest of the class filed toward the door.

Mr. Robbins stood in front of his desk, arms folded across his chest, watching my consternation with a bland expression of indifference.

I started right in as soon as the last student disappeared around the corner. "What the hell is this all about, Mr. Robbins?"

He spoke with the calm, forthright sort of baritone he used when lecturing. "I'm not sure I know what you're talking about, Miss Shaefer."

"The hell you don't." I slapped the crinkled paper on his desk. "Why'd you give me an F on this?"

"The meaning is you failed the assignment, Miss Shaefer." Unruffled, Mr. Robbins answered without a hint of sarcasm in his voice. "I found your poem tasteless and without merit. Try to do better next time."

"What?" My brain tried to sort out his response.

He waited, stone-faced.

It didn't make any sense. I tried again. "Excuse me, but you gave a B minus to Frankie Jones for writing about hooking a worm onto his fishing pole. Is that what you consider deeper merit?"

"Franklin's poem was finely crafted with excellent meter. You could learn by its example."

I couldn't believe what I was hearing. "Meter, my ass! It was a free-verse poetry assignment. I turn in a piece about the exploitation of women, and you say it's without merit? Do I really have to explain the poem to you, or should we skip all that and go straight to the principal?"

"I think you'd better watch your language, Miss Shaefer." He walked toward the classroom door, looking a touch ruffled.

Fine. I was more than ruffled, and on a roll.

"Where do you think you're going? I deserve an explanation for this. My poem was better than ninety-nine percent of the crap you received."

That wasn't ego talking. I'd dated a college-leveled poetry major for over six months. I sat in on readings with his friends. They became *my* friends. I'd had my own poems critiqued by people who ate and drank the craft and passion of poetry. I knew good poetry from bad poetry and could define both in ways the teacher had yet to hint at in his basic-level lectures. This was an easy A, plain and simple, and it was ridiculous I even had to discuss it.

"That's really for me to judge, Miss Shaefer." He pushed the door to close it. "I wanted to keep the entire school from hearing our conversation, that's all."

Once the door shut, Mr. Robbins turned toward me. A pencil-thin smile formed on his face, a cocky, self-assured grin of confidence betraying his indifferent tone.

"I think it's safe to say that you're on your way to failing this class, Miss Shaefer. In fact, I'm sure of it."

A chill ran through me. I blinked at him, thrown off-guard.

"Are you threatening me, Mr. Robbins?"

He seemed amused at the idea. "Threatening you? I'd get in a lot of trouble for doing something like that, Miss Shaefer. English is a subjective class, and I'm allowed to give subjective grades, based on my own subjective standards. And I'm afraid, right now, based on those standards, you're just not going to cut it." He shrugged, indicating that nothing could be done.

I kept my mouth shut, my mind circling around his words like a lost airplane. He'd called my bluff and had thrown out a promise of his own. In my mind, I could hear myself whine and beg. I could break down and cry, tell him I'd be good, or throw a hissy fit.

Not in a million years.

"You have only yourself to blame, you know," he continued. "Picking fights with the other students on day one. That trashy costume you call clothing. You're a real discipline problem. I moved from Chicago many years ago to get away from teaching people like you. I have no interest in trying to teach smart-aleck punks who have no interest in learning."

I glared back at him in hopeless defiance. I hoped he'd finish soon, before the desire to throttle him overwhelmed me. Of course, that would only make matters worse.

He stepped behind his desk, his head low, tone solemn, like he was delivering a eulogy. "You think you can smart off and start fights and do whatever you want, and then somehow your teachers will just let you slide by. Unfortunately for you, I'm the only one teaching senior English, and that's not going to happen." He stopped and leaned forward, his calm manner of speech cracking.

I took a step back, reeling at the intensity of his fury.

His face turned red, and he stopped himself to catch his breath. "If you drop out, you'll have to commute to La Grange over the summer to graduate. That's a forty-mile drive, one way. Not a lot of fun, but acceptable. If you stay, your GPA will suffer, and you'll still have to commute. The point is, it would be best for both of us if you quit my class now."

Somehow, I got my head back on straight while he rambled. Hatred I could deal with, at least I knew where I stood.

I put on my bravado and charged ahead. "You're being absurd. I'll just take this to the school board."

He chuckled at my threat. "What are you going to tell them, Miss Shaefer? That the senior English teacher won't give your incredibly clever work a passing grade? That I can't recognize sheer genius when I see it?"

He removed his glasses and wiped the lenses with a white hand-kerchief he'd pulled from his breast pocket. "You don't know much about our school, or our town, if you think that will work."

All pretenses at humor stopped, and he leaned forward, setting aside the glasses and placing both hands flat on his desktop.

"I'll tell you what will happen," he spoke between clenched teeth. "They'll open your file. They'll see your suspension for fighting. They'll look at how you're dressed. Then they'll laugh you right out of the room. And if they bother to call me in to explain myself, I'll find a reason, and I'll make it stick. They'll accept it."

He stood and straightened, placing his glasses back on his face and straightening his lapels as if recovering from a minor scuffle not worth his time. "They'll believe me because they don't want little punks like you in this school any more than I do. So tell the school board. That would be the best thing to happen to me all year."

I couldn't think anymore. I just stood, sinking into oblivion while he finished. I continued to lock eyes with him, head up, but it didn't matter. He knew he'd won in every way that mattered.

Mr. Robbins pulled the chair out from his desk. "I don't think there's anything more you need to say, Miss Shaefer. When you're ready to admit that you can't handle my class, I'll sign your dropout slip. Good day." He sat and returned to his work.

I'd been dismissed.

SOMEHOW, I stumbled to the cafeteria and stepped through the line in a zombie-like state before the despair welling up within me burst forward full force. I stared dumbly at my food, wondering what I could possibly do to stop the inevitable. But I already knew I had no chance. I had as much choice as a fish in an aquarium. No options. Fi-Fi Shaefer blows chance at a college English degree due to failing the class in high school. *The end.*

I could commute, but I would need parental approval to do so. And convincing my mother would be impossible. She wouldn't believe me, anyway. This stank of exactly the type of story I'd tell to get transferred out of the school or to force her to move. Just the sort of thing I'd do to get back at her.

And Mom would gamble with my grades. I knew that. I could already hear her accusing me of failing on purpose, just to prove my story.

I sank deeper, trembling. The room lost its edges. My lunch smeared out of focus from the buildup of tears.

A drop splattered on my tray. My hand shook as I touched the wetness, realizing it was a tear from my own face. The tremor built up my hand and through my body.

"Oh, shit." Tears flowed. I covered my face with both hands while I wept like a little baby. And I couldn't stop.

Worse, I heard a voice at the table.

"Fi-Fi? What's wrong?" Chip had sat down across from me. I wanted to crawl away and die.

"Go away!"

I wiped a denim sleeve across my face. I couldn't see very well, but he wasn't listening to me, anyway. He just continued to stare.

One kid at the table next to us glared hard at his tray. The girl next to him shifted her eyes in my direction and grinned.

"Great. I'm the afternoon entertainment." I grabbed a napkin and wiped tears away. Chip watched me in open shock. I glared back. "Enjoying the view? Get the hell away from me!"

I could hear a couple of snickers from somewhere around me. Chip looked hurt. "Hey, I just wanted to know. Maybe I can help."

"Yeah? Great. I'm fucked, and you can't help. Happy?"

I stood, pushed aside my untouched tray, and stormed away from Chip. I stepped through the foyer and out the double-door entrance. Nobody stopped me. Because of the beautiful late September weather, we could go outside as long as we remained on the school grounds.

Sure enough, the sun shone brightly. *Good for the sun.* I stepped across the grass, the light stinging my eyes. My jewelry jangled. A couple of students played Frisbee nearby. Clinty and his followers huddled across the lot using each other's bodies to hide the joint they passed. He glared at me and snarled then returned to the important business of getting stoned.

The cool breeze chilled me, and my teeth chattered. I reached an open area of lawn and sank down with a tired sigh. I considered ditching the rest of the day. It wouldn't hurt my other classes much, provided Mr. Robbins hadn't started some sort of club in the teacher's lounge with everyone out to get me. Of course, I could wind up getting suspended again. Kick me out of class for skipping class; leave it to the Board of Education. No wonder failure seemed inevitable.

A pair of Payless tennies approached me. I looked up the jean-clad leg.

"Oh, shit, Chip. Go away." I sighed. I didn't have the strength to chase him off or run.

He plopped down next to me while I rubbed my tired, wet eyes.

One thing I'd already learned about Chip, he'd get an idea into his head and couldn't be deterred, no matter how hard you applied the sledgehammer.

Right in character, he said, "I'm not going anywhere until you tell me what happened."

I sighed. "You know, you're real sweet. But in case you haven't figured it out, you're getting yourself in trouble just by hanging around me. Do yourself a favor and get lost." My stomach fluttered, and I feared I'd lose my temper again. I clenched my fists and couldn't talk for a long time.

"Look." Chip's matter-of-fact tone jarred me from my self-loathing. "It must make you feel unique to think you're the only unpopular kid in school. If you think I have a reputation to blow, believe me, hanging out with you has gotten me more recognition in the last two weeks than I've had my entire life. You think it's bad to be the center of attention, try being invisible for a while."

I sat for a few moments, absorbing what he'd said. Then, I repeated, "Why are you doing this?"

"Because whatever the problem is, you don't deserve it. And because you kicked the shit out of Clinty, so maybe I admire you for that, because I never could."

He hunched down in the grass, placing all his weight on his feet, his knees folded up near his shoulders. "You know, I watched the fight. I just stood and watched while they pinned you against the locker, knowing that Clinty was about to take it to somebody else. Some other nobody at the wrong place at the wrong time. No matter what happened, I was going to stand and watch. When you did what you did, I guess I felt pretty bad."

I sighed, and, when I spoke, my voice dripped venom. "Don't go around wearing your heart on your sleeve, Chip. Somebody will tear it off and squash it."

"Well, maybe so, but I'm not going away until you tell me what happened. So if you really want me to get lost, there's only one way to accomplish that."

I glared at him, fighting the desire to scream.

He looked back in utter calm, maybe even a little amused at my behavior.

Even in my current state, I couldn't take my anger out on him. In no way did he deserve it, and I knew he only wanted to help. So I put my head into my curved arm, taking a deep breath and putting a lid on my frustration.

I sat up in the grass and started talking. He listened. He didn't comment or judge; he just let me pour out my rage, without interruption. Because of that, I told the entire story in a drained monotone.

His enthusiastic face slowly bleached white.

I finished, "...So, if you want to go over there and kick the shit out of Mr. Robbins, I'll be happy to watch, and we'll be even."

Chip's blue eyes flared icy anger. "Don't patronize me. I'm holding my hand out, and you're chewing it off."

"I warned you!" I took a deep breath. "I'm sorry. You really are sweet, Chip. You're the only one in this town who even gives a shit about me. And I'm grateful. But you can't do any good."

"There has to be something you can do. Do you think the school board would really back his play?"

I shrugged. "How should I know? You think I've ever actually had to report anyone before? You live in this town. Does it *sound* like something that could happen?"

Chip shrugged. "I'd like to think common sense would prevail, but..." He shrugged and shook his head.

"Well, okay, then. I can't risk getting kicked out of school on an answer like that. So I guess I have to write off the school board idea."

We sat and stewed. I'd gotten past the anger and frustration. Failure still loomed over my head, but at least I could get through the rest of the day.

Chip, however, appeared to be thinking. His face held a look of such intense concentration, I could almost see smoke coming out his ears.

After a while, he shook his head and seemed to dismiss his train of thought. "C'mon, Blue, we'd better go back inside. Try not to worry about it. Things could turn out all right after all."

Blue? Where'd that come from?

But exhaustion bore down on me, and I let the matter go for now. "If you don't mind, I want to stay outside for a couple more minutes."

Chip gave me one last look. "Okay, see ya."

I curled up in the grass, letting the breeze and the sun comfort me because I could find comfort nowhere else.

CHAPTER SIX

PERIONNE – NOVEMBER 1990

Jeff Crimley watched Perionne Park's roller coaster chug through the darkness, then return to the launch shelter. The piston burst of hissing brakes cut through the silence. No passengers exited. No expectant crowd waited to board.

The train chugged over the track; Jeff turned his head to watch. First, a near-vertical ascent, drawn out to maddening slowness, then a suicidal dive straight to the ground.

No one screamed. No one laughed.

In his mind's eye, Crimley saw the kids and teens who should be riding, getting tossed about and shaken as the coaster plummeted through the corkscrew to the finish of the ride. Happy screams.

Crimley shook off a chill, watching the train charge forward for yet another solitary run.

One last adjustment before packing away for the winter; one last chance to catch the small problems before they turned into big ones.

Crimley perched on the edge of the stool, seated in the control booth overlooking the boarding platform of The Whirlwind. The brakes were turned on full, set to jerk the coaster to a jolting slow-down at every turn. So far, the coaster performed with its usual shakiness. Someday, he'd figure a way to smooth it out, but not in the dead of night, not right before winter.

Flipping a switch, Crimley released the brakes and launched the cars again.

The coaster charged forward like a fighter in training, ready to go one more round.

The little hairs on the back of Crimley's neck stood at attention. The only bad thing about working in the dark was the eeriness. Except for him, there wasn't a soul—

"Gotcha, Crimley!" Hard metal pushed against Crimley's shoulder. He yelped, jumping out of his seat and spinning around. He caught the metal object in his hand, his fist drawn back to attack the assailant. As recognition sank in, he stopped his action short.

"Gunther. You sunuvabitch! I oughta pound ya for that."

Gunther grinned, his white teeth gleaming in the dark. A hint of malice behind Gunther's blue eyes made Crimley pause.

Gunther's cackle sounded genuine enough, though. "You shouldn't make it so damn easy. Ya get working on this train and ya go into another world. I've never seen anyone get off on a kiddy ride like you do."

Crimley smiled, unable to deny it. He shook off a chill as Gunther folded his arms over the control booth railing and leaned forward. Something in Gunther's obsessed stare bothered him. Neither man could claim to be on the up-and-up, but Crimley had never sensed any instability in Gunther.

Before tonight.

Crimley wanted to explain away the bad vibes he felt as simple nerves. But now he wondered if he wouldn't regret agreeing to this nasty business.

As co-workers, Gunther and Crimley became fast friends. Gunther swept the coaster deck every hour or so. Last week, he visited the control booth, where they sat and sipped a couple of Cokes together.

That's when Gunther let Crimley in on his scheme. Crimley was willing enough to join, provided Gunther agreed to his one stipulation, a stipulation he'd maintained his entire life; no one got hurt, and, certainly, no one died. If Gunther wanted him along, Crimley'd be no part of any nastiness.

Now, looking into Gunther's predatory gaze, Crimley tried to shake off the feeling he'd made a huge mistake. One he might have to take care of.

Gunther let out a shuddering sigh. "I'm tired of Perionne. We're goin' forward with the plan. We pull this off, neither of us will have any more worries."

Crimley shrugged. "We just better not get caught."

Gunther cackled, a hard gleam returning to his eyes. "Who's gonna catch us? The Perionne P.D.? They're barely equipped to handle jaywalkers, let alone bank robbers."

"Guess you're right."

Gunther's eyes narrowed. "You still in?"

"'Course I'm in. I told ya I was, didn't I?"

"Then you got the car?"

Crimley produced a set of keys, dangling them from his fingers. "Just like I said."

"What is it?"

"A '76 Thunderbird. Four doors, just like ya asked."

Gunther snagged the keys. "'76? That's a fourteen-year-old car. You sure it runs well?"

Crimly nodded. "V-8. Clean interior. Purrs like a kitten. And it's plenty fast enough to blow us right through this town."

"Color?"

"Yella."

Gunther paused, unable to contain a worried expression. "We're going to rob a bank with a *hot* yellow ancient T-Bird? You couldn't find anything else?"

Crimley suppressed his own apprehension. "Hell, no. Look, you wanna tour the town, I got a great station wagon. You wanna blow through town like a bat outta hell, the T-Bird's gonna do it. You've got my guarantee."

The coaster skidded to a halt before them. Crimley wanted to run it again. Instead, he turned his attention back to Gunther. Crimley explained, "The car's parked on I-69 north of the first Michigan rest stop, 'bout ten miles up. Just like we agreed. Jim still going to drive?"

"I think I can guarantee his cooperation."

"He ain't gonna fuck around, is he?"

Crimley didn't like the calm, maniacal grin dominating Gunther's face. "Don't worry about Jim. I'll see to it that he don't. I gotta go. See ya."

As Gunther vanished into the night, Crimley shivered, but not from the cooling night air.

MOST PEOPLE WOULD THINK TWICE ABOUT PAYING a visit to a household at 11 p.m., particularly unannounced. But tonight, Gunther's obsession propelled him up the well-tended pathway to the roomy porch.

The modest single-story house shone with a coat of new white paint, even in the moonlight. As he strolled past the front wooden gate, Gunther could make out the dug-out strips of a new garden bordering the lawn, and jealousy raged within him.

The domestic tranquility galled Gunther. His old "buddy," Jim, with no more skill or talent than Gunther, enjoyed a home all to himself. Jim had married Jessie Beauchamp, quiet and beautiful. Not because of an unwanted pregnancy or desperation, but after careful planning and considerable success. So knocking on Jim's door late at night to bring a little chaos into Jim's life brought a secret glee to Gunther's soul.

The porch light snapped on, and the door opened. Gunther smiled down on the petite blonde framed in the doorway. "'Evening, Jessie. Jim here?"

Jessie stared back with wide, frightened brown eyes. "Just a sec, Gunther. I'll get 'im. You wanna come in?"

"Nah. I'll just wait here on the porch." Jim had a front porch swing, and he owned his house.

Gunther helped himself to a corner seat and flopped down. The breeze had picked up with the settling of evening.

Jessie still eyed Gunther. "Care for something to drink?" Her words held a nervous edge. The scowl on her face undermined the polite gesture, but Gunther didn't care.

"I'll take a beer, thanks." Gunther showed his teeth to her, an over-large, toothy grin he knew made people uncomfortable.

Jessie's scowl vanished, replaced with a robotic smile. She disappeared into the house.

He could hear Jim's voice from inside. Gunther sat back and enjoyed the night air. His steel arm clanged against the metal bench beneath him. *Tomorrow, I'll get what's due me.*

But first, he needed Jim's cooperation.

"Gunther, what the hell you doin' here?"

"'Evenin', Jim." He looked up at the broad, youthful man standing before him. An imposing figure normally, Jim rose to his broad-shouldered six feet-four inches in response to Gunther's presence. Jim wore a full beard and mustache that, in general, would be parted in a kind smile. Jim offered no such smile to Gunther tonight.

Jim shifted his weight from foot to foot. "You dare to come

around here in the dead of night, scaring my wife?" He spoke in a lowered voice, though his tone indicated intense anger. "I already told you, I don't want nothin' to do with your crazy schemes. I'm not doing it, so just get out of here."

Gunther grinned back at Jim. His gaze roamed over the property. "Been working hard on the lawn, I see. Even in the dark, it looks thick and lush."

"You're not here to talk about my lawn. And I'm not playing this game with you."

The front door swung open.

Gunther smirked at Jessie, who stepped onto the porch, carrying two beer bottles. "Hello again, Jessie. I was just telling Jim here you and he's fixing the place up real nice."

Jessie looked down at the porch, her lashes obscuring her piercing green eyes. She extended the bottle toward Gunther.

Jim took the other bottle, refusing to make eye contact with his wife. "You just enjoy. I'll be back in the kitchen if you need anything."

Jessie paused. When neither man said anything further, she vanished through the front door.

Gunther chuckled, enjoying the tension. "Yessir. House is looking real good, Jim. Must be getting ready to start a family. Ain't that right? Seems like I heard that."

"Gunther, I don't care what you heard. There ain't no amount of money that will make me be a part of this. I don't need it. We're doing just fine."

Gunther shook his head. He intended to rub Jim's nose in as much shit as possible. "Five glorious years of marriage, right? Got the good job, the good house, oh, and a Buick Regal in the driveway, I see. Gave up the stock car driving. Well, that was just a craze in your youth, right? Still, you were a hell of a driver. I remember watchin' you."

"Stop it, Gunther. I already gave you my answer."

Gunther nodded his head in mock acknowledgment. "And please allow me to respond, Jim. Y'see, it ain't that easy."

Jim stepped forward, engulfing Gunther in his shadow. "It *is* that easy. Now, get the hell off my property, or I'll call the cops."

But Gunther refused to be intimidated. "You either hear it from me, or I tell Jessie all about it."

Jim rolled his eyes, the beginnings of a smile, not a friendly one, forming on his lips. "What are you talking about? You can't threaten me."

Gunther took a swig of beer before continuing in a mocking conversational manner. "Oh, I'm not here to threaten you about helping me, Jim. Just warn you, man to man. Keep your damn hands off Lily."

The look of shock on Jim's face erased Gunther's earlier humiliations of the day.

"Are you crazy? I've never touched Lily Mills."

Gunther let his eyebrows rise with a mock indignant look. "Hey, whoa now, buddy. That's not how Lily told it. You remember. About a year ago, shortly before I met her?"

Jim placed a hand on his waist and puffed out his chest. "What kind of bullshit is this?"

Gunther shrugged. "Now, why you gotta be that way? Lily told me all about it. She ran into you at the Cat's Cradle. You two snuck off to the back room and started playing pool. No one else was back there, so you locked the door and ended up on the pool table."

An angry scowl disfigured Jim's face, and Gunther slapped Jim's arm, then chuckled. "I tell ya, it's amazing some of the things a woman will tell her man, whether he wants to hear them or not. Really, Jim, taking advantage of a drunken woman."

"It wasn't like that. Jessie and I'd had a fight." Jim spoke with great care, spacing out his words. "Lily and I played a few rounds of pool. Drank a few beers. She kissed me once. But we stopped and that's it." Panic overcame his stone-like features. "What did she tell you?"

"She didn't tell me nothin', Jim. And she won't tell Jessie nothin', either. If you cooperate." Gunther waited for his words to sink in.

Jim grabbed Gunther by his shirtfront and pulled him close. "You're bluffing. You can't possibly think you can hold something that petty over me."

Gunther turned his head and took a swig of his beer, ignoring the grip on his shirt. He fought back the urge to swing his bottle and smash Jim's face. The power Gunther now held over Jim, the mental anguish he'd brought to the bigger man, counted for more than the momentary satisfaction any physical blow would bring.

Gunther flashed another humorless smile. "I'll tell you what I do know, Jim. My girl is pregnant. And she'll say or do just about anything if it will help her child. She's certainly willing to take nothing and make it sound like something." He reached down, pried open Jim's unresisting fingers, and straightened the rumpled shirt with exaggerated gentleness. "And I'll do anything, too. With or without your help."

Jim's shoulders slumped, and he sank onto the swing.

Gunther resumed his original seat on the opposite end. "Now then, would you care to reconsider my offer?"

The words came out of Jim as little more than a whisper. "What time?"

"Tomorrow. Two o'clock. Don't be late." Gunther fished into his pocket and pulled out a pair of keys. He handed them to Jim, who held them loosely in his fingers.

The front door swung open.

Jim's hand snapped shut around the keys. He spun around on his wife.

"Is everything al—"

"Jessie, get in the house!" Jim ordered.

Jessie jumped back.

Jim spoke in a softened voice. "Get in the house, honey, please. I won't be much longer."

Jim watched his wife turn and retreat through the door. Gunther sensed an aching agony burning through the man. "Damn you, Gunther. What do I have to do?"

"Well, that's the kind of fire we need."

Gunther leaned forward, closing the space between them. "Take your car to Darby's Drag Racing Arena."

Gunther relished watching the shocked scowl cross Jim's face. He nodded. "That's right. The old track where you used to drive every Wednesday night. Just like the glory days. Go to the east parking lot. It'll be deserted, but you'll find a yellow '76 Thunderbird with a souped-up engine. Park your car in the lot, but don't park it next to the T-bird. Put it five or six spaces away, any direction. Leave your car, take the Thunderbird. Got that?" Jim nodded.

"Pick up Crimley and me at his house. From there, we go straight to the bank. You wait in the car while Crimley and I take care of business. If you play it cool, we'll get away without a hitch. Then, drive us back to the racetrack and we hop back into your car. From there, we catch the exit to I-65 and drive easy as you please ten minutes north to Michigan. You drop us off the first exit past the state line."

"Then what?"

Gunther shrugged. "That's our problem. Ya drive back home, kiss the wife, make up some bullshit story about a late meeting, I don't care. That's the deal. That's the plan. Agreed?"

Jim nodded. "Agreed, you bastard. But in the meantime, I don't need you hanging around bothering me or my wife. So get the hell out of here."

Gunther stood. "Not very neighborly of you, Jimbo. But under the circumstances, I guess I can live with it. I can live with a lot of things. I hope you can, too."

Gunther was satisfied all would go according to plan. He threw his head back and finished the last swallow of beer then stepped into the darkness, leaving Jim sitting on the porch, head still bowed, stewing in helpless anger.

Gunther'd already gotten some of his power back.

CHAPTER SEVEN

Later that week, Chip asked if I wanted to sit in on a *Dungeons & Dragons* game with his buddies. He had plans for a big Saturday night session. I'd known people in Broad Ripple who were into roleplaying games, but I'd never played one. I'd seen D&D mocked on *Buffy the Vampire Slayer* reruns. It involved lots of maps, papers, and oddly shaped dice.

I checked my calendar, twice. Both times, I had nothing else going on, so by the end of the week, I'd agreed to show up.

I hoofed the several blocks to his house, feeling safe enough in the late afternoon. Chip's house evoked the family-centric quality of the town; two stories, constructed of solid red brick with white panel highlights, a design that could have been from the 1930s, the 1990s, or any era in between.

The white picket fence surrounding the home (actually painted white and made of pickets, the cliché comes from *somewhere*) had seen better days. Even in the coming darkness, I could make out many spots where the worn wood shone through the pale coating.

The wooden planks surrounded a lush green lawn and a cobblestone walkway that seemed mandatory in this town, even in our own yard.

I stepped onto the roomy, bare porch, once painted a dark green but now faded and sun-bleached, and knocked on the door.

Chip answered, a wide grin appearing on his face the moment he saw me.

I returned the smile.

"You're here!" he exclaimed.

"Uh, yeah, I sort of promised I would be."

We stood looking at each other in comical silence until he snapped out of his daze to step away from the door. "Sorry. Please, come in."

A tiny foyer led directly to a coat closet. Beyond, carpeted stairs rose up to a loft. From my vantage, I could make out a desk and computer system set up to look out over the railing. A large oak bookcase dominated the far wall.

Beyond the stairs, we stepped into the unimpressive glory of the living room. All the essential ingredients; couch, chair, and coffee table, with off-white floors and walls tastefully, if not remarkably, decorated in the modern standards of blasé suburbia.

I lingered in the room, taking longer than necessary to check out the minimal surroundings. Something bothered me, something just on the wrong side of obvious, but I couldn't put my finger on it.

A handful of photos hung on the wall over the couch.

A larger portrait showed Chip at age ten or so. A blonde woman in her mid-thirties embraced him. Her glistening brown eyes matched the contented smile on her clear face. Behind them stood a large, hulking monster of a man wearing a blue suit. He grinned into the camera. Large dark curls topped his head, and he draped beefy hands across the both of them. The flash of the bulb added a shine to his clean-cut features and reflected the only hint of light in his dark eyes.

I shuddered and turned away from the photo, repressing sudden anxiety.

A small group sat in the connecting dining room. A group of fellow Perionne High School peers. Colleagues.

All wearing glasses, staring at me in hushed expectation.

Six guys.

Six geeks. And me.

Had Joey seen me, he would have kicked my ass on the spot.

One overweight, jolly guy, introducing himself as Phil Jenson, stood up from the head of the table and extended a beefy hand. He pumped my hand vigorously, making my entire body shake.

"You're the girl who kicked the shit out of Clinty! I don't know whether to shake your hand or bow down and worship you."

"Apparently, you're shaking my hand, but feel free to bow down later," I quipped.

A number of nervous chortles erupted all around the table.

I grinned and felt myself flush. How could I not feel honored at such adoration?

Another guy, this one much skinnier and with a more confident air toward the opposite sex, stepped forward and pulled an empty chair out, motioning me to sit.

I dropped down into the proffered seat, grinning at everyone watching me.

Chip presented me with a piece of paper, my "character sheet." He'd created the character for me that afternoon, a "pretty basic" one since I'd never played the game before. I looked the sheet over. Columns of numbers and strange abbreviations.

Chip explained the character was a "tenth level barbarian woman with a big sword and no magical powers." My job: use the big sword on the bad guys, strictly in the realm of the imagination, of course. Sounded easy enough.

Most of the group played magic users, characters requiring a more intricate understanding of the game, so my job was to make up the balance in combat situations.

Though I often floundered, someone would always volunteer information, explain a statistic, hand me an odd-shaped die to roll. As a unit, the group embraced me, eager to make me one of their own. Quite a difference from how I'd been treated since I'd arrived in town.

Before long, I absorbed myself in the *Lord of the Rings*-type aspect of the adventure.

An hour into the game, I laid eyes on Dad Farren in the flesh. Chip's dad would have intimidated me with the sheer massiveness of his bulk, even if I *hadn't* been sitting when he entered the room. Dressed in a red plaid button-down shirt, his face now covered in graying dark whiskers, he towered over everyone.

In all fairness, he spoke with refined quietness and gripped my tiny hand in his massive one with practiced gentleness. In spite of this, a shiver ran through my spine. I expected him to growl any moment, and clear the table of books and maps with one swoop of his massive arm. He kept calling his son "Eugene" but, with a name like "Fiona", I wasn't about to comment. He checked on us occasionally, bringing sodas and snacks, but otherwise leaving us alone as he *thump-thump-thumped* up the stairs, presumably to work at his desk up in the loft.

He chatted with us briefly during one break. I learned he provided tech support for a fairly large accounting firm, and that his firm had discussed taking on Shaefer and Gerrold. My mom's office wanted someone local to handle their payroll, provide accounting software, and oversee their mainframe. Mr. Farren commented on Mom's professionalism.

I swallowed a response, not inclined to engage a man who, for whatever reason, made my "Spidey-Sense" tingle.

As we joked and played, hours disappeared. Chip "dungeon mastered," narrating the action and refereeing battles. Working as a team, we tried to solve Chip's puzzles and "win" the adventures, but, as the night wore on, we grew progressively slap-happy. My boundaries dropped, and I turned flirtatious, character-to-character, with Phil.

I, Daria, the barbarian warrior from Corinthos, stumbled upon a magic crystal embedded in one of the dungeon walls. Being the only person strong enough to pry it from the wall, I claimed ownership of the crystal. So I carried around a magical charm, dangling on a chain between ample bosoms that bore no resemblance to the real me. I carried in my possession a mysterious object that did "gods-knew-what," a problematic situation inviting trouble.

Phil played a powerful sorcerer who could identify the crystal for me. I asked for his help, putting an intimidating inflection to Daria's words.

Phil huffed in a deep character voice. "Why should I, Magtog the Great, help a barbarian wench the likes of you?" He waved his arms with theatrical flair. "I, Magtog, who can turn sand into diamonds, bring forth cleansed water from the tar pits, and heal all my wounds with but a single touch. What have you to barter with that is of any interest to my greatness?"

My eyes locked on his and I responded with utter seriousness. "Tell me the secrets of the crystal, and I'll be your sex slave for the night."

The entire room erupted in laughter.

Phil flushed red from forehead to neck, broke eye contact, and let his head drop toward the table into his forearm. But he laughed the whole time.

I cracked up myself, and, soon, we were all wiping tears from our eyes.

Chip stared at me, mouth hanging open, aghast.

I winked at Chip, then watched Phil struggle to return to character as the high and mighty Magtog.

"Uh...I, Magtog the Great, will consider your offer." A moment later, he said, "It's a deal."

Chip shrugged. "Great." Then a twinkle in his eye hinted that an amusing idea occurred to him.

"Magtog" recovered some of his previous bluster. "But I'll only tell you what you want to know if I've had a good time."

I quickly referenced my character sheet. "Listen here, wizard. I have a dexterity of sixty-five and a strength of seventy-three. I think you'll find me adequate. The only real question is, can your wand measure up?"

A frown fell over Phil's puffy features. "Well, my dexterity is low, because, you see, when you're a wizard, you generally don't need—"

Chip interrupted. "Magtog, roll your dexterity."

Phil threw the odd-sided dice across the map, squinting at the result. "Uh, I failed."

"Okay," Chip said. He turned and addressed me, a sheepish grin spread across his face. "Daria, at about three in the morning, Magtog is asleep, snoring, and uh, finished, passed out on this sleeping gear. No matter what you do, you can't revive him."

"Ah. So, uh, how am I?"

Chip blushed but kept a straight face. "How bad was your roll, Phil?"

Phil shook his head. "Pretty bad."

I sighed. "'Magtog the Great,' indeed!"

The group broke out into hysterics.

Chip pointed at Phil. "Magtog, for the next twenty-four hours, you're unable to cast a spell over level three."

"Level three? But I'm a tenth level..." He stopped, shrugged, and grinned. "Oh, hell. It was worth it. Let's find something I *can* do right and identify that crystal." Phil rolled the dice again.

I reached for a potato chip. "Daria stands up and yells, 'This one's done. Bring me another!'" I batted my eyelashes, yes, batted my eyelashes, at the guys staring back at me.

I sighed and grinned. Boys!

CHAPTER EIGHT

The game broke up late in the evening. With the bad guys slain and the good guys counting the leftover treasures, we moved as a group into Chip's living room. He took a moment to say goodbye to a couple members of the gang.

I still had troubles with names, opting to wave and offer a "see you later" to their retreating forms. To my surprise, I'd had a lot of fun and didn't want it to end.

Phil had driven his own car and intended to hang out for a bit. He offered to drive me home if I wanted to stay later, and I happily accepted.

The rest of us followed Chip up the wooden stairs, *clomp-clomp-clomp*-ing the entire time, through the roomy loft. As we passed, Mr. Farren grunted, his face magnetized to the monitor.

Like father, like son.

Chip led us down the hall and into his tiny bedroom. Somehow, the four of us who remained all packed onto his double bed, hip to hip to hip to hip. Chip introduced me to his pride and joy, "My own hand-built dual-core, dual processor system with two gigs of memory, one terabyte of hard drive space in a raid configuration, a

PCIe video card, one physics card and a sweet twenty-four-inch LCD widescreen flat panel monitor." I took that to mean state-of-the-art. I nodded, hoping I looked appropriately impressed.

This prompted him to continue. "I compile my own Linux kernel, too, but run Windows for the games." I still had no idea what he was talking about, but he sure *meant* it.

The computer came to life with the shift of his mouse. He started off showing a couple of sci-fi movie trailers to Phil and couple of others who hadn't seen them yet. While the trailer ran, he opened a second window, fiddling with a DOS screen, and explaining to me how he and Phil had made it a practice to hack into local company databases for kicks. Not actually monkeying with the data, just getting in and out. I shrugged. Everyone needed to rebel.

Don't I know it?

Chip had just conquered a watershed goal, hacking into the First Bank of Perionne, and accessing the current balances of several friends and relatives.

Cool. Now we're talking. "So," I teased, "why's a nice kid like you busting into bank records?"

He shrugged, but red crept into his cheeks. "I wanted the challenge."

I watched over his shoulder as he called up a sci-fi blog and posted a message about some supposed nonsensical moments in the *Battlestar Galactica* finale, a thread of perplexed emails apparently extending back more than a year. I shuddered. As the nerdiness ramped up, I knew I'd have to excuse myself.

Phil, by no means a tiny guy, also had no sense of personal space. Neither did the red-haired geek on the other side of me. Arms and shoulders brushed innocuously against my chest. The bed provided convenient close quarters for hard-up guys copping an incidental grope. I gave Phil, at least, the benefit of the doubt. I liked the guy. He, at least, couldn't help his considerable bulk.

Chip worked, poised over his keyboard, I saw a glint in his eyes. I sensed he occupied a time and space where he truly belonged.

"And now," he said, "let me show you my webpage." The browser window dissolved to his personal page. He rose and waved a hand for me to sit.

"I don't want to." I'd dabbled with creating my own page a couple of years ago. Low-res photo, bio paragraph. A webpage struck me as too much effort for too little result, and mine suffered the same case of terminal boredom as most of the others. Besides, Facebook was much easier.

"It's easy," he insisted. "You know how to web browse, right?"

I stepped forward and yanked the mouse from his hand.

"Let me drive, smart ass." I squatted into the chair.

The home page declared,

The Ghost of Gunther Webpage

Beneath the text was a highly detailed rendering of a wraithlike figure waving a bloody hook for one hand. I noted a scanned photograph of Gunther Stalt, identical to the one in my Xeroxed article. The text read:

— — —

Webpage created by Chip Farren. Click Here to leave me an email!
*** Click Here to Join the Ghost of Gunther Discussion Group!*
*** Click Here to View the Article Archive!*

— — —

On the one hand, Chip's research could prove handy for the big test in Hap's class next week. On the other..."Damn, man," I said. "You really *are* obsessed."

Chip answered, "Actually, Blue, you'd be surprised. I have thirteen hundred people participating in the discussion group."

In a town of six thousand. Clearly, a significant demographic shared this insanity.

Phil chuckled. "Boy, *is* he obsessed. That's the word for it." He leaned forward, a bed spring squeaking in protest. "He had me up 'til three in the morning last month configuring the chat site."

The conversation quickly digressed into computer hard drives and blips per second and the latest micro processing speed-zoids, or something. The four geeks lost me pretty quick, and the warmth of the combined bodies became oppressive. Rude or not, I had to get out. Besides, the little geeks had gotten lost in the world of *Dr. Who* and technology. It would be some time before they even noticed I'd slipped away.

LEANING against the stair railing overlooking the living room, I stood in somber thought, enjoying the solitude. Ambient light from the small kitchen lit the ground floor.

The solidity of the real-wood floors made for a comfortable place. Still, something didn't set right with me. I remembered puzzling over it earlier. The walls lacked significant décor, save a couple of small family pictures. The furniture in the living room consisted of a piecemeal arrangement. Up in the loft, a computer on a fancy redwood desk near a large bookcase of mismatched oak.

A large shadow crossed through the open doorway to the pantry. A silhouette blocked most of the light from the kitchen, and I found myself standing in almost complete darkness.

I heard a creak.

A chill ran up my spine, and I knew without looking that Chip's father had stepped through swinging doors and into the living room. I suppressed the shiver.

His smile was friendly enough, and he waved his thick, beefy hand my direction before retreating back to the kitchen.

I swallowed, trying to shake off my trepidation. Chip's dad couldn't help his imposing presence. Naturally, his bulk intimidated me, but I needed to get past this issue. I gathered my courage. They say the best way to conquer a fear was to face it. At least, that's what I told myself as I clomped down the wooden stairs.

Walking through swinging doors, I saw Chip's father sitting at the breakfast bar, pouring a fresh Sprite for me. I thanked the courtesy gods that he didn't pour yet another Mountain Dew. Like I wouldn't be bouncing off the walls enough. I'd vowed hours ago to swear off that green piss for another month, at least.

He motioned to the barstool near him. "I kinda suspected you were going to take a break from all that."

"Uh...yeah, I suppose." I hadn't considered a conversation with Chip's dad a preferred choice, but, until Phil remembered he'd promised to take me home, I pretty much had nothing better to do.

I took a deep breath and made eye contact, determined to break down the barriers for Chip's sake, if not my own.

Mr. Farren looked to be in his late forties. The dark hair atop his head showed some gray at the temples and maintained the same tight curls I'd seen in the earlier portrait.

He folded his arms across the table. "My son gets to talking about computers, and, to me, it's another language. And I'm no dummy when it comes to computers, either." He grinned, showing large, white, even teeth.

I nodded, unable to think of a reply in the deadening silence. I shifted on the stool, trying to ignore his open scrutiny. That's when I noticed the annoying, rhythmic thump from my own fingers drumming against the tabletop. "Sorry." I halted the drumbeat and resorted to watching bubbles float through the ice of my Sprite glass.

As if picking up the thread of an old topic, Mr. Farren said, "You know, your hair is quite something."

I shrugged. "Actually, it's considered retro in Indy. Very eighties. Not a bad thing, just not exactly edgy, either. It's all black leather and piercing these days. But I prefer the color."

He grunted and sipped from his own Sprite. "I bet you have to take a lot of shit for it, don't you? Take my wife, God rest her soul." His eyes traveled upward for a brief moment.

"If you were her daughter, she wouldn't allow it. You know how it is. She was born and raised here in this town. Everyone cut from the same cookie-cutter mold." Mr. Farren shook his head. "You're lucky your mother allows you to find your own way."

Keeping my voice neutral, I answered, "I appreciate what you're saying." He knew nothing about me, *or* my situation, but, in his own way, I sensed he was trying to reach out.

Then the missing piece slipped into place. In my head, I could practically hear a "clicking" sound. Mrs. Farren had died. She wasn't at a friend's, or staying with family, and they weren't separated. She no longer inhabited the house.

The barrenness, the haphazard furniture layout, the pure functionality, suddenly made sense. No plants, no floral patterns, no candles, no *softness*; no trace of a woman's touch. All her decorative touches had probably turned worn and tattered over time, or broken, or stored away. Piece by piece, Chip and his father had removed almost all memory of what she'd brought to the home, except a single picture hung in memoriam. What remained were the awkward traces of a single Dad, clueless to decorum, doing his best to provide a home for his only son.

A profound sadness fell over me.

Mr. Farren spoke in a solemn tone. "Years ago, I guess it's been almost eight years now, Chip wanted his own computer. Of course, he had no way to afford one, and using mine didn't give him the hours he wanted to explore programming to the extent he needed to, even then."

Mr. Farren shrugged. "What could he do? He was only ten, but he pleaded and begged. He collected aluminum cans, glass, he mowed yards, raked leaves, anything to raise the money. After three months, he presented me with $150 in change." He chuckled at the memory and shrugged his shoulders.

"He knew what he wanted, even when he had no way of reaching his goal. So I bought it for him. What else could I do?"

When I didn't volunteer a response, he shoved on. "I suppose I could've refused him. He'd be just like most of the people in this town, but instead I think he's unique. Know what I mean?"

I grinned back. "I suppose I do."

"See, my son, he admires you very much. For the most part, he just lets people pass by. But you caught his attention right away. He could sense something different. So much so he told me about it. He's also told me a few things about what happened to you at school. With the teacher and the fight and all. For what it's worth, I think it's a bunch of shit."

I kept my stone-neutral expression, but, inside, my head spun. After the grief from my mother, the outrageous hatred from Mr. Robbins, I didn't know how to respond to an adult, a *parent*, jumping to my defense.

He continued, "It's a sad fact, though, that in this town, you're going to get that sort of treatment all the time." He sighed and shook his head. His voice welled with emotion. "A lot of people here, they'll keep at you and try to knock you down until you get *proper*; 'til you cut your hair, put on a decent skirt and show up to the church pitch-in with your side dish."

He took another gulp from his drink. I sensed I'd better not interrupt. "This town doesn't change for nothin'. They keep at you and at you, so that even five years from now you'll still be getting an earful."

I wanted to comment about the earful I was getting now but instead said, "I have no intention of being around here in five years."

Mr. Farren grinned, as if we'd made some sort of connection.

"When Chip graduates, he's getting out of here. I'll send him away to college. Doesn't really matter which one. There's plenty of great engineering schools to choose from in Indiana. I just want him get clear of this place and not look back."

I shifted in my chair while he rambled on. "I don't want to see somebody who thinks a little differently change just to please the town. You do that, you've been beaten in any way that counts."

Yes! I wanted to shout, dance, and high-five the old guy.

I did none of those things. The whole thing still creeped me out. I couldn't decide if my feelings originated from Mr. Farren himself, or just the idea of talking to a *grown-up* who understood my problem.

But then again, what did I know about how *caring* parents might feel? Especially a dad?

The now-empty glass slipped from my hand, tipping onto the table. Ice cubes slid across the surface. I fumbled with the cubes and dropped them back into the glass. I stood and wiped my hands on my blue jeans. I never returned his gaze, which I felt penetrating into me. "I've gotta check on the guys upstairs."

"Sure, go on."

I walked through the doors into the darkness.

I sat on the couch in the living room by myself. Mr. Farren must have sensed that I wanted to be alone because he didn't follow me. I heard him puttering around for several minutes until a door opened upstairs, and Chip's friends descended to the foyer.

Strange, for the first time, my blue hair and jewelry struck me as stupid and shallow because an adult expressed approval. Baffling.

CHAPTER NINE

B ut not nearly as baffling as when I arrived at school Monday morning.

I stepped into a room full of chatter, the class buzzing with the conspiratorial pitch of fresh gossip. The entire class stood or sat around one student.

Clinty.

My apprehension kicked to high. Clinty no longer commanded just through the power of intimidation. This time, for once and truly, he held the people around him captivated with his every word. The look of joy on his face spoke volumes.

I took my usual seat in the front row, pretending indifference, but my ears all but jumped off my head to catch every word.

"The cops paid a visit to Goody-two-shoes Robbins over the weekend," Clinty gloated. "Seems he won't be teaching the rest of the semester, at least."

I turned in my chair to face him. As much as I hated to address Clinty directly, this was too important. "What did he do?"

Clinty glared, but answered, anyway. He, too, must have decided the news of a faculty member's downfall warranted a temporary cease of hostilities. "Looks like Mr. Robbins fled Cincinnati five years ago to dodge multiple DUI charges. Took this long, but somebody finally recognized him. Now, he's suspended."

I sighed. "Suspended. Why are they keeping him at all?"

A small girl, seated toward the front but on the other end of the room, piped up. She wore her blond hair in a pair of short-cropped pigtails that bobbed when she spoke. "The school can't fire him. At least not yet. Not until after a trial." Her pigtails wiggled with the nodding of her head. "Mr. Robbins is saying he's innocent. So they can't fire him until he's found guilty. But from what I hear, the description in the police report is an exact match. They say he ran over a little kid."

After dropping this bomb, she looked down at her desk, looking properly mortified.

"That's not what I heard," Clinty chimed back in. "I heard he drove over his grandmama. Ran her over dead."

One of Clinty's toadies added to the confusion. "I thought he just skipped town. That's why they can't fire him yet."

"Doesn't matter," the pigtailed girl insisted. "The suspension's just the beginning. He's through here. And good riddance."

At this point, Hap called us to attention.

My head spun at the news.

Mr. Robbins; arrested, suspended from teaching. Had my hopeless predicament taken a sudden turn for the better? Had I somehow managed to dodge a bullet fired straight at my head?

And the story made so much sense. Given all the unjustified anger he'd displayed toward me, it only figured he'd have other skeletons in his closet.

～

I SAUNTERED into my late morning senior English class to see a tall, balding man occupying Mr. Robbins' chair. Probably in his late forties, his large Coke-bottle glasses made him appear older.

The bell rang, and he scowled at us. "When the bell rings, class, we open our books and close our mouths."

The new teacher's voice droned loudly over the classroom, in sharp contrast to his nerdy, studious appearance. The buzz in the room quieted.

The teacher rose to his full height, a thin, but authoritative, presence.

"As many of you who have taken my class before may know, I'm Mr. Tyers from senior composition. I've been asked to fill in for Mr. Robbins, who has chosen to take a sudden leave of absence for the rest of the semester."

I chuckled and then choked as multiple sets of eyes glared at me. Embarrassed, I stared down at my desk.

For a moment, I wondered if I'd do any better with Mr. Tyers than the first time around with Mr. Robbins.

As class continued, I decided I at least had a shot. Mr. Tyers balanced a stern disposition with clear instructions on his expectations. He wanted homework turned in on time with no excuses. Book chapters read with no excuses. Tests passed with no excuses. Writing assignments turned in following the proper format, as shown in our textbooks. Did I mention no excuses?

By the end of class, I decided I had nothing to lose by approaching him. I stayed behind after the last student shuffled out the door.

Sitting behind Mr. Robbins' desk, he eyed me with practiced patience, folding his hands and placing them on the paper-strewn surface.

"Can I help you with something, miss?"

"Shaefer," I started. I held out the stack of my crumpled assignments I'd been carrying around in my backpack. "Fiona Shaefer."

"Ah, yes, Miss Shaefer. I noticed your name in the grade book. I'm afraid it's the standout of the bunch."

"Yeah. Well, I'm sure it is. Look, Mr. Tyers. Can I be direct?"

"Please."

"I know this is an unusual request, but Mr. Robbins' situation is an unusual one as well."

"You shouldn't believe everything you hear, Miss Shaefer," Tyers interrupted.

I paused while he returned an unreadable stare.

I took a deep breath and tried again. "Fair enough. But the rumors I've heard sort of confirm my suspicions."

I placed the papers on the desktop before him. "I'm not demanding that you change my grades. But here're my assignments. Just look them over again. I think Robbins may have had a personal issue. With me."

He raised his eyebrows.

I hurried on. "I don't believe my work is as bad as the grades would make you think."

He lifted the first page, "'American Idol Finalist,'" grunted, shook his head, and then placed the paper down.

I thought I detected a crack in his stone-like façade, perhaps the slightest hint of a smile.

Or I could have imagined it.

He lifted the entire stack of papers in one hand and opened a side desk drawer with the other then dropped my work down into it.

He refolded his hands across the top of the desk while meeting my gaze with studied indifference. "I think, given the circumstances of Mr. Robbins' sudden departure, it might be worth giving your work a second reading for a fresh perspective."

"Thank you, sir." I used my most respectful voice. I knew my only chance of winning him over was to play the innocent victim angle to the hilt.

And why not? I am *an innocent victim.*

I stepped toward the door.

"One thing, Miss Shaefer." I paused in mid-step, turning my head toward him, trying not to look too hopeful.

He continued, "I want you to know that, if I do find Mr. Robbins graded your material with clear prejudice, I will not hesitate to bring this matter to the attention of the school board. I'll probably only end up speeding up a process that is already underway."

Keeping my face as neutral as I could, I nodded and left the room.

The moment the door shut behind me, I let out a whoop of triumph probably heard the full length of the corridor. Heads turned, but I didn't care.

I tossed my backpack over my shoulder and raced down the hall, dodging anyone in my way.

Wait until I tell Chip.

MUMBLING AROUND CHEWED CRUST, I exclaimed, "It's chust too goo to be twue!" I paused to swallow my bite and washed it down with more milk.

Chip listened in patient nonchalance as I talked between mouthfuls, relaying all my lucky breaks since the day began.

Pizza practically flew into my mouth. For the last several days, I'd eaten almost nothing, my stomach too upset to really deal with food. Today, I'd hopped into the cafeteria line and ordered doubles of everything. Even before Chip approached what had become "our" table, I'd been wolfing down the largest bites I could handle.

I paused to wipe my face with a napkin and take a deep breath. I was all smiles. "I can't believe Mr. Robbins could be so holier-than-thou when he was dodging the cops. Incredible."

Chip studied his nails as he answered. "You're right about one thing. It *is* too good to be true."

Alarm flushed through me, and I dropped the fry I'd been holding into its little divider. "What do you mean? What have you heard?"

No longer able to keep his poker face, Chip grinned. "Let's just say a certain report was faxed to the Perionne Police Station over the weekend. And, although it was electronically dated and time-stamped Cincinnati, it didn't technically come from there. And for the record, it was about a man who ran out on his parole for multiple DUIs. That's all. No hit-and-run, no one killed at any accident scene."

He rolled his eyes. "Just some shmoe fleeing house arrest. The man they're really looking for is about a foot shorter than Mr. Robbins, and the hair color is all wrong." Chip frowned, staring into space at an imaginary document floating before his eyes. "Otherwise, the description's pretty close."

Is he saying what I think he's saying? I dropped the pizza and wiped my hands, though my eyes locked with his. "What are you talking about? Stop being so coy and explain."

Chip shrugged, though he squirmed a bit under my command. "I predict Mr. Robbins will fight this. He'll hire an attorney, who will trace the fax back to the original file. They'll find these discrepancies, sooner or later. Probably sooner. But not before the gossip has ruined him."

His story picked up steam, and he leaned forward.

"Meanwhile, the police will wonder who mistyped the information. They'll want to make an example of somebody, so they'll check the original send file and see the information was entered accurately, and arrived correctly, everywhere else."

Chip took a casual sip of milk before continuing. "What they won't know is that someone intercepted the police fax before it printed off at the Perionne precinct. In fact, someone intercepted *all* the reports last week and read over them, waiting for something to come through that could be used. Once the DUI was found, that same someone changed certain details and facts, and then sent the revised report on to the Perionne Police Station."

He stabbed a fork at his own pizza, his face calm, except for the trace of a smirk in the corner of his mouth.

I couldn't speak. It all made sense. At no time did I doubt the truth of what he said. I'd been too lucky for this to be dumb coincidence. While I believed in poetic justice, did it ever really arrive so perfectly positioned, and so timely, without a little outside prodding?

Chip had changed a police report to get back at Robbins.

My mind reeled as Chip continued his narrative. "Those details are moot, though. Robbins'll never come back to Perionne High School. Or if he does, Tyers will be after him for what he did to your English papers."

I should have known. I should have guessed.

"Shit!" The curse hiccupped out of me, both a whisper and a scream. "Did you...Chip, you hacked into the police station?"

As if giving a lecture, Chip's voice took on a droning quality. "It's simple enough. I just had to find the backdoor program and key it to—"

"I don't give a shit about that. You didn't think this out. What do you think will happen if the police find out about you?" For the first time, it hit me that I shouldn't be speaking these things aloud.

I drew close to him, hissing between my teeth. "Do you know what they do to people who hack government institutions? Ever since 9-1-1, the feds take a *particularly* dim view of this sort of thing."

"You didn't seem so concerned when I took an unauthorized tour of the bank files."

"That's different. You didn't *do* anything to those files."

Chip shrugged. "Doesn't matter. No one will ever know."

I clenched my fists to keep my hands from shaking. "Famous last words, Dillinger! You think Mr. Robbins can't figure out who could have done this? You think half the school hasn't noticed you, and

Phil, and me, all hanging out together? You want to do me a favor? Don't be a criminal. You don't think like one."

His face betrayed hurt. "No, really, Blue, it was nothing. Just your entire future."

The momentum dropped out of my lecture, as if I'd driven over an ice patch in the middle of July. I flushed at the realization that my friend, my dear, dear friend, knew the stakes, but proceeded, anyway. To save my ass. To him, that victory made it worth the risk.

Chip leaned close, eyes flashing, his voice barely a whisper. "First of all, I don't *care* if he knows or not. His word won't be worth shit in a couple of days. He could tell the police the honest truth, if he's able to figure it out, and the locals won't give him the time of day. Don't give people too much credit, Blue. They're lazy, and they accept the obvious explanation." Chip's voice cracked with passion.

"Why?" I had to know. "You don't do this all the time...for other people?"

Again, he looked stung. "Because I can't stand the thought of anyone getting away with an attitude like his. It's wrong, whether it happens to you, or Clinty, or anyone. I had a chance to stop him, so I did."

I could hardly talk. "You could get in a whole lot of trouble if you get caught."

He shrugged. "I won't get caught. Besides, I couldn't let you down again."

"Thank you." Overwhelmed, I stared down at my tray full of cold lunch, trying to collect myself.

I picked up a cold fry and tossed it in my mouth, rolling my eyes and shaking my head. "Listen to me. Preaching to you about breaking the law. I've already been in this town too long."

CHAPTER TEN

Jim wiped the sweat from his brow with the back of his hand. How had he gotten into this? Their yellow Thunderbird crept along Main Street. He pulled the car next to the curb in front of the First National Bank of Perionne. He almost kept driving.

The bank stood in sharp contrast to the archaic structures on each side, a brick frame with modern curved corners. Jim looked around. The street shone with unseasonal sunny sharpness, bringing glorious warmth to the pedestrians bustling about their mid-morning activities, making the idea of stealth pretty much moot.

Gunther and Crimley looked ready to go, hooded and gloved, prepared to spring into action.

Jim tensed behind the steering wheel, trying to ignore the lump in his throat. His entire future depended on whether or not these maniacs were clever enough to pull this heist off without getting caught. He didn't like the odds.

He craned his neck to take in Gunther's panting form in the back seat before settling his gaze upon Crimley, who sat up front. "Don't screw anything up," he growled before pulling the blue knitted ski mask over his face. "If the cops come chasing me, I'm pulling over. I'm not dying in a car wreck."

Gunther grunted, shoving a pistol handle-first over the passenger seat to Crimley. Gunther's breath sounded sharp and fast in the confinement of the car. "Dammit. Can't load this. Put the cartridge in for me."

Crimley's eyes, the only part of his face peering out through the slot of the mask, rolled in exasperation. He cocked his shotgun and flipped the safety on before laying it across his lap.

"Hey. That thing's pointed at me!" Jim said.

"Safety's on. Hold your horses while I take care of Gimpy's pistol. Ain't nothin' gonna happen for five seconds." Working around the confines of his gloves, Crimley grabbed a loaded cartridge from the glove box and snapped it into the pistol.

Jim shut his mouth, but kept a wary eye on the gun.

Crimley reached back and shoved the pistol into Gunther's eager hand. "There ya go. The one-handed special. Just point and shoot."

Gunther slid the pistol into the right pocket of his tattered jean jacket. "You ready, Crimley?"

"All set. Let's do it. Remember, no one gets killed."

In unison, Crimley and Gunther popped open the car doors and sprinted toward the bank's glass double doors.

Jim lowered his forehead to the steering wheel, fighting back stark terror. He could do nothing now, but wait.

CRIMLEY AND GUNTHER burst into the lobby before the small group of people had a chance to react.

Crimley ran a beeline for the front counter.

Gunther held back, waving his pistol at six customers cordoned in the roped-off queue. "Everyone on the ground! Now!"

The women screamed, dropping paperwork, and men stared with their mouths hanging open.

As Gunther danced around them like a tribal wild man, the customers fell over themselves to drop prone on the floor.

Crimley sprinted through the swinging side door partition that led back to the teller's area. He barely had a moment to recognize the blue of a uniformed guard across the lobby before the figure blurred into motion. With practiced ease, Crimley locked in a critical shot and then dropped his aim low.

He fired; the air crackled.

Red flesh tore from the guard's thigh. He stumbled, teetering off balance and falling face-first on the floor, the gun flying from his hand and skittering across the marble tile.

A scream erupted from one of the women lying on the floor.

Crimley kept the shotgun trained on the bleeding man standing between him and the row of tellers.

From under the wounded man, a puddle of blood spread, slowly creeping across the marble floor.

Gunther's yell cut through the room, trying to overpower the shrill screams of the hysterical customers. "Don't anyone fuckin' move! No heroes. You hear me? I said don't move. Lady, shut up!"

Crimley ignored his partner, now pointing his gun at the first teller. "You. Open your drawer. Quickly. Move it."

Crimley watched, eagle-eyed, as the teller's shaking hands struggled with a ring of keys. His gaze fell upon an empty money sack in the storage space beneath her station. "Stop. Reach down. Grab that sack. Not too fast."

Behind him, Crimley heard Gunther's screaming voice. "Dammit, lady, I told you to shut up!"

Crimley risked a glance toward the lobby. He saw Gunther bent over the queue, waving his gun at the tearful older woman.

He glimpsed the combat-crazed gleam in Gunther's eyes and saw a man who had been pushed too far, like a predator animal. Crimley sensed fear and imminent death in the air. He needed to take control of the situation.

Crimley almost yelled Gunther's name but caught himself. "Hey! Calm down. Just watch them. We've got it under control."

"She'd better shut up, or she gets it." Gunther stepped over the rope and stood over the sprawled woman, who still whimpered.

Crimley heard a sudden thump that brought his attention to the teller next to him. In a shaking panic, she'd dropped the bag, and now stood watching him, wringing her hands.

"Hey! Pick up the sack."

The teller leaned over and gripped the satchel.

"Open it up. Let's see the inside. Looks good. Now, open your drawer and put the money in. Quickly!" He shouted. "Hurry the hell up!"

The teller yanked her drawer open.

"Just the loose money. No bound cash. I'm not stupid. I know about marked money. So don't dig too deep."

The teller shoved loose cash into the bag by the handful.

"That's good. Now, walk to the next one."

The woman gripped the satchel with both hands, trying to control her shaking fingers. She crab-shuffled to the next station.

"Open it."

"I...I can't. I don't have the keys." Her eyes closed, and her voice took on a high, whining beg. "Please don't shoot me."

Crimley didn't like her answer. "Don't fuck with me. Who can open it?"

An older blonde woman with graying streaks in her hair stepped forward from the gathered group of tellers in the middle of the room, approaching slowly, arms raised over her head, a ring of keys hooked over her index finger.

Crimley trained the gun on the approaching woman.

Her blue-eyed gaze remained steady. "I'm the manager." She spoke in an even tone. "I'm holding the keys to all the drawers. I'll get the money for you." Her voice continued in calm conviction as she approached the swinging door, even though Crimley's gun, pointed straight at her head, never wavered.

Crimley gathered this was not her first experience with a bank robbery. *Even better. The last thing I need is some teenage moron freaking out on me.* He prodded the young girl next to him with the end of his shotgun. "Give your boss the money bag, then get on the floor. Quickly!"

"Are they fucking with you?" Gunther called.

The manager reached out to unlock the drawer, but her hands shook, and the key ring fell.

"Pick it up!" Crimley's voice echoed through the bank.

"I knew it!" Gunther called. "We need to show these fuckers we mean business."

A shot shattered the air; a woman's hysteria cut off in mid-cry.

Crimley's blood turned to ice.

He whirled to face the lobby, no longer concerned about the money bag. He saw a woman pinned under Gunther's feet, a pool of blood forming under her body. "Damn you, Gunther! You killed her."

"Goddam right." Grinning madly, Gunther pointed his gun at a young man in a three-piece business suit. The man lay face down, eyes squeezed shut, mumbling to himself.

Gunther called out, "They fuck with you anymore, this one gets it next."

Crimley gawked at the mad scene before him, unable to move for several precious seconds. He stared at the pool of the woman's blood flowing across the marble floor.

My fault, puttin' my lot in with that psychopath. Damn it all.

Then, clarity returned, and Crimley leveled the shotgun at the manager with renewed purpose. Now wasn't the time to dwell on what couldn't be undone.

"Pick up the keys! Now!"

The manager grabbed the keys, but her hands trembled too much to work them.

"Give 'em to me!" He snatched the key ring from her and motioned her aside.

Gunther continued to scream at the prone, terrified young man on the floor. "Goddamn right I shot her! I'll shoot all of you if you don't shut up!"

Crimley unlocked the drawer and pulled up a large stack of loose money. He called out into the lobby. "Be cool! I've got it!"

While Crimley worked, Gunther's voice continued to reach him.

"You wanna' fuck with somebody? How about this?" A second shot rang out.

Crimley swore, realizing too late the unforgivable part he'd played in setting a crazed maniac loose on innocent victims, but his hands never stopped manipulating a third drawer. He shoved a large pile of money into the bag.

Gunther's voice reached Crimley as he sealed up the bag. "Guy kept mumbling and praying, like God could stop a bullet or something. I guess it didn't work." Gunther's evil cackle resonated through the building.

All Crimley could think about was getting Gunther out as fast as possible.

Gunther continued to taunt. "Anyone else wanna start something?"

The bag bulged. Crimley had planned to empty all of the drawers and the vault. No way to do that now. "We're getting the hell out of here."

"What? Why? We're not done."

"Yes, we are. We've got plenty." Crimley jogged through the swinging partition. "Let's move! Go! Now!"

They bolted through the doors, across the short cement path, and into the waiting car. The Thunderbird's tires squealed, and the car sped down the road.

~

Jɪᴍ sᴛᴇᴇʀᴇᴅ with one hand and pulled his mask off with the other. He took a sharp turn on Main Street while releasing a hissing breath. They had to go another half a mile to the town limits, where they could access the dirt roads.

Crimley tore off his mask and twisted his body to scream at the man behind him. "Goddamn it, Gunther! You shot two people! You killed them!"

"Hold on! Red light!" Jim gunned the car across the yellow line, blowing past the waiting cars and through the intersection, narrowly avoiding a collision with a pickup truck. Then, Crimley's words sank in.

"What?" Jim shouted. *Please tell me I didn't hear them right.*

"So what?" Gunther said. "You shot the guard."

The inside of the car exploded in screaming chaos, but only one fact sunk into Jim's shell-shocked mind. *People died today because of me.* Somehow, his body responded automatically to the task of manipulating the car through traffic and keeping them alive. Unable to take the noise of the other two, Jim bellowed his own warning. "Shut up and hold on!"

The car roared up the street; Jim jerked the wheel to the right, steering the car onto the dirt road. "Here we go!" Jim floored the car, opening all eight cylinders of the T-Bird's power.

The car shot forward like a rocket, pushing Jim back into the seat with familiar velocity. So far, no one chased them.

"Perfect!" Gunther cackled. "By the time Perionne's finest gets organized, we'll be in another car and out of town."

"Gunther," Jim yelled, "did you kill someone, you son of a bitch?"

Crimley answered with a voice of shocked mourning. "Two people. Shot 'em in cold blood."

Gunther slammed his arm against the back of the seat with a leathery thump. "Fuck you, Crimley! You shot the guard."

"Oh, God." Jim groaned.

"I shot him in the leg, you dumb asshole! He's still alive."

Jim jabbed an accusing finger at Gunther. "You got me involved with murder, you sonofabitch!"

The seats shook. The car had drifted off the road, and a thousand pounds of speeding bulk tore through dirt and side-brush. Crimley gripped the wheel and eased the roaring beast of a car back on the road. "Careful. The way you're driving, we'll be pulled over for speeding before they even know who they're chasing."

"They won't chase us. A cop starts after us, I'm pulling over."

"You are not!" screamed Gunther. "I'll blow your brains out right here if—"

"That's enough from you," yelled Crimley.

Jim needed to pay attention. The dirt road they followed ran parallel to the paved road leading to the highway overpass. Flashing red sirens caught and held Jim's attention.

"Crimley, Gunther, duck!"

Jim cut the wheel hard left, turning off into loose dirt and brush. The car veered away from the blockade of cars and officers stationed at the on-ramp; the robbers focused their attention on the oncoming traffic moving from the other direction.

The ride grew bumpy, but Jim controlled the car's path, testing old reflexes he thought had left him years ago. For the next three miles, Jim guided the T-Bird as it tore across the countryside, keeping a true course across the dusty land. He waited for the squealing of sirens that never came. They'd escaped the police, at least for now.

Crimley spoke first, unable to hide the awe in his voice. "Who'da thought they'd get a roadblock up so fast? Looks like the Perionne Police Force doesn't take kindly to a couple of their citizens getting murdered. Just the fire up their ass they needed to get those road-blocks in place, pronto." He directed his next words at Jim. "You saved us back there. Thanks."

Jim ignored the gratitude. "Here's the turnoff. Everyone hold on."

Jim skidded the Thunderbird off the dirt road and across the parking lot of the derby arena. He pulled the car into a spot near his own. The doors popped open, and the three men jumped out.

Crimley and Gunther ran up to Jim's car and waited expectantly.

Jim looked from one to the other. "No way, deal's off. I can't even get you onto the highway. You might as well turn yourselves in. I'm done."

"Jim," Gunther shouted, and pointed his handgun at Jim's head. "You're done when we say you're done."

"Shit!" Crimley swatted the shotgun handle down on Gunther's good hand.

Gunther yelped, and the pistol dropped to the ground.

Crimley brought the shotgun up and rammed the stock into Gunther's chest.

Gunther fell back against the car, pinned for the moment.

Crimley held the gun between them. "That's enough!" In a flash of motion, he pressed the edge of a knife against Gunther's throat.

Jim could only watch, mouth hanging open.

Gunther tensed and froze.

"I said, *'that's enough,'* little man. Think you're tough, 'cause you shot a couple of defenseless people? Well, I'll slit you from ear to ear, and leave yer body for the crows."

Gunther glared but held back. He took a deep breath and answered in a slower tone. "Okay, Crimley. You win."

There was a long, tense pause between the three men. Jim watched, wide-eyed, while Crimley glared at the now-cowering Gunther.

"All right," said Crimley. "For starters, no more pistols for you. Second, we're burying the guns and the money."

"Why the hell we doing that?" asked Gunther.

"Because I win, and we're doing what I say." Crimley lowered his knife and offered Gunther a contrite smile.

He pounded Gunther on the shoulder. "We can't get out of town now. We have to ditch the money and come back for it later. Relax, Gunther, I have an idea. Jim, pop the trunk, then get in the car, both of you."

Responding to Crimley's authority, Gunther and Jim ran to the Buick.

Crimley loaded the weapons and the money bag into the trunk and slammed it. He then hopped in the back.

Jim pulled out of the parking lot and onto the main road, this time in his own car, with two unwanted passengers crouched on the floor of the back seat.

"Okay," Crimley said, "drive back to town. Nice and easy. We'll need to stop and pick up supplies for tonight."

Jim drove without comment, trying to bury his fear and concentrate on the task at hand as if his very survival depended on it.

Because it did.

CHAPTER ELEVEN

SOMEONE CALL THE DOCTOR! GOT A CASE OF LOVE BI-POLAR! My eyes snapped open to the awesomeness that is Katy Perry screeching from my iPod alarm clock. STUCK ON A ROLLER COASTER! CAN'T GET OFF THIS RIDE!

I groaned, realizing, belatedly, that today was a Saturday and I'd forgotten to turn off my alarm. Katy went on a few more seconds about her boyfriend being hot and cold, yes then no, in and out, wrong when it's right.

Bitch, then moan, I added in my head as I hit the off button.

Well, I was up now, even if I wouldn't define my current state as "awake."

I flung aside the covers and wandered into the living room, still wearing my oversized T-shirt, stifling a yawn and trying to blink the sleep away.

I wonder if Mom would notice one less cup of coffee?

The smell of fresh-brewed coffee had drifted over from the kitchen. Mom had set the timer to auto-brew at six every morning, but with today being a Saturday and ninety minutes past brew time, the life-giving broth might stew another half hour or more before Her Majesty stumbled out of bed.

I considered the pros and cons and instead poured myself a glass of orange juice. In Mom's head, coffee might stunt my growth, even at age seventeen. I didn't even like coffee, just loved the smell. Plus, I wanted to deny some of it to Mizz High and Mighty snoozing down the hall.

And yet, I didn't.

Screw the school routine, anyway, or I'd also still be sleeping. And because I was a good girl last night, I actually made it home at a reasonable hour.

Well...11:30 was a reasonable hour, compared to how I used to prowl around until well after midnight.

My thoughts fell to the other prowlers who still stalked the streets of Broad Ripple without me. With an ache in my chest, I wondered what Joey was doing. And if he missed me as much as I missed him.

I spied the desk in the corner of the living room, with Mom's computer on top. Technically, the computer was for both of us, but she used it ninety-nine percent of the time. I usually checked my Facebook and email on my cell phone or at the computer lab at school.

Since I was grounded from my phone through the weekend, and no one was awake to kick me off, I stabbed the power button and filled the room with the humming of the cooling fan.

The 'puter was about three years old, and it never booted Vista up particularly fast, but it ran well enough once it ground through the almost-five-minute startup. I made good use of this time by wolfing down a bowl of Frosted Flakes, and I settled in front of the screen just as the machine relinquished control over to me.

I brought up Facebook and typed in my account. I hadn't been on in almost two weeks. I was greeted to the usual plethora of notifications sorted by subcategories, but my attention riveted on my friend count, which had dropped by one.

I knew it would eventually happen. We were no longer together, and promises made in the past meant nothing in the temptations of today. *But so soon?* I brought up Joey's home page, and the Add Friend button stared back at me, telling me I'd been removed.

I scanned five new messages in my inbox. Surely, he had the courtesy to send me a Dear Jane before cutting me off at the knees. Surely, even a *self-obsessed little shit* like Joey, poet extraordinaire, would take five minutes to lessen the pain and leave some sort of final thought. Something even as trite as "we were great together but it just wasn't meant to be" would have been preferable to a "no comment."

One of the five messages in my box, from my friend Zadora, who hung out with us at the café, caught my attention with the header "RE: Joey." I took a deep breath, bracing myself as I clicked the message.

Hi, Feef!

Sure miss you on reading night! As you know by now, Joey decided to make a clean break. He told us last night not to say anything to you. Screw him, right? Ay, Caramba, gotta hurt bad, Chica! I'm sorry. He's in a bad way, but we'll keep him out of trouble — we owe you that much.

I always liked you, Chica, but you two were poison. Best thing for you was to get the hell out of here. I know you don't see it that way, but take it from this senorita (at the ripe old age of 22 lol) forget about him and move on. You have a special heart, Chica, find someone worthy of you. You deserve it.

Zadora

I sat for, well, I don't know how long, staring at the words on the screen, delivered like a long-distance, glowing electronic punch. I waited for the shock to wear off and wondered if I would cry once it did. *The cowardly shit couldn't even write me himself; I had to receive a pity note from someone else.* Because that's all Zadora could do now was feel sorry for me, the poor Chiquita high school kid dumped by her stoner boyfriend. And because she knew Joey for the shit that he was, she tried to provide the closure she knew he wouldn't.

Soon, the words blurred away in predicable tears, but what surprised me was the lack of resonance down in my gut. I'd known this was coming and had been bracing myself. Now here it was, and in reality...maybe it wasn't so bad.

Today marked a new beginning, a fresh start. Except for one thing, *I hate it here.*

Classmates out to kill me, teachers out to flunk me. But on the bright side, all the computer geeks want to be my friend.

The first real sniffle came, just audible enough to catch *someone's* attention, the just-rising Queen of the Abode herself. "Fiona? Are you okay?"

I clicked the window shut with one hand as I wiped a sleeve across my face with the other. If the first sniffle was audible, the second one echoed through the house. *Dammit. Last thing I need to hear right now is 'I told you he was no good for you' from the Prophetess.*

"I'm okay, just...saw something sad on YouTube." I heard the distinct gurgle of coffee being poured. Mom wouldn't venture far from the kitchen without a full mug, loaded with sugar and creamer. Her addiction to caffeine bought me almost two minutes to dab at my face and dry my tears.

She wandered in, dressed in her white silk robe and vanilla slippers, which happened to match the shag carpet. Though still bleary-eyed, her suspicious gaze fell upon me. She sank into the black leather couch near the computer. "Are you sure you're okay?"

I mustered up a smile. "Couldn't be better. Just a little tired."

"It's not Joey?"

Somehow, I froze the smile on my face. "No idea, Mom. Haven't checked in with him since we got here."

"It's Joey." This time, no question. She took a deep breath of self-righteousness, which I cut off.

"Mom, *please*...can we not do this? It's over, I won't be contacting him again. You can take that away as a victory, and we'll just skip the part where you rub my nose in it. Just this once."

I waited, bracing, and could almost see the mental switching of gears in her head as she took pity on me and changed topics. "Actually, I have good news. And because you didn't have your cell phone, I couldn't tell you last night. Joke's on me, I guess."

I bit back my comment. If she could be nice, so could I. She extended my silver flip-top phone at me. I let it drop into my open palm and wrapped my fingers around it. "Thanks for that, but I gather that's not the good news?"

"No, hon. I found a job for you. In fact, you start today."

Uh-oh! "A job? Today? Doing what?" I'd spent a couple days during my week of suspension looking for a job to earn a few bucks, but, with school already in session, most places had filled their quota of weekend and evening help. I'd tried the video store, some retail clothing places, even an ice cream store.

"One of my new clients, Ted Adams, he bought the Southern Chick'n Stop fast food place down the road." I had, in fact, tried the Chick'n Stop a couple of weeks ago, but the impatient, fat manager with the rattling keychain attached to her side made it clear in no uncertain terms they had no open spots.

I repeated this to Mom, as if I had to justify that I might have missed this golden opportunity. She nodded and waved her hand to brush it aside. "Well, since then, he had to let a few people go, and now he needs help. He said you can come in later this morning to fill out the paperwork and watch some videos."

Actually, I was hoping to avoid fast food. I'd worked both at a deli and a secondhand clothing store in 'Ripple, and there was no comparing the two.

Okay, well, as far as fast food goes, the Southern Chick'n Stop could be pretty tasty. Maybe I can land a spot behind the counter instead of back in the grill.

A twinge of something akin to gratitude tugged at me, but I shook it off before it could stick. I reminded myself that Mom just wanted my commitment to someplace I could be while she worked overtime at her office. The job amounted, in her head, to a glorified daycare where they paid me instead of the other way around.

Still, that glorified daycare meant extra spending money, something Ms. Stingy usually divvied out sparingly and only after much pleading on my part. So this job thing definitely had an upside.

I nodded and rubbed the last of the sleep from my eyes. "I guess I'd better get dressed and head over. Thanks, Mom."

And I meant it.

WALKING the few blocks to the Chick'n Stop took about half an hour, just like anyplace else in this town. Mom offered to give me a lift, but, as it was warming up into another hot day, and I wanted to enjoy the sunshine while we still had it; I decided to hoof it.

Besides, I wasn't *that* anxious to get started.

Dressed and showered, I grabbed a slip of paper on my way out the door where I'd jotted Chip's cell phone number. I'd guessed, correctly, that I'd be able to add it to my phonebook soon. Skipping along the sidewalk, I fired off a quick text message to him.

    C got a job Chikstop start 2day ttyl B.

I hit SEND, set the ringer for vibrate, dropped the fliptop into my denim jacket, and then forgot about it. I waved at Sylvia, still rockin' and knittin', bless her pointy old head, and broke into a light jog.

I arrived twenty minutes later, a bit after 10:00, still feeling good but glad to step into the AC for a while.

I approached the front counter, in the corner, away from the small group of customers and three open registers. The two dudes and one girl behind the counter all looked about my age, or close. One gave me a quick, impatient glance before turning his attention back to the customer rattling off his order.

Standing behind them, a puffy-faced fat girl turned my way. She blinked dark, beady eyes at me, and I realized this was the same manager I'd spoken two a couple weeks ago, the one who'd told me they had no positions open.

She came nearer, taking off her headset. By way of greeting, she said, "I told you last time we don't have no open spots."

Ugh, she remembered me. But then again, my bright blue hair beacon *and* sparkling personality rendered me virtually unforgettable. "Actually, I'm already hired. I'm supposed to watch videos today."

The glare she gave me made it quite clear how little she thought of being kept in the dark about new hires, particularly those she'd already shooed away. "You're the fresh meat? Fona something?"

"Fiona," I corrected. "Shaefer."

"Okay, come back this way. We'll get you set up on the videos." She indicated the swinging door set into the counter. The manager passed the headset off to a tall, skinny dude back by the deep fryers and grabbed a clipboard up from behind the counter. She held the clipboard up with the self-importance of a health inspector paying a surprise visit. "Birthdate and soc'?"

I rattled off my birthdate and social security number.

She tapped on the touch screen of the closest register on the counter.

I waited patiently, then impatiently, as the seconds dragged on. I could see various windows opening and closing but had no idea what was going on.

Finally satisfied, perhaps two minutes later, she scribbled a note on her clipboard.

"Everyone clocks in on this register," she said. "You enter your birthdate and soc' to clock in; enter it again to clock out. Simple." She waved a beefy arm at the swinging door leading to the back of the store. "Follow me, fresh meat."

We walked up a narrow path past the grill. The aroma of just-cooked southern fried chicken patty, so pleasant from the counter, transitioned into old grease and caked-on raw poultry juice. My nose twitched. I wondered if I'd ever want to eat here after this, or if I'd get used to the smell.

I followed her back to a tiny rectangle of a break room, dominated by a small table and restaurant chairs scattered in disarray. A ten-inch TV with a built-in DVD player sat on a high shelf facing the table. I noted the manager's office against the far wall, recognizable by the heavy steel door with the inset horizontal slot-shaped window.

"Have a seat, fresh meat. My name's Kim, by the way."

I flashed my most disarming smile. "My name's Fiona, by the way." I'd considered adding that everyone called me Fi-Fi but didn't have the energy. Fiona, for today, at least, would be preferable to fresh meat.

To my surprise, Kim laughed. "Spunky. I like that. Don't worry, fresh meat. You'll lose the title in a couple days." She reached out and clapped me on the back, not hard, but I flinched, anyway. Kim creeped me out, and I couldn't help but cringe at the thought of working with her. She took her job and the power it brought her *waaaay* too seriously, which meant she didn't have much else going for her.

I waited while Kim disappeared into the office.

She reappeared moments later with some DVD cases. Behind her, a short, older man, maybe thirty, balding and graying at the temples and well into inflating the spare tire around his middle, also emerged from the office. He smiled at me and extended his hand. "Hello, Fiona, my name's Teddy. I'm the owner-operator of the Perionne Southern Chick'n' Stop."

I met his hand with a firm squeeze. "Hello, sir."

"Your mother told me about your job search just in time. We lost a lot of kids when school started, and we really need the help. Welcome aboard." I smiled at the warm welcome, noting that Kim would do well to follow his example.

"Thank you, sir. I'm anxious to start."

I stood there a few moments while Teddy's gaze traveled over my form, top to bottom.

"Well, I can't say I'm thrilled about the hair, but, if you work the counter, you'll have a hat on, anyway. No nail polish, rings, or any other jewelry when you're on duty. We can't have anyone losing something while handling the food.

"Cell phones stay in your locker when you're on the clock. I won't tolerate texting or phone calls when you're supposed to be working. I expect you to take ownership of whatever task we give you, even if that's scrubbing the urinals. You are always polite and courteous to our customers, no matter how rude they might get. And absolutely no profanity anywhere on the property, whether you're on duty or off."

I nodded. So far it all seemed reasonable, even though I'd have to take extra precautions to watch my damn mouth.

Teddy extended a clipboard at me. I glanced down at the W-2 and various forms and rules. "The training videos will go into a lot of procedures, but those are my rules of the road. Any problems so far?"

"No problems, sir."

Teddy nodded. "You can fill those out while you're watching the videos. Better settle in, it can take three hours or so. Oh, you have unlimited drink refills throughout the day."

I grinned at that. "Even the sweet tea?"

"Of course. Ready to get started?"

I grabbed a cup and turned in the direction of the counter. "Just give me a minute to fill up, and I'll be ready."

I worked my way back to the drink station, dodging metal fry baskets and cardboard boxes cluttering the aisle. *Maybe this won't be so bad after all.*

I was *so* wrong.

CHAPTER TWELVE

Twenty minutes later, I was taking notes about FILO, the first-in, last-out rule of storing food in a walk-in freezer. I'd already been interrupted five times by other workers cutting through on their way from here to there and wanting to say hi to the "fresh meat," so I was only about ten minutes into the video, such as it was.

As I stared at a badly acted scenario demonstrating the various ways to pollute your food with salmonella, Manager Kim waddled through, past the office and into an area I hadn't entered. She returned moments later, dragging behind her a large, oversized duffel bag. She placed it before her like Indiana Jones returning with the buried treasure. "Kill the video, fresh meat. Duty calls."

"What's up?" I asked, stabbing the stop button on the remote.

"We had two people call in sick today, so we're short." As she spoke, she unzipped the top of the duffel, exposing a bulbous, golden polyester chicken head with an open, bright orange beak. The gold polyester cut off at the neck, extending out to shoulder pads of white foam.

I stared at the smiling chicken head, my mind screaming out a three-alarmer. "You *can't* be serious."

Kim returned my appalled gawk with a sadistic grin. "As a heart attack, fresh meat. We're offering free samples of our new Mocha Shakes with each combo meal during lunch today."

"And this concerns me, how?" The sarcasm bubbled up in spite of my best intentions.

Manager Kim reached into the bag and pulled out a sign, a home-made sign consisting of a two-foot-long stir stick intended for mixing exterior paint glued to a rectangular piece of plastic. Across the face, I could read letters stenciled from a kit at an office supply store,

Try NEW! Chicka-Delicious
Mocha Shakes 11-2!

I stared, aghast, at the chicka-retarded sign. As words continued to fail me, Kim offered, "I made the sign myself."

"Nice," I croaked then grabbed my sweet tea, sucking deep from the cool, comforting brew.

"Lunch rush is hitting, and we need Chicka-D outside by the road waving the sign. And you've just been volunteered."

"Okay, I get it." Her tone and evil grin told me she'd entertain no argument. At least, from the looks of it, no one would recognize me inside the costume.

I waited for the blindfold and cigarette. "What do we do first?"

"Lose the shoes. Socks only." As I kicked off my tennies, Manager Kim hefted the foam chicken head between her hands and held it above my head. A weight of snug foam dropped on my shoulders. The light dimmed, and sound closed in around me.

I could hear my own breathing, panting in the confines of the foam. Luckily, I wasn't claustrophobic, or I would have been in trouble before we began.

It took a few moments for the light to find me through the mesh portal that, I was pretty sure, filled the gap of blackness in the mascot's open beak. I could see fairly well, at least directly in front of me, through a porous round portal about eight inches in diameter.

Still grinning, Manager Kim held the chicken body suit to my eye level, looking like a pair of warm golden footie pajamas with orange leggings, from which dangled a pair of oversized three-pronged claws for the footies. And these PJs zipped up the back.

"Okay." I heard Kim's voice through the layer of foam. "Take a big step forward into the leg."

I did, and my left foot sank into a thick wrapping of polyester.

She helped guide me into the costume with practiced ease, her voice rattling off the "rules" of the mascot secret society which I must obey or risk the terrible consequences. No talking in public under any circumstances. No bending at the waist; I couldn't see if my head might hit someone. Bend only at the knees. No chasing children, no hugging them. Let them come to you and hug you.

She rattled off a bunch of other things that had nothing to do with standing on the side of the road waving a sign. After she wound down, I asked the one question on my mind, "How long?"

"You can't be out there longer than forty-five minutes. I won't lie to you. It's in the high eighties now, and that thing is going to heat up to a light simmer, about forty degrees higher than wherever you are." She briskly turned me in place so she could zip me up. "So it'll get uncomfortable." She pulled the costume closed with one fast yank. I lost half my light, again, and the foam closed tight with even greater stifling urgency. "Be grateful you're the first today."

"Why?"

"Because the costume's dry now. Someone else will put it on right after you to finish lunch rush. After you've soaked the inside with sweat."

"Yuck!" I tried not to think about it. Nausea at this point would be a *very* bad thing.

Manager Kim walked down the cluttered aisle.

I started to follow, but one oversized claw stepped on the other, and I stumbled. I reached out and braced myself against the side of the walk-in freezer then continued after her, consciously taking larger-than-normal steps. That seemed to work okay.

I chugged through the grill area, exaggerating my movements as the manager had instructed me, shadowboxing into the air. *Hey, I'm stuck with it; I might as well have some fun.* Through my portal to the outside world, I saw the fry cook nod, raising his spatula in a mock salute.

Kim held the door open as I stepped through to the counter. "Duck, Chicka-D. Low door." She warned me just in time.

I emerged from the counter area to the combined squeals and yells of every kid in the place. "Mom! Look! Chickie!" "I'm gonna give him a hug!"

I barely made it onto the dining floor before I felt several small collisions about my abdomen. I had to crane my head uncomfortably down to see the small girls grappling my waist and legs in various death-hugs.

I reached down and patted each child on the back, waiting patiently as, one by one, they released their grip and ran back to their parents. One ten-year-old boy, clearly too old for that hugging nonsense, followed after, holding up his hand. "High-five, Chick!" I swatted at it, and he nodded and walked away, apparently satisfied. "Stay cool!"

"This way, Chicka-D," cued Manager Kim, heading toward the entrance. I relaxed my neck, now able to center her in my portal of vision, and followed.

I spotted someone familiar out of the corner of what I could laughably call my peripheral vision. Actually, he sat in the booth closest to the door, or I wouldn't have noticed.

Chip held a cup under his chin, sucking through a straw on one of the coveted new Mocha Milkshakes. I detoured, stepping toward him, and pumped fists in his direction.

This caught his attention, and he gazed in apparent confusion. I *so* wanted to laugh or say something, but I caught myself. I waved a frantic hand, or (wing?) toward him.

He stared at his own hand, as though an alien thing, then extended it, palm facing me, swaying his arm back and forth a couple of times in a feeble return of my greeting.

I turned back toward the door.

Kim stood in the doorway, gripping the paint stick attached to the sign face, which rested against her bulging polyester pants. "This way, Chicka-D, time to go play in traffic." She chuckled at her own joke.

Ducking slightly, I stepped out into the blazing noon sun. The portal-shaped window to the outside in my headpiece radiated a disc of intensified light. The individual holes in the mesh took on greater definition, and, more importantly, I could see the sidewalk, parking lot, and grass leading to the edge of the road.

And, more disconcerting, I felt the air within the tight space warming up.

As we approached the sidewalk, Manager Kim's hand gripped my shoulder. "Step," she cued, warning me of the downward drop to the blacktop. "Big step," she said, helping me cross the drainage ditch in the grass. I took three tough shuffles uphill to get to the sidewalk running parallel to the main street.

Near the side of the street, traffic noises from the steady stream of passing cars crescendoed. A car cruised by and honked, making me jump. A second car, driving the opposite direction, also emitted a friendly beep. I suspected I'd get used to it pretty fast.

Kim leaned in close and had to yell to be heard. "We'll get you in forty-five minutes! Here's the sign! Just walk back and forth and try to have fun!"

Have fun, yeah, right! I grabbed the sign in my mittened hand, not easy. As the next car raced past, the sign, like an aerial flap pointed the wrong direction, caught the windfall, and tried to jump from my hand.

I gripped that sucker two-handed to keep it from flying off. I turned to tell Kim the wind might be a problem, only to see her stomping away.

Resigned, I paced back and forth, waving the sign up and down over my head. A car flew past and honked. A second one honked. I realized they would *all* honk. *Just not much going for entertainment in this town.*

Occasionally, a car in the lane closest to me would honk, then slow, turn, and pull into the store. Other times, a car in the lane across traffic would slow as they honked then skid-brake into the turn lane and pull into the parking lot.

Those are my *customers! Holy crap, this works!*

As cars pulled into the parking lot, I did a quick release of one hand from the sign to flash a quick thumbs-up. The passenger would usually reward me with a second friendly toot.

I started hop-walking back and forth, in a long, pacing trail along the sidewalk. Instead of simply turning, I'd jump in the air and spin in place, shaking my "tailfeathers" as I landed. This almost always resulted in a passing car honking. *Not a bad workout.*

And, for a while, I had fun.

After another while, I stopped hop-walking and slowed to a standard walk.

And after a long while after that, I started noticing how much I was panting and how *damn* hot it was in this stupid thing.

That's when the thought hit me that I had no idea how long I'd been pacing out here. I knew that time had a tricky way of being relative when paired with hard work, and it could have been anywhere from five minutes to over half an hour. All I knew for sure was that the sweat had built up around my neck and dribbled down the back of my collar and into my blouse. Moisture soaked my bra. The foamy polyester basking in the sun roasted the denim of my jeans and burned my legs.

The panting in my ears took on a more urgent intensity.

A Mitsubishi Spider honked, then slowed, pulling up near the curb. I woke up, realizing I'd been daydreaming. Some buffed guy behind the wheel turned in the seat where he'd pulled up the sports car. "Look alive, chicken!" His Barbie doll girlfriend giggled nonstop.

I raised the sign and ran after him. As the tires squealed, I swatted the sign through the air in an indignant pantomime.

A couple cars driving the opposite direction honked in apparent appreciation.

I continued my patrol with renewed enthusiasm. *I can do this. Forty-five minutes isn't that long. I must be just about finished by now.*

Right?

Except...

I turned and looked back at the restaurant, blinking sweat from my eyes as I peered through the portal. The cars in the drive-thru wrapped around the building, a segmented serpent of hungry customers. The parking lot, practically full, continued to receive a steady stream of cars from both the road where I patrolled and the strip mall beyond our parking lot.

But the rules were clear. I couldn't be out here more than forty-five minutes. *Surely they wouldn't forget about me. That would just be...wrong!*

Right?

I swallowed back my fear with a throat that suddenly hurt. I slid a dry tongue around in a dry mouth.

How long had I been out here? I had no idea. My prideful inner self started giving me hell. *They're keeping track inside. So don't be a wuss, and do your job.*

I raised my hand to lift the sign. *When had I dropped it to my side?*

I couldn't lift the sign.

The sidewalk in front of me blurred. I blinked rapidly to clear sweat from my eyes. I realized I wasn't feeling the sting of sweat, and, no matter how much I blinked, the sidewalk wouldn't snap back into focus.

I turned toward the grass decline. I took a couple of wobbly steps toward the building, felt the stupid sign drop from my hands, my feet get tangled up, and my body pitch forward like some bright golden Humpty-Dumpty.

Padded and cushioned, I don't remember the fall hurting much. Then, everything went black.

CHAPTER THIRTEEN

The world returned some time later. I could feel myself splayed face down in the drainage ditch, my clothes soaking, in total darkness. The timeout gave me a burst of energy, or so I thought, and I fought to stand up.

I shoved against the ground with both hands, feeling the costume rise into a push-up position. Warm water poured from the back of my head into my face. Light streamed through the portal, but my strength gave out in one arm, and I toppled sideways.

Grunting, I kicked at the ground, and succeeded in rolling over.

I flopped onto my back. On the positive side, light shone through the grill again. But I couldn't get up.

I heard a distinct change in the normal sounds of the passing vehicles. One, I could sense, pulled close, then skidded to a stop nearby. *Help is on the way!*

I heard the laughter of an approaching man, and a second person calling, maybe from the car.

"Greg, what the hell are you doing? Let's go, man, we're going to be late!"

"Hold on, this is priceless."

The silhouette of a head and shoulders blocked part of the light. I opened my mouth to speak, but I had no voice, no words of pleading would come out of my mouth.

I waited. He waited. I could see arms reach up, holding a device in front of his face.

No, he isn't!

I heard the click of a camera shutter.

Laughter, then someone shouted at me. "What a loser! You should be in a turtle costume!"

I heard a more distant shout, vaguely familiar from a million miles away. The shithead hovering over me cut off his laugh and looked toward the restaurant, at least, I think it was the restaurant. I heard footsteps run off, followed by more laughter, the squeal of tires, and the acceleration of a car driving away.

More cars honked, passing by, but I also heard distant footfalls running toward me from the restaurant.

"Blue! Oh, my God, it *is* you, isn't it?"

Chip? I must be hallucinating...

Except there he was, moments later, recognizable, even though his face leaned in close and cut off most of the light. "Hold on, I'm going to get you out of this..."

A woman bellowed from a distance, accentuated by the thumping stomps of Manager Kim approaching. "Sir? You can't open the costume here, sir!"

"She may be dying in there!"

"We'll get her inside right now, sir, if you'll help me, but we can't unzip her out here."

"Blue, can you hear me?"

I couldn't answer, but I waved my hand, and, a moment later, he gripped it in return.

His other hand traveled up my arm and positioned itself under my shoulder.

I pulled myself into a sitting position.

My face burned as if on fire, and I felt old sweat dripping down
the crevices and contours of my body. A wave of nausea passed

through me, and I closed my eyes. *If there is a God, He will* not *let me puke inside this costume!*

"Sir, I can get her, thank you."

"You need my help. I don't think she can walk on her own."

A second pair of hands grabbed a hold of my other arm. "Fiona, if you can hear me, squeeze my hand." Through the layers of material, I gave her fingers a tentative squeeze. "Okay, count of three, we're going to lift you to your feet."

She counted, and I rose, through no action of my own. "Okay, just step as we go, and we'll guide you."

Somehow, walking mechanically, gripping Chip's hand for dear life the entire time, I was guided and prodded back across the grass and over the cement. I ignored the honks and callings, though they sounded more urgent and mocking than ever. I closed my eyes, waiting for the burning on my head to stop, realizing I had no fresh sweat beading on my forehead or in my eyes. I knew, distantly, that wasn't good.

Somehow, I ended up back in the restaurant. The raised voices of Kim and Chip roused me from a stupor. Chip wanted to stay at my side, and Kim was reading him the riot act for trying to step behind the counter. Kim called out a name, and Chip pried his hand loose from my death grip.

A second body slid under my arm, and they dragged me back into the break area.

"Hold her up," Kim ordered, and she slipped behind me while some other body stood in front and gripped each of my upper arms. I heard a fast *zip*, and a blast of cold air attacked my back. The sopping-wet polyester dropped from my chest and gathered along my arms. The hot air escaping made an audible hissing sound, replaced almost instantly by a sharp cold chill.

"Oh, my God!" the guy in front of me gripping my shoulders exclaimed.

Another pair of hands grabbed the costume head on either side, and pulled. Again, a vague sucking sensation, and harsh, brilliant light hit my face at the same time a blast of cold air attacked my head and shoulders.

I saw, not just one person standing nearby, but two dudes, and the girl I recognized from the front counter area. I'd officially made a scene. And I didn't much care.

And then my legs gave out, and bodies rushed forward to hold me up, and then lower me into a chair. "Jesus, look how red she is!"

I closed my eyes, waiting for the room to stop spinning. Someone held a straw under my mouth.

A timid woman's voice spoke near my ear. "Here, drink this, but slow..."

I sucked a huge gulp. The liquid hit my mouth like tiny paper cuts, and I immediately coughed it up.

Everything dropped away for a while.

I woke up to swaths of ice cold against my face and shoulders, opening my eyes against a white cloth. The chilling weight of an ice pack lay awkwardly across the front of my chest.

"What the hell's going on here? Back to your stations! Stacy, you stay. Kim, you, too!" I recognized the voice of owner Teddy, though the severe tone was something new. People were shuffling and leaving in a turmoil.

I reached a hand up toward my face.

Still in the seated position, I pulled the cold towel down and looked up into the girl's kind stare, her blonde hair pulled back and framing a pretty face. Her large blue eyes reflected clear concern as she observed me.

She smiled and extended the large cup of ice water. "Here, try again." Though she spoke softly, her voice reached me. "Slowly, this time. You need to replace all that liquid you lost."

I sipped, and, even though my mouth still hurt, I could swallow. And after a couple swallows, I could breathe deeply again.

"How long?" I heard Teddy snap.

"I'm not sure," Manager Kim admitted. "We were so busy. Did you see the numbers? The customer count was off the chart, so—"

"How long?"

"Maybe an hour, seventy minutes at the most, but we were too busy to—"

"Are you crazy!" The bellowing response cut off any further protests from Kim. "Seventy minutes in this heat! She might have died, and that would have ended our great lunch in a *very* bad way, wouldn't it?"

"I'm sorry sir, I just thought—"

"Obviously, you weren't thinking! I ought to put *your* ass in that costume and send *you* out for an hour, except we both know you couldn't fit in it!"

"I'm sorry, Ted."

"Clock out and go home! I'll call you later and tell you whether you're coming in tomorrow to work your shift or to just turn in your keys. Get out of my sight!"

I patted my face with one of the no-longer-cold cloths. I winced. My whole face felt sunburned wherever the towels touched.

I craned my head to see Kim walk out of the room, but she refused to look at me as she mumbled under her breath.

I coughed, and my mouth filled with snot, an improvement over the dryness of minutes earlier. I swallowed the phlegm down with another mouthful of water.

I reached for my sweet tea, still on the table from when I'd watched the videos. I found I actually had the strength to hold my own cup and sucked on that. The sugar-brewed liquid tasted *so* good.

The room stopped spinning, and I looked over at Teddy, seated in a chair across from me, arms folded across his chest defensively, watching me.

Worker Stacy had vanished, and I realized I must have zoned out again. He looked upon me with what appeared to be genuine concern. "How are you feeling?"

"I think...a whole lot better." I'd found my voice, so I guess that proved the truth of what I said. I pulled my hands out of the yellow feathered sleeves and struggled out of the body suit. Even through the denim, I felt the frosty air hit my sticky-wet legs as I pulled them free of the chicken legs. The costume fell in a yellow heap next to the staring, lifeless head, looking in many ways like some sort of bizarre mafia murder.

"Just leave it," Teddy said, even though I had no intention of cleaning it up.

Bracing my hand on the chair behind me, I rose onto shaking, wobbly legs and waited for balance to return.

Teddy rose, watching me closely as I popped open the locker where I'd stashed my denim jacket. "I don't even know what to say."

I nodded. "Just imagine how *I* feel."

"How *do* you feel? There's a Med-check down the road if you want me to drive you there."

I shook my head. I just wanted to get the hell out of there. I took a couple of steps. My legs shook, but I wasn't in danger of falling, and the second step was easier than the first.

I turned the corner and spied a hand-washing sink, complete with a small shaving mirror. I gasped at the red-faced horror that stared back at me. I looked as if someone had fired a blowtorch a couple inches away from my face; my entire complexion shone a dull pink with highlights of red around the eyes and lips. I turned on the cold water and splashed my face over and over, trying to placate the screaming nerve endings of my tender skin.

I grabbed a paper towel and dabbed it over my face, which only scratched and irritated my skin. I stared at the shocked, sick face reflected back at me.

"You're welcome to come back Monday after school and finish those videos if you want."

I glared at the humbled owner standing nearby. "I like you all right, Teddy. But I wouldn't hold my breath on that happening if I were you."

"Take a day to think about it."

I nodded and turned my back on him, walking up the aisle. If I said anything more, things might get ugly.

He called after me. "Don't worry about clocking out! I'll take care of it."

Furthest thing from my mind, but I didn't say *that*, either.

"Can I give you a ride ba—"

"Goodbye!"

I paused long enough to top off my super-sized sweet tea, the very least they owed me, and made a beeline for the door.

I stumbled across the blacktop and into the grass when I heard someone calling after me.

"Blue! Wait up!"

Chip? I turned and saw him coming up the grass toward me. "Oh, my God!" I reached out. "Thank you *so much!*" As he stepped forward, I wrapped my arms around his waist and held on tight.

His arms draped and clasped behind my back, and his chin nuzzled the top of my head.

"You really saved my ass. I guess that's two I owe you," I said into his shirt.

He planted an affectionate kiss on top of my head. "It wasn't just your ass I was trying to save. I prefer you all in one piece."

Ewww, my hair is still pretty sweaty. For that matter, I was a walking, talking damp rag. But he continued to hold me. *And scoring points every moment.*

A couple of passing cars honked. I giggled as he flinched. "Oh, let them honk, I'm used to it."

We separated moments later, continuing to walk in the direction of home.

I pressed the cool side of the sweet tea cup to my forehead. My scalp started to itch. My other hand was enfolded in his. "What were you doing there? I mean, I'm glad you were, but did you really hang out for over two hours?"

"Well, *yeah*," he said, as if stating the obvious. "I got your text message and wanted to come see you, wish you luck, that sort of thing. I hung out for a while and ate lunch. Just when I was getting ready to give up, you came out in the chicken outfit, or I was pretty sure it was you once you waved at me."

"Good to know you received my telepathic message."

He chuckled. "Something like that. Anyway, I figured I'd better hang out, and I'm glad I did. I kept looking out the window to see how you were doing. After about an hour, I told the manager you probably needed to come in, but she said they couldn't spare anyone while they were so busy."

Chip shook his head and released an exasperated sigh. "Stupid bitch."

I flinched. An expletive from the Chipster was a fairly singular event.

"And somewhere between one glance and the next, that's when you fell. I told the manager I was going to get you, and, of course, she chased after me, suddenly all concerned."

The sidewalk dipped sideways and blurred out of focus. I stopped, waiting for the dizzy spell to pass. Chip's hand squeezed tight, and I pressed down to keep my balance.

"Take it easy. We'll take it slow. I'll make sure you get home okay."

I nodded, glad for his support.

We sorta forgot to release our hands the entire walk home.

I'D NEVER SEEN Mom dote before, but she was hovering around me the moment I cracked open the door, guiding me by the shoulders to the recliner. "Oh, my poor baby, I'm so sorry!"

Okay, who are you and what did you do with my real mom? But I let her seat me then pull the handle so my legs dangled above my head. I flinched at the sight of a white washcloth lowering toward my face then closed my eyes as the cold cloth soothed my still-tender face. *Aaah, now just leave me alone for the next ten years.*

Her hand stroked my head in the lingering silence. I had neither the energy nor the desire to ponder my strange day. I'd practically drifted off to sleep when she spoke. "Ted called and told me what happened."

I tugged the ends of the washcloth and let it drop across my chest. "I've thought about it, and I don't want to pursue legal action. I'd rather just let it alone."

Mom moved to the couch and turned to face me. "Legal action? Why would you want to do that?"

I shrugged, assuming a mock tone of deep thought. "Oh, gee, I don't know. Negligence, endangerment, at the very least they broke one of the super-secret mascot covenants, if not a few laws regarding the safety of a minor. Something there must be actionable, but you'd know better than me."

Mom threw her hands in the air. "I told him I was reluctant to have you go back, but he told me he fired the manager responsible for your incident. He's willing to throw in a twenty-five-cent-per-hour raise if you'll come back and just forget about it."

I shrugged. "A twenty-five-cent raise doesn't mean anything. Nobody had time to tell me what I was making before sending me out to get slow-roasted."

"But he's trying to make it right. He assured me it would never happen again."

"Teddy trained the manager on duty, and, best I can tell, he sat hiding away in the office through the entire lunch rush. *He's* ultimately responsible for what happened to me."

Mom drummed her fingers on the arm of the couch, the *thump-*

thump-thump emphasizing the level of her impatience. "Jobs are *so* hard to come by now. I want you to reconsider."

"Mom, do you think what happened to me was some sort of fluke? That they never get crowds at lunch time? That some other kid's never been stranded out there? Now that I think about it, those other workers seemed to know *exactly* what to do to take care of me."

Mom released a slow, hissing breath as she considered my words. "So this is the thanks I get when I try to help you?"

"Mom, I can't go work at a place that treats their employees like that. Please, I need you to support me on this. I'll find another job."

But I could tell my words had no effect. She'd already made up her mind. Even as she stewed, she was going over the old rant in her head, which I could hear as plain as day. *Good for nothing, ungrateful daughter, after all the sacrifices, yadda-yadda-yadda.*

But she said none of those things. Instead, she slapped the arm of the couch and stood. "Fine. Quit. I give up!" With that, she stormed out of the room.

I sighed and pulled the cloth, no longer cold, across my face.

That makes two of us.

CHAPTER FOURTEEN

Jim watched Jeff Crimley run from the shelter of the car toward the locked gate of Perionne Amusement Park, using the illumination from the headlights to see through the heavy rain.

Crimley fiddled with his maintenance keys until the gate swung open.

Jim eased the car forward.

The car door opened, and Crimley settled into the back seat behind Jim. Glancing into the rearview mirror, he saw Crimley wiping his hands across his wet face, trying to clear his vision. "Damn. Just our luck."

Jim finally asked the one question he'd dreaded voicing all day. "What are we doing?"

Crimley and Gunther had kept Jim cruising the back roads of town all day. They spent several hours driving randomly and getting nowhere, though they did stop long enough for Gunther and Crimley to break into someone's tool shed and run off with a couple of shovels. Now, as it crept up on 10:00, they directed him to the amusement park. Jim knew he couldn't deflect Jessie's suspicions once he returned home. With a tightening in his gut, he wondered about his chances of getting home at all.

He drove slowly along the walking path. Except for the twin beams of light in front of him, the park remained shrouded in total darkness.

Jim knew from previous visits that the roller coaster stretched dead ahead. He squinted through the windshield, peering at the blacktop, which now split off in two directions, straight ahead and to the right. He barely managed to keep the car on the footpath.

"Take the right split," Crimley ordered.

He did as instructed.

Eventually, his headlights revealed a large domed cement structure. He recognized it as the rear wall of the Pirates of Perionne boat ride.

"There." Crimley pointed to a back doorway. "I can get us in there."

Jim turned the car into the mud, centering the headlights on the plain metal door.

Jim fought a growing panic. The memory of all the gangster films he'd seen flooded his brain, movies in which the criminal masterminds inevitably decide the hired flunky has outlived his usefulness and must now "disappear."

"Okay," said Gunther, "It's your plan, Crimley. What's up?"

Crimley shifted in his seat. "Relax, Gunther. We can't be seen with all this money right now. But we gotta make sure no one else finds it."

Gunther cackled. "So we're going to bury it inside the ride?"

"I knew you'd appreciate the joke," Crimley said. "The buried treasure under the buried treasure. No one would ever think to look for it in a place like this. We'll take enough cash to lay low in Michigan for a few weeks. Then when the heat cools down and they think we're long gone, we just sneak back into town and pick it up."

Crimley directed his next words to Jim. "You won't have to worry about a thing."

Because I won't be around to worry? Otherwise, why tell me? They know I can steal the money. The moment the thought came, Jim knew himself for a coward. He'd never return here, no matter what. But would Gunther and Crimley take that chance?

Jim drew a deep breath and put on his bravado. "Go on, then. Get your burying done and over with."

Gunther reached across his lap for the door handle.

"Why don't you come with us, Jim? It'll go a lot quicker with three people digging."

"Hell, no, Gunther. I'm not going to have any part of this. You already got me in deeper than I wanted to be."

The fury he'd fought to keep buried pushed forward. Jim twisted in the seat and stared Gunther in the face. "Now you get your ass in there and hurry it up. Then, I'm dropping you off, and I don't expect to ever see you again. Got me?"

During this exchange, Jim peripherally registered that Crimley had already opened the car door and ran to the building. Now, he struggled with the keys and the maintenance lock to the back door of the ride.

Gunther shrugged, returning Jim's glare with a deadly calm of his own. "Suit yourself. I need the keys to get in the trunk. Then you sit tight. Don't even think of moving 'til we get back. You got me?"

Gunther shifted forward, and Jim could see a glint of madness reflected in his eyes. "If you take off and we get caught, we'll tell the cops all about your part in it."

Jim let out a shaky breath. "The one thing on my mind is getting you two out of my life." He turned the ignition off and handed the keys behind to Crimley.

The rear door opened then slammed shut. Gunther's silhouette moved away from the car. Jim closed his eyes, focusing on the gentle patter of the rain on the roof. *Here it comes. One shot through the windshield, and I'm done.*

For the next couple of minutes, Jim calmed his breathing and listened to the rain.

A flash of red lit the back of his retina, followed by the percussive boom of thunder. Jim's eyes snapped open, and he shrieked. *I don't want to die. I don't want this to be my burial ground.*

The car shifted. Gunther had opened the trunk.

A few seconds later, the car rocked from the sharp slam. There was a knock on the window near his ear. Jim jumped and bit back another whimper.

Gunther's angry voice reached him from the outside. "Open the goddamn window!"

Jim rolled the window down and blinked into the spitting rain.

"Here!" Gunther dropped the ring of keys in Jim's lap. "Listen to the radio or something. But stay put!"

Gunther ran toward the building. He probably knew Jim for the coward he was, knew him with such confidence, he'd let Jim keep the keys to his freedom, positive he'd be too terrified to leave. Perhaps he'd live after all.

GUNTHER STEPPED through the back door of the ride carrying the two shovels in his hand. He brushed a sopping forearm across his face, redistributing the wetness just enough to clear his vision.

He heard a series of loud *click-clacks* overhead, and then the room lit up, showing the small pirate island before him. He stood on a sandy islet surrounded on three sides by the now-silent moat-track leading to a set of double doors.

A wicked-looking pirate mannequin wearing an eye patch loomed close, ready to pivot toward the next boat full of riders. Nearby, a black cauldron sat upon a small rectangular wood porch in the center of the islet. The rain pounded on the roof of the chamber, creating loud and oppressive echoes within.

The side door in the back wall opened. Crimley stepped through, juggling his ring of keys. "That should give us the light we need." Gunther could make out a control room about the size of a broom closet over Crimley's shoulder.

Crimley looked grim-faced. "We got some work ahead of us. Best get started."

Gunther dropped both shovels in the sand. "Here. Help me lift this."

Together, they moved the black cauldron and the framework to one side.

Gunther extended his hook, pointing. "If we bury it right here, and put the black pot back on top of it, we'll have a perfect marker for when we come back."

Crimley nodded. He picked up a shovel and pushed it into the ground. "We should dig down about four feet or so to make sure the money's good 'n buried."

Gunther grabbed the second shovel. He latched his prosthetic hook to the lower part of the wooden handle and pressed the business end of the shovel into the ground using the strength of his good arm. "I'll keep up well enough. Don't worry about me."

They dug together in silence for several minutes until they created a pit large enough for the both of them to stand side by side, burrowing about half a foot.

Gunther continued digging, even when he saw Crimley stop, sweaty and tired. A surge of minor triumph coursed through him. *Another endurance victory for the handicapped man.*

He could sense Crimley's puzzlement. "Gunther, are you sure draggin' Jim into this was a good idea? He doesn't seem up to it. He may be long gone for all we know."

Gunther chuckled. "Just leave ole' Jim to me. I've got him under control."

Crimley sighed. "You're some piece of work."

Gunther stood to his full height, gripping the shovel in his good hand. "What do you care? I got you the driver, just like we agreed."

Crimley stared him down, clearly not intimidated. "Oh, you did a *lot* of things that had nothing to do with our agreement."

"What are you talkin' about?"

Crimley pointed an accusing finger. "You've made us both accessories to murder. That, *partner,* was not a part of the original deal."

Oh, that. He'd forgotten about the killings, and he shrugged off the accusation. "You think I ever robbed a bank before? I just...went nuts when I had the gun in my hand. It's over now. We were leaving town, anyway; now we'll have to leave the country. What difference does it make?"

Gunther waited, wondering how far Crimley would dare to elevate this. Instead, Crimley sighed and said nothing, apparently choosing to keep his thoughts to himself.

AFTER ANOTHER HOUR OF HARD, sweaty work, both men were up to their waists in the hole. They'd removed their jackets long ago. Plenty of time for Crimley to fume over the danger Gunther had put him in.

Crimley finally tossed aside the shovel, bracing himself to finish the unpleasant work ahead. "Okay. This should be more than plenty."

He watched Gunther drop his shovel. "Yeah. I still don't get why it had to be so deep. I mean, there's no way anyone is going to find the money."

Crimley reached his hand into his pocket. "You can never be too sure."

Gunther turned his back to climb out. Quiet as a cat.

Crimley pulled out his pocketknife, unfolding the silver blade.

Gunther shook his head. "Yeah, well, this should be deep enough to discourage any—"

Crimley pressed in close, slamming Gunther against the side of the hole and thrusting the knife between his ex-partner's ribs.

"I needed a big enough hole to bury *you,* you crazy bastard."

Gunther sagged against the hard-packed earth.

Crimley pulled the knife up and out, then took a half-step back. *I need to get out of here.* He realized his mistake too late.

Gunther growled, apparently still having some fight in him. He made a sweeping motion with his arm, catching Crimley off guard.

A distant stab of pain penetrated the red fury of Crimley's anger as Gunther's prosthetic hook sunk in his chest, but he aimed his knife at Gunther's gut, jabbing with all his strength.

"Traitor!" Gunther moaned. "I'll kill you for this."

Crimley pulled the knife out and thrust again, not caring where he hit, as long as the blade penetrated.

Gunther's fingers locked around Crimley's throat in a death grip. The hook twisted in his chest. Crimley pulled up in an automatic reflex, ripping a huge hole in Gunther's exposed belly as they fell.

Before they hit the ground, darkness overcame him.

CHAPTER FIFTEEN

A huge boom of thunder woke Jim from his doze. He twisted the knob to light up the overhead dash and look at his watch. *It's quarter 'ta one, for Chris' sakes.* He'd sat with the engine running and the radio on for three hours, and the rain kept on pouring. He turned the high-beams on, illuminating the metal door in yellow light. *This is crazy.*

The only thing left to do was the last thing he wanted to do.

Mustering his courage, he got out of the car and bolted for the entrance. The door to the ride swung inward, and he scanned the brightly lit treasure scene.

They had moved the cauldron. His eyes focused on the hole in the midst of the island for several seconds before his brain realized its existence.

The hole spread out deep and wide, but from his vantage point, Jim could easily make out the two unmoving figures lying inside, smeared in liquid red.

"Oh, hell!" Jim rushed forward and crouched down, then hopped in.

He stared at Gunther's back for a moment before he latched onto

Gunther's shoulders and pulled him up. Gunther fell over, unresisting, into a reclined position.

The crazed eyes continued to stare ahead.

Jim gripped Gunther by the hair and placed two fingers at his neck to feel for a pulse. *Nothing. Damn it!*

A rush of lightheadedness froze him, and his mind locked. *How could things have gone so horribly wrong?*

A groan of misery reached his ears as if from a great distance. He turned his head to stare at Crimley, who struggled to sit up.

Crimley's eyes blinked open, and cleared in recognition. "Help me. Hurry." The weakness of Crimley's voice shook Jim from his stupor.

Jim abandoned the staring corpse and crawled to get closer to Crimley. "How did this happen?"

"Help me, Jim. I'm dyin'."

Jim rose to his feet, staring down at the torn and bleeding man. The gaping wound in Crimley's chest bled freely, soaking the front of Crimley's T-shirt.

Jim took off his denim jacket and wadded it into a ball. He shoved it against Crimley's chest. "Here. Hold this, and press down hard, you hear me?"

Crimley nodded.

Jim gripped him by the shoulders, then pulled him up and propped him against the edge of the hole.

"Stay right here." He muttered a string of curses. *That's a dumb thing to say. As if Crimley can move.* He grabbed Crimley's shovel and tossed it up, then pulled himself out of the hole.

He stared at the moneybag lying on the ground near the edge. The thought of touching the bag revolted him. With a swift kick of his boot, he sent the moneybag flying, landing atop Gunther's corpse. "There ya' go, ya' son of a bitch. I hope it was worth it."

Jim grunted and cursed, but, with quiet efficiency, he buried Gunther's body and the moneybag in the dirt.

During the process, Crimley kept fading in and out of consciousness, but the man didn't complain. Jim knew Crimley would not live through the night without help.

He lifted Crimley out of his corner of the hole and carried him out to the car.

"Here," Crimley said, reaching out and handing Jim the keys. "Turn out the lights in the control booth. But make sure the room looks the same."

Jim nodded and ran back.

In less than half an hour, he finished the burial. He glanced at the platform underneath the cauldron that hid the freshly turned dirt beneath. Jim scattered the decorative doubloon coins around as best he could. On a boat ride in the dark, it would look good enough.

He found three small dots of blood near the door, still wet, which he wiped clean with a handkerchief.

Jim threw the shovel in the trunk and got into the car, driving back toward town, uncertain what to do.

Crimley stirred next to him and called out. "Jim! I need to get to the hospital. Please, hurry. I'm gonna die."

Jim gunned the engine. He could reach the emergency room in three minutes.

"Jim, come on, I'm..." Crimley passed out again.

Fighting back a growing dread, Jim pulled over and checked for a pulse. He could barely find it. "Crimley? Crimley! Oh, no."

Jim buried his face in his hand. The rain continued to pour. *I can't go to the hospital. I can't keep Crimley. I can't stay here with a body in my car.*

He strained to come up with options. *Crimley's as good as dead; why should all our lives be ruined?*

The answer came to him in sudden clarity, along with a cold determination to see it through.

He got out of the car, walked to the passenger side, and yanked at Crimley's shirt.

Crimley slumped sideways, fell to the shoulder, and landed with a thud. A grunt escaped his lips. "Jim, don't do this…"

As Jim tried to stand, Crimley reached up, pulling at Jim in desperation.

Jim cursed and pulled his jacket out of from the clawing grip of the dying man. He popped the trunk and threw the jacket inside.

"Jim!" The voice calling out in the rain seemed to find new strength. "Don't leave me!"

A flicker of compassion lit up deep inside. "I'm sorry, Crimley. I truly am. But you did this to yourself. I won't pay for it the rest of my life."

Jim climbed back into the car. He took a deep breath, mentally shutting out the quiet voice of his conscience begging him to turn around before it was too late. Instead, he hit the accelerator and drove off into the rainy night.

CHAPTER SIXTEEN

Without Joey-like distractions, I absorbed myself in schoolwork. For pleasure, I read my books and fiddled with my poetry, basking in the theoretical freedom to smoke, drink, and party at will. At the same time, I patted myself on the back for not doing any of those things. I chalked it up to my newfound self-discipline.

Miz Leona Shaefer, Super-Attorney, drummed up enough business to keep her in the office after-hours an average of four nights a week. But not tonight. "I'm taking a short trip. I need to wrap a few things up in Indy this weekend."

Seated at the dinner table, I tried to keep my voice casual. "Can I go with you?"

She shook her head. "I'm checking into a hotel room and eating out. I'm spending the rest of my time at the old office building. It's not a vacation, Fiona."

Before I could argue, she pointed at my plate. "Eat your vegetables."

I stabbed a fork into an unnaturally hard carrot. "Yes, Mommy Dearest. It's the least I can do after all the minutes you spent defrosting this delicacy in a pot of boiling water."

She opened her mouth to fire off what was sure to be a scathing retort when the phone rang. I rose from my chair before she could move. "I'll get that."

The wireless headset laid free of its cradle on the edge of the counter I stabbed the "Call" button. "Hello?"

"Hi, Blue."

"Chip! Great timing. I just finished eating." I waved at Mom, who shook her head in disgust and picked up our dishes.

As I made small talk, I watched Mom dart around the house to set up shop in the living room. She barely glanced at me as she strolled by to turn on the TV and then grabbed a stack of paperwork.

I hurried into my room with the cordless to keep the conversation private.

I curled up on the bed and made myself comfortable, determined to put off my algebra homework as long as possible.

Chip chattered in my ear. "So how long do you think before Perionne Park closes?" His voice filled with a casual curiosity, as if he presumed I had some stake in the question.

It took me a while to recall the dilapidated old amusement park I'd seen on my way into town, and I hadn't given the wannabe-Disneyland another thought.

"Why? Is the Board of Safety looking to shut it down?" I rolled over and got comfortable.

"No, Blue. The park closes every year when it gets too cold to support business. Last year, they'd already ended the season by this time."

"From the road, it looks deserted."

"Oh, no, not at all!"

I held the phone away from my ear to save my eardrum from his enthusiasm.

"Perionne Park's been doing great business since it opened."

As much as I wanted to give Chip one hundred percent of my attention, just about anything else was more interesting than Perionne Park.

Chip droned on. "It'll probably be around long after you and I have left here."

That deserved a response. "Well, it will certainly outlast *me*, since I graduate next May, and am fully prepared to do a disappearing act immediately afterward."

Somehow Chip sounded put off by my lack of excitement. "Clearly you mock what you don't understand. We're pretty proud of the park around here."

When I added nothing to the conversation, he continued. "Every year, we try to guess how many more weeks we have before it closes."

"Mmm-hmm. That's very interesting. No, wait, I'm wrong. It's not interesting at all." I grinned at the mouthpiece, expecting a big laugh at my amazing wit.

Instead, Chip ran right over my sarcasm. "The Pirates of Perionne is one of the best rides of its kind. It's a pirate boat ride. Kinda slow, but it has outstanding mannequin effects. I've been hoping to one day use some of the imagery in a video game."

I grinned again. His dorky excitement had a certain charm that made it hard for me to make fun of him. But I still tried.

"We-ell," I said. "Let me check my busy social calendar. Hmm. You know what? I think the idea of us, you and I, together at the town park would be mind-blowing, just to see the looks on everyone else's faces. Okay, it's a date. *If* you think you can handle it. Tell ya what. I'll spike the hair extra high and break out my leather miniskirt and high-heeled boots. I'll put on my prowler girl costume just for you, Chip. They'll think you won a contest at the local strip club."

"Ah..." Chip floundered.

I showed no mercy. "You *do* have a strip club around here, or do I presume too much?"

Chip ignored the question. "Maybe you should just put on what you normally wear."

"Ha! Chicken shit. As if *that* will save you." I propped myself on an elbow. "Listen. Mom's going back to Indy for the weekend. Let's head straight to the park after school, and we'll make an evening of it. Maybe Saturday we can catch a movie."

"Sounds good. I guess it's a date."

WALKING home from school the next evening, shuffling across the sidewalk to the house, I saw the old woman. Sylvia slowly rocked and stared out at the street.

As I passed the house, her head craned to follow me. She squinted in open scrutiny. I walked along the stone bricks cutting though my lawn, trying to pretend her attention didn't give me goosebumps.

Her hands wove her knitting needles in an automatic motion through the off-white something spread upon her lap, the same something she'd been working on the day we'd met. The intensity of her gaze sent a chill through me.

She spoke in a rasping whisper that didn't quite carry across the yard.

I fished in my pocket, looking for my keys, debating whether or not I should pretend I didn't hear her.

Like they had a mind of their own, the keys slipped from my hands and bounced across the cement and into the lawn.

"Young girl, come here, I say!" She must have known her voice reached my ears this time; no sense in denying it.

I stepped onto the grass, retrieved my mutinous key chain, and trudged across my lawn to trade words with my creepy neighbor.

Her cloudy eyes reminded me of nonfat milk. Kinda opaque white with a bluish tint surrounding them.

Hands in pockets, I stared at her, waiting.

She rocked back and forth, a half-smile curling her thin lips.

"I hear you are beginning to settle into our town." Her voice grated on me like crinkled sandpaper, and my legs itched from the contact with the dried stalks of what used to be a lawn.

"Oh. I didn't know we had any mutual friends."

"I hear things."

I waited, but she didn't elaborate.

I was not in the mood to play "cryptic comments" with her. "Look. Not that it's any of your business, but I'm only committed to this nut house until graduation." I fidgeted where I stood. Being around this old woman made me want to have a cigarette, a habit I'd hoped I'd given up when I gave up Joey.

Sylvia settled back into her knitting, her gaze dropping down, away from me. "Where would you say, then, that you belong, young lady?" Her hands moved, continuing in their mundane repetition. Her rocking remained constant.

I shrugged. "Chicago, Los Angeles, New York. Any big city. Even Indy will do. Someplace with good music and lots of people. Someplace relevant."

"Strange to want to leave. When I was a girl, growin' up in Perionne, I didn't want to ever move away."

For a wicked moment, I entertained asking if she grew up with a car or if she rode to school on horseback. I resisted the urge. Instead, I reached down and plucked a piece of dead grass. "Times have changed."

She nodded and continued her knitting. "Kids leave for the city while the city folk, why, they turn around and hightail it out to us. Everyone's restless for something different. Nobody's satisfied. Hmmm."

Just when I thought she must have lost her train of thought, she started up again. "My boy wasn't ever satisfied." She looked up, shaking a bony finger at me like I'd been personally responsible for her "boy's" selfishness. "Always restless. Always wanting more."

"Boy?" How old might Sylvia's son be now? Quite possibly a grandfather himself.

I couldn't figure out how Sylvia's legs didn't give out from all the rocking she did. The woman must be in her early nineties, yet her hands were as nimble as her feet.

Sylvia took a deep, shaky breath. "Thing is, my boy never left the town, either. Been restless his whole life, but he's never seen more than the twenty miles of Perionne. I told him one time he should git'. But he never did." She stopped knitting and looked me straight in the eye. "Paid for it, too."

Okay, now I want to run home and slam the door.

Sylvia shook her frail head. "Nope, he never left. Shoulda tried harder to kick him out. He mighta thanked me in the end."

"Where is he now?"

She continued rocking. "He's around. Here and there." I contemplated the latest cryptic comment. A strong breeze blew across the yard, rustling my jacket and causing a bunch of leaves to flurry over the cracked pavement. "He's around," she repeated, her words almost lost to the wind blowing across my ears.

The chill from the resulting gust cut through my denim jacket. Now I was *cold.* "Look, Sylvia, I'd better get going. I have a test to study for."

Sylvia perked up. "Test, you say?"

"Yes. The midterm for American Folklore's going to have a lot on that Gunther guy everyone gets so worked up about."

"You're studying Gunther," she said, her eyes reflecting intense interest. "Learning about the ghost, are ya?"

"Sort of. The teacher doesn't believe the stories, but we're learning them, anyway."

Her eyes flashed anger. "Thomas Haplin is a young fool. You take heed in what you hear about the ghost. The ghost of Gunther is real, girlie. Seen him myself several times. Never sneer at things you don't understand." She waved a tangled knitting needle at me. "You remember that, an' you'll live to be older than me." She cackled in that freaky way again.

Oh, Lord, I hope not! "Yes, ma'am," I answered, backing away.

She nodded and dropped her gaze back toward her knitting, apparently satisfied she'd confused me enough for one day.

I stepped across the crunching leaves and angled toward the door of the house, my sanctuary. Only after shutting the door behind me did I breathe a sigh of relief. I wiped cold sweat from my brow, even as I told myself not to get worked up about the delusions of an old woman.

THAT NIGHT, I curled up on Mom's leather chair in the darkened living room, the single spotlight lamp behind my shoulder illuminating the stack of papers on the coffee table before me. Mom had crashed early, a little after eight, to be fresh for her weekend trip.

Outside, the wind howled, rattling the windows and shaking the blinds with unusual ferocity. I unfolded the handout, trying to read the first article regarding the legend of Gunther Stalt. I'd barely glanced at the material since the first day of school.

This afternoon, Chip had tried to assure me that the test would probably not focus on Gunther all that much. After all, Gunther remained the homegrown legend, discussed over and over, year after year. An easy "A" for the rest of the class.

The first blurry Xeroxed article, dated July 15th, 1991, offered an overview of the November 10th incident of the previous year, encapsulating the events of the daring daylight robbery at Perionne National Bank. Since the money was never recovered, it remains the only unsolved bank robbery in the town's one hundred and thirty year history. Remembering that Hap had said something to the same effect, I ran a highlighter across this sentence and turned the page.

The next article showed a copy of the front page of the *Perionne Gazette* the day after the actual robbery. The headline read, ***TWO DEAD IN DARING BANK HEIST***.

I read the story, trying to absorb the facts. All in all, the crime was pretty cut and dry. They botched it. Crimley calling out Gunther's name, for instance, struck me as tragic and comical at the same time. How did Gunther manage to disappear without a trace?

I turned the page and found myself staring at an article dated a week later, providing a bullet-point overview of the robbery and its after-effects, while reminding the community about a theoretical getaway driver.

So the questions remained. Had Gunther died? Where had the stolen money disappeared to? Did Gunther manage to get past the roadblocks and take it across state lines, or was the money still somewhere in town?

I rubbed my eyes, checking over my outline, certain I'd snagged all the facts regarding the legend.

I sighed, turning the handout pages to Section Two. These articles involved the various, and numerous, sightings of the "ghost of Gunther Stalt." I held between my fingers a stack of thirty pages. No longer fit for the front page, the *Gazette* buried these bits of gossip on the middle or back pages. Based on Hap's assessment of the ghost sightings, I treated the stories the same way.

Since the robbery, witnesses claimed to see an apparition with a hook for a hand in various cornfields and alleyways around the town, often witnesses of questionable sobriety or mental capacity. I stared again at the Gothic sketch of a wraith-like comic-book ghost reaching off the page.

I flipped to the next article, a three-part series of interviews with Gunther's mother, in which she admitted to hearing her son's voice from the Netherworld. He apparently whispered in his mother's ear, telling the deep, dark secrets of Perionne society. Strange and bizarre stuff; the reporter assured us much of it was unsubstantiated gossip that could not be printed in the article.

But the accompanying photograph of Gunther's mother, with her familiar features, made my head spin. I stared at the image of Sylvia Stalt, already ancient back in 1991. Her listed address, even at the time? *Right fucking next door, thank you very much.*

The door rattled from a sudden gust of wind, making me jump and emit a squeaky gasp. *Good going, tough girl.* I walked through the darkness to shut the blinds and block out the moonlight.

Through the slits, I could see the empty rocking chair on the porch next door, swaying back and forth. I shut the blinds on the eerie scene, trying to shake off a chill that wouldn't leave me.

CHAPTER SEVENTEEN

I spent the rest of the week anticipating my date with Chip. I surprised myself at how much I looked forward to it. As I slogged through my classes, Friday evening lingered on my mind. I counted the hours 'til I could put the schoolwork away and spend quality time with my buddy outside of a school setting. Even the backdrop of a broken-down amusement park beat the hell out of the cafeteria.

Friday finally blew in on a not-too-bitter early October breeze, carrying a billow of dark clouds that overcast the sun. I'd wrapped my leather jacket over a bundle of clothes, stashed them in my locker, and, after school, changed in the restroom.

The jacket fit snugly across my chest and cropped across my ribcage. I wore a tie-dye T-shirt that extended a bit farther down than the jacket. A rim of skin showed around my waist, revealing the top of my hip-hugging blue jeans. The high-heeled black stripper boots and a pair of cheap sunglasses, hiked up over my forehead, and my super-spiked blue hair completed the scandalous image.

I sauntered down the hallway, where Chip waited for me, his

back against a row of battered lockers. He straightened when he saw me, and I couldn't help but enjoy his bug-eyed gawk.

Chip took my hand, and we gabbed about nothing much while we hoofed it to the park.

Once there, Chip sprang the eight bucks for a pair of enter-all passes, little bracelets of plastic clipped around our wrists.

I held out my wrist and grinned at the shocked expression of the woman in the ticket booth. I guess she didn't appreciate the latest in skanky 'ho fashion.

Chip and I strolled along the main paved walkway. The groups and couples shuffling back and forth gave us a wide berth. Chip pretended he didn't see the stares and gawks, and I ignored them. In my peripheral vision, I spied Clinty and a couple of his gang draped over a park bench like damp laundry. As we walked past, they turned to glare at us.

I couldn't help it; feeling their eyes upon me, I strutted, putting an extra swing to my hips. I recognized several of the gawking faces, boys I'd seen in the halls, or doing chores in the yard.

The walkway appeared to loop in a gradual curve, circling the park. Chip leaned close. "What first?"

I'd already spotted five variations of the "spin-and-barf." We hadn't eaten yet, but I wasn't ready to shake up my intestines. Spotlights brightened the roller coaster framework. Craning my neck to take in the coaster, immodestly called the Whirlwind, I could only see a portion of the first drop, which rose high above us. The train reached the top of the hill, and we could hear the sudden acceleration of the wooden cart. The *click-clack* of the rails increased, and the car dropped over the abyss. Loud, distant screams echoed with the plunge.

I dipped my head toward the Whirlwind. "Oh, come on, Chip, I'm a big coaster fan. I hit King's Island and Holiday World at least twice a year. This is *bound* to be a disappointment."

The walkway forked toward the coaster line. Chip shrugged. "I've ridden those coasters, too, and I actually prefer the Whirlwind. It's older and in disrepair, which actually gives it an advantage in offering thrills."

I squeezed his hand. "Popcorn, ice cream, and a threat to life and limb. What more can a girl ask for? Oh, wait, I guess I shouldn't ask until I get the popcorn and ice cream." I grinned.

His fingers tightened on mine. A flush ran up my body, and I felt oddly like Prom Girl Barbie on her date with Quarterback Ken. *Strange.*

We reached the back of the line, and a few hostile faces turned toward us. No comments, but some of the twenty-something guys leered openly, and I saw someone's girlfriend elbow her companion for gazing too long. I untangled Chip's fingers from mine, and slipped my hand around his upper arm, gripping affectionately.

Up ahead, I recognized the friendly face and dumpy profile of Phil, Chip's D&D friend. Phil held hands with a petite redhead I didn't recognize. They leaned against the metal bar partition in the long line for the first car.

Phil waved at us from across the line, and I waved back.

The redhead, taken aback, gave Phil a perplexed look.

He whispered a few words to her, and then she smiled at me. The cars loaded up, and we eased forward.

We shuffled our way around the partition and caught up with Phil and his date.

"Hiya, Fi-Fi!" Phil reached out and gripped my arm. "I want you to meet Mary Rowan. Mary, this is Fi-Fi Shaefer, the new girl I told you about the other day."

"Ah..." Mary glanced around. I tried to ignore the turning faces, the watching eyes, the barely heard whispers all around us.

Mary waved in my direction and I waved back. Her bright red hair and pretty face worked to her advantage. She carried her stocky, compact body with exactly that sort of demeanor that screamed "loving and loyal, serious relationships only."

I tried not to instantly hate her. To her credit, when she spoke in her hard Indiana drawl, her voice sounded genuine and unchallenging. "Hi...Fi-Fi. Yer every bit as flamboyant as I've heard. And Phil told me 'bout your run-in with Clinty."

I raised my eyebrows.

Mary hurried on. "I'm real sorry about that. Must not 'a given a good impression of our town." She spoke with a sincerity that made me blush.

"I don't hold the town responsible for the actions of one bully."

We stood in an awkward silence, which she eventually broke. "Perionne ain't bad. We just take a while getting used to some types."

I nodded.

"I won't jump to conclusions if you won't." Though I remembered all-too-well the attitude I wore the first day of school. Not *whether* there'd be trouble, but rather who would it come from, and how soon.

Rather than jumping at my challenge, Mary continued in her apologetic tone. "We're not exactly throwing Clinty a ticker-tape parade. In fact, that fight earned you a little fan club."

I shook my head. I didn't want to argue, partly because she was Phil's friend, and I liked Phil. "Forget it."

Phil interrupted, clearly anxious to change the subject. "So has Chip taken you on The Pirates of Perionne boat ride yet?" I saw a mischievous gleam in his eyes.

"Ah, no; why?"

"We're doing that next," Chip said. I could feel his entire body bristle through my hand on his forearm.

Phil chuckled and moved closer to me. "Be careful with him on that. It's, like, his personal obsession. In an unhealthy kind of way. I don't even think he realizes the ride's just an excuse to make out."

I smirked. "Oh, well, maybe I can enlighten him."

Chip pulled me forward, away from the couple. "Come on, Blue, the line's moving."

Playing up the moment, Phil cupped his hands to his mouth, calling out. "He's weird. He thinks that pirate ride is the greatest thing ever created. Check out his notebook. Sketches, notes, diagrams. Weird, I tell you. I mean, I thought *Catwoman* was a pretty good movie, but...okay, maybe that makes me weird."

I raised my eyebrows. "Maybe?"

Phil grinned. "But this is a whole other level."

"But, Phil," I said, "I'm told it's one of the best rides of its kind."

"Blue!" Chip sounded betrayed.

On a roll, I barely noticed. "And the mannequin effects are truly outstanding."

Phil laughed. "Did you believe him?"

I shrugged. "I just figured it was a pickup line."

Chip hunched his shoulders. "It wasn't!"

I turned to look at him. "Relax, dear. It's *okay* that it was a pickup line."

Phil made a twirling motion with his index finger pointed to his head. "He even tried to hack the blueprints. Threw a hissy when we found the blueprints were pre-Internet."

Mary's quiet voice interrupted us. "That's enough."

I tugged at Chip's arm, pulling him against me and speaking with a seductive purr. "Golly, Mister Farren, is the ride as good as all that? I'm always up to trying a new good ride! *Meow!*"

Mary called. "Phil, the line's moving."

Chip waved at the departing couple. "Sorry to see you go."

I wiggled my fingers at Phil and Mary. They pushed forward with the crowd, and we walked the opposite direction.

I strolled after Chip, who stomped ahead, pulling away from me.

I caught up to him and grabbed his hand. "So, Chip, how come I keep hearing your name associated with the word 'hacker?'"

"Oh, lay off already!" He yanked his hand away. The bitter undertone in his comment took me out of teasing mode.

"Hey, come on, we were only kidding." The way he'd withdrawn from me stung more than I'd expected.

"He was being an asshole," Chip said. "And you were egging him on."

I stepped in front of him, forcing him to stop. I couldn't believe the pout hanging on his face. "We were *kidding.* Come on, will you lighten up? You're *supposed* to be silly."

Just when I thought I'd be stuck with a sullen date, Chip's mood changed, like he flipped an internal switch. He reached out and put his hand over mine. "You're right, Blue. Let's forget about it."

Satisfied that my irresistible charm had won him over, I practically skipped alongside him while we closed the gap in the line.

He grinned in my direction. "Did you see the folks watching you talk with Mary Rowan? If that keeps up, you'll be getting invitations to the sleepovers in no time."

"Now who's teasing?"

We entered the gate for the second car, and I saw the loading and unloading process for the first time. I found something oddly disturbing about the cars.

"Where are the bars? I only see a leather strap."

"Bars?" Chip's eyes squinted.

I watched while the couple in front of us pulled the single belt across their laps and clamped the end into a metal hook attached to the side of the care. "Oh, you mean the restraint? This coaster doesn't have one. The safety commissioner was supposed to oversee the installation of modern harnesses three years ago."

"And?"

"Perionne hasn't had a safety commissioner in office for five years."

"You're not serious!" But nothing in his tone suggested amusement. I turned toward him in indignation. "I'm going to go sliding all over that seat. There's room for three of me in there."

"That's because you have no butt to speak of." His inflection never changed, but I could see a twinkle of humor in his eyes.

I swatted his arm, but without anger. "That's for peeking. Is that any way to talk to a lady?"

Chip chose to ignore that opening. "Relax, Blue. I'm here to protect you."

"Yeah? So why am I not filled with confidence?"

The train pulled forward. I could see the couple, still laughing, their faces flushed, struggling to remove themselves from the car.

I tried to be a good sport but, in spite of myself, I cringed when the coaster pulled forward, and I saw the wide seat I had to step into. Chip, not exactly a bulky guy, dropped down into the rickety wood car and slid onto the ripped red upholstery seat.

Biting the bullet, I dropped down next to him. His arm slipped across the back of my shoulders. Our clones could have fit on either side of us, and the four of us would have been quite comfortable.

Chip reached over with the leather strap, pulling it across our laps and tucking the eye over the metal hook attached to the train just outside the seating compartment, giving the belt a hard, meaningful tug.

"Oh. Oh, *hell*, no!" I tugged at the strap, examining the slack...the *gaping* slack...across my lap. "Chip, I'm serious. This won't hold me."

"Blue, relax. After all, you've ridden the *big* coasters at King's Island and Holiday World. This is bound to be a disappointment."

"Oh, you! Fine, I promise I'll never use your words against you again. Let's just—"

The car jerked forward, and I fell back. A gust of wind flew into my face, and the rest of my complaint vanished down the back of my throat as the coaster chugged away into the darkness.

The car shook when the train tipped up the incline, and I dropped back against the seat, my feet flailing in open space, just out of reach of the floor. I heard more preliminary screaming and the monotonous *click-clack* as the coaster started the ascent.

I had no leverage.

Sheer terror jolted through me.

My left hand gripped for dear life against the side of the car. The other hand found a wad of Chip's shirt. "Shit!"

I turned to see a wide grin on Chip's face.

"You're enjoying this, you pig!" But I grinned back, elated and terrified all at once.

Chip squeezed my shoulder, and I could feel his legs press toward the floorboards. "Hold on." He kicked down and secured his feet. I pulled against him to wiggle firmly into the seat just as the car's *click-clack* slowed, indicating the coaster had reached the top of the hill and righted momentarily. I pressed my legs against the interior. The rest of my body braced for the inevitable plummet.

I caught an aerial view of the town, splayed out across the distant horizon, a tiny spot of suburbia dotted along a stretch of highway and farmland. Under different circumstances, I might have enjoyed the sight.

The bottom dropped out beneath me, and wind whipped into a vortex across my face.

I heard a whisper blow over the air.

Bluuuue...

Icy terror caught in my throat. My breath seized up.

The train dropped into a violent descent.

Fierce velocity pressed against me. *Click-clack* sped into a deafening *clatter*.

The strap dug into my abdomen, burning. Flutter winds darted up my legs.

I could no longer feel the seat under me. I flew through the darkness, my screams mingling with the euphoric terror of the other passengers.

My sunglasses, forgotten until that moment, spun off my head, never to be seen again.

The coaster dipped out of its first decline and charged uphill. I slammed into the seat, the pressure forcing tears from my eyes. They streaked across my face, and I didn't dare let go to wipe them away.

Up and down, and up, the coaster threw me around, rendering me bruised and breathless.

I hated it.

I loved it.

Then, we hit a corkscrew, plummeting into total darkness.

The world twisted, turned inside out, and then righted itself.

The coaster fell like a tornado, a constant, spiraling decline.

We spun into the forest, and the wind called me again, stinging my face.

Bluuuuuuuue...

I raised my arms and screamed through the final dizzying moments.

Brakes screeched, jarring us to jolting halt. Spent, I squeezed my eyes shut, feeling the car chug along the last few feet of track at a more conventional speed.

My throat hurt, and I couldn't find my voice.

The next thing I knew, Chip scrambled out to stand on the wooden platform, reaching down toward me. I placed my chilled hands in his.

He pulled me up and out of the coaster.

I leaned against him, dazed and giggling like a madwoman. I could feel solid planked floor beneath my shaking legs, and I clung to Chip.

He put his arm over my shoulder, although he was none-too-steady himself, and we stumbled to the exit.

I finally found my voice. "Wow. I mean...fucking wow!"

Chip panted his response. "It's only great because it's a safety hazard."

CHAPTER EIGHTEEN

If Chip wanted to prep me for a slow ride, I could not have been more ready. I still had trouble willing my trembling legs to hold my weight. And so, with a hand grasped on either shoulder, Chip led me, unresisting, down the sidewalk path to the Pirates of Perionne.

No more than five people stood in line waiting to get onto the boat ride. Chip took me off the path to a set of wooden stairs. A wood-carved handrail split the middle of the stairs to create separate enter/exit lanes. We descended down the "enter" side, which led us to a circular cement platform in the midst of a small manmade lake. Surrounding the cement base, a motorized, rotating, circular wood porch guided the tiny boats in and out of the enclosed track.

Two attendants scrambled across the rotating platform, one helping couples and families exit out of the floating capsules, the other running a squeegee over the plastic interior and guiding the entering groups to their ride.

We stepped onto the rotating platform. In spite of my shaky legs, it only took a moment to adjust. As we walked across the platform, Chip took my hand.

Our shoes made loud clomping noises on the wood.

Chip stopped at the edge of the dock and handed me into the slippery plastic of the boat interior. I squatted down, and he dropped directly behind me.

Nice!

I generally enjoyed this sort of Tunnel of Love thing as a lark. As Phil had indicated, mannequin boat rides provided the perfect backdrop for a little snuggling, and I needed some snuggling in the absolute worst way.

I leaned back, placing my head on Chip's shoulder.

His arms enclosed either side of me, fingers brushing across my stomach. I reached down and enfolded my hands in his.

A shiver ran up my spine, partly from a chill and partly from something else. His body shifted, and he pulled me against him into a more secure embrace. His hands trembled in mine.

Chip's warm breath brushed against my ear. "Better?"

"Much, thank you, sir." If I were a kitten, I would have purred.

I saw a sheepish grin on his face. I grinned back, and then settled against him, caressing his warm hands. Now that the adrenaline rush had run its course, I'd become tired and droopy-eyed.

The boat disengaged from the rotating porch and propelled forward toward a double-door entry. The image of a pirate, black patch covering one eye, grinned at us before the nose of the boat forced the doors open, splitting him down the middle. The doors closed behind us, and the boat drifted into total darkness.

The sound of rippling water soothed my me, though my nose wrinkled in an involuntary response to a moldy odor riding upon the too-humid air.

I heard a click, and spotlights from overhead snapped up to reveal a huge mock pirate ship before us. The room erupted in the sound of cackles and screams and a hearty pirate "Yo-Ho-Ho" song echoing through the chamber. A large crew of stuffed pirate mannequins took turns attacking our boat as it floated past.

I smiled, amused to hear the warped musical tones, the telltale sign of an audio tape still on active duty long past its intended use.

"Argh! Is that a gold ring yer' wearing?" a "pirate" called out, swinging a plastic sword toward the boat in an arc that passed harmlessly overhead.

Giggling, I craned my head back. "Maybe he means my belly-button ring. But I think I left it at home. Care to check?"

Chip's body tensed, but his fingers tightened around my hands. "Not right now, Blue."

Oh, well.

Another pair of doors split, and we floated into a new chamber. Hedonistic tropical music assaulted my ears while the boat encircled an island.

A pirate chased a blonde damsel across the beach, the distorted music muffling the whirr of the crane carrying them both along a track. Other pirates fended off dark-skinned natives, sword-to-spear. Arms and legs gyrated and rocked in amusing fencing action.

I drifted, content to let the scenes unfold around me. On the verge of falling asleep, I watched with a sort of detached fascination.

We floated by a sandy lagoon supporting a wooden-planked deck, covered in glittering doubloons.

A cackling pirate, standing next to an ominous black cauldron, emitted a shrieking "HAR!" at us.

The soundtrack, set to eleven, jarred me from my slumber and, startled, I pressed back against Chip.

The pirate leaned forward, pointing a short sword in my direction, still shrieking too loudly, "Git yer own gold, matey! This be all mine!"

It continued to cackle at high volume while the boat floated out of the room and into the night air.

A shiver ran over my body from the chill.

Or perhaps something else.

I sat up, now fully awake and annoyed. I adjusted my jacket and shirt, let the attendants think what they wanted, and waited patiently while Chip rose up from behind me and stepped up onto the rotating plank.

I reached up with both arms, gripping his outreaching hands.

He braced himself, allowing me to stand and rise to my feet. Then, his hands dropped to my waist. He lifted me out of the wet boat and placed me down onto the platform. I sighed, sad it was already over.

Still holding my hand, Chip led me up the stairs, oddly somber and quiet for the next several moments. "So what did you think? Wasn't it great?"

"Well, I think you owe me a hotdog."

We stepped back onto the walkway. Chip chuckled. "It's a deal."

I slowed my pace, feeling somber. "Seriously, Chip, the last date I had in Broad Ripple, my ex-boyfriend escorted me down an alleyway and tried to get me to do shots with him. As if he needed to get me drunk to do whatever he wanted." *Yikes, did I just say that out loud?* "And I'm *so* sorry, I'm talking *way* too much. Let's go get that hotdog."

Chip stared at me, blank-faced. "I'm sorry, Blue."

I shrugged. I decided at that moment to stop feeling sorry for myself. "The ride was fun. The evening's been great, Chip." I reached my arm around his back and pulled him into a half-hug. "You're a good friend. And I really need one right now."

He looked down at me and smiled, draping his own arm across my shoulders. "We losers have to stick together."

I giggled. "That's right, no one's running us out of town as long as we watch each other's back."

"You're going to be okay, Blue."

I sighed, suddenly very tired. "Besides, you mentioned a movie tomorrow. I think the new Vin Deisel just opened."

"Please. I've let my testosterone shots slip."

"Or we could just go to the theater and see what's playing. I don't really care what movie we see. As long as I'm with you."

A smile warmed my entire face. "Thanks."

ADVANCING TOWARD HOME, we walked in darkness along the sidewalk. We held hands, occasionally chatting.

We passed beyond Sylvia's porch and stopped in my front yard. The house loomed in complete darkness before us.

Chip shrugged nervously and squeezed my shoulder. "I'll come by tomorrow around noon. I'll see you then."

I grinned. "Looking forward to it." I reached out and clasped both his hands, glancing at him in expectation. "Chip, I had a great time."

He smiled back. "Me, too. Goodnight, Blue." He paused a moment, then disengaged his hands and turned away, walking off into the darkness.

I swallowed back disappointment. His fidgeting, hesitating, awkward responses throughout the night screamed inexperience. *Patience, Fi-Fi. It's not lack of interest.* Still, a final goodnight kiss would have been the perfect ending.

I stepped carefully across the cement stones leading to the house. My mother had already left for her trip. Only darkened windows remained to greet me.

Like a slap, the harsh white brightness of the front porch light next door struck me in the face.

What in the—

I turned toward Sylvia's house, holding a hand out to ward off the blinding light. I blinked away spots, waiting for my vision to clear.

I called out, irritated as hell. "That was *not* nice, old lady! You'd better—"

My eyesight cleared, and the vision of Sylvia, still sitting and rocking in her chair, halted the complaint in my throat.

I stole a glance at my little Indiglo digital watch, 11:42 p.m.

I stood, paralyzed with shock and fear, watching the rocking silhouette. Her head rested at an awkward angle against the side of the chair. She continued rocking even with her eyes closed.

I called out. "Ma'am?"

She didn't move. Best I could tell, her body appeared stiffened in the chair, like a pile of dry mulch. A sudden wind gusted between us, rustling the new-fallen leaves.

I walked across the yard, closing the space between us. "Sylvia," I called again.

I stepped onto the porch, fighting a sudden urge to run. *Please, God, don't let her be dead!*

I turned away, gazing at the closed door that held the sanctity of my home, and then turned back.

A musty smell hit my nose, overpowering even the cold fresh air.

Sylvia was gone.

The chair stopped rocking with an abruptness that made me jump.

The wind blew and leaves rolled across the porch. I blinked, telling myself she'd never been there, that I had imagined seeing her. *Maybe I passed out and dreamt...*

But then, a gravelly voice whispered, "Guntherrrrrr..."

A shudder passed over me like an electrical current. I couldn't shake the dreadful feeling that I had seen her.

The wind howled, and an eerie voice floated on the breeze. "Bluuuuue..."

In spite of myself, I shrieked and backed away from the porch. *Nothing more to see here.*

I bravely walked away, trotting, *not running, dammit!*, to my house.

I shut the door on the wind and the old woman's porch.

I switched on all the lights, hurrying down the hallway and into my own room at the end of the hall. I stripped off my clothes, dropping them on the floor, and pulled a long T-shirt over my head. Settling under the covers, I waited for the shakes to pass. But it took a long time.

CHAPTER NINETEEN

Staring at the reflection in the bathroom mirror, I'd just finished brushing on a thin coating of blue eyeliner when the doorbell rang. I glanced at the reflection of the clock, quarter to twelve.

Chip had arrived early, but I already looked dazzling. Hair combed, slight spike, mascara, faint color on the eyes and lips so I looked less rebel and more cutie, but in a subtle way. I applied a touch of Cinnaminx, my favorite scent, to my neck.

I gave my reflection one last cheesy smile, admiring the magic of whitening toothpaste, then stepped into the hallway. I left the eyeliner and makeup scattered over the bathroom marble top. Hey, Mom was gone; fuck it.

I opened the front door into bright sunshine and Chip's smiling face. He thrust a huge bouquet of blue carnations toward me.

Startled, I took an involuntary step back into the house.

The carnations followed after me. A hopeful glow lit Chip's expression. "Here. I want you to have these." He deposited the huge bouquet into my arms.

I cradled them in a reflex action.

The perfumed fragrance overpowered my nose, and I could only imagine the dumbstruck look on my face. I continued to stare at the flowers in my arms, still unable to find my voice.

But Chip's words reached my ears. "Do you like them?"

I backed into the room, my head spinning, but I found my voice. "Come in. Shut the door, please."

Water...you're supposed to put these in water. I turned on my heel, taking mechanical strides toward the kitchen. I could hear his footsteps following me.

I reached up, popping open a white-stained cupboard, looking for a vase I knew I wouldn't find. *When was the last year either Mom or I had gotten a bouquet of flowers?*

I spied a wide-mouthed Taco Bell Go-Cup. I dropped it onto the counter.

I stared at the sink, not wanting to look up. I fought down the conflicting waves of pleasure and fear rising in me. I'd flirted and fished to gain his interest, but the unexpected gift of flowers had just thrown me off balance, not a place I liked to be.

I struggled against the inclination to wrap my arms around his neck, shower him with kisses, and let hormones take their course.

Exactly the way I'd surrendered to Joey.

I couldn't let that happen again, not without being sure.

I turned toward him, shaking the bundle of flowers at him like evidence to a crime. "What is this? What do you think you're doing?"

His smile vanished, replaced by a frown of confusion. "I...uh, thought you would like them. They're a gift."

"A gift?"

I deposited the flowers on the countertop next to the Go-Cup and drew a shaking breath, collecting my thoughts.

The absurdity of the situation pushed forward in my head. *Chip the suitor arrives at the door to woo his maiden fair.*

But I was anything but a fair maiden.

My feelings must have shown on my face because he tried to step away from me. I put a hand on either side of his head, locking my eyes with his and stepping close, making him look down at me. "Don't do this, Chip."

"Blue, what are you—"

"Don't try to turn me into a Mary Rowan, or some other dipshit proper Perionne girl you think you can court and win over."

I panted, and I knew he could feel my hands shaking, but the words poured out of me. "Do you have chocolates for me? Are you going to start writing me sweetheart notes? I'm not going to change for you. I'm not going to change for anyone. I'm not the good girl who gets the flowers. I'm not going to the church pitch-ins or the girl's-night-out slumber parties. I don't want the bullshit. I don't want it from Phil, or Mary, or *most* of all, you."

During my tirade, Chip's expression changed from upset to angry. "Wait, just a second. What the hell's gotten into you?"

What the hell *had* gotten into me? Well, *I* knew what I meant. I just didn't know if I could explain it.

He reached up and took my hands in his. "Look, I'm sorry the flowers upset you, Blue. I bought them because I like you, and I wanted to show you."

"Stop it."

"No, *you* stop it."

My jaw clamped shut.

"Look, I don't know who this fuckhead was from your home town, but, clearly, he messed with your mind in some horrible way, and now I'm stuck with the collateral damage. I don't expect you to change. God, I don't *want* you to change. You're unlike anyone else I've ever met, and that's *why* I like you. And if I buy you flowers today and chocolates a few days from now, it only means I want to show you that I like you. That's all."

I could feel his hot breath across my cheek, and I knew he could feel mine. His sincerity penetrated my fear. I realized that it wasn't Chip keeping me from enjoying this, but my own silly paranoia.

I took a deep breath, centering myself, and then continued more calmly. "You're right. When I first met Joey, he was so sweet, so smart, and...full of bullshit. He'd take me out to dinner, and write me poems, and buy me jewelry, and then..."

I broke off. I couldn't go there. Not yet. "No bullshit, Chip. Not from you. Joey may have been the worst, but he wasn't the only one. When someone wants something from me, they butter me up first. I get the gifts. I get the compliments. I give my heart away. Then the other shoe drops. If that happens again, I'll be *so* hurt and *so* disappointed. And I want you to leave now if that's what you're doing."

Chip took a deep, somber breath, returning my angry glare with a stone-faced stare of his own. He replied in a calm, unemotional tone. "I'm not going anywhere. And I already told you why I bought you the flowers."

I dropped my arms, letting my hands travel from the sides of his face, then reaching down and placing them back in his. "The thing is, I already trust you. You're my friend, and we've always been up-front and honest with each other."

A hint of my cinnamon scent reached my nose, a reminder that I'd been doing my part to pretty myself up and get into date mode, so who the hell was I to come down so hard on him?

The realization of my own actions hit, and I knew I needed to let him off the hook.

"So let me see if I get the hidden meaning behind your...*gift*. You want me...and you want to know what I think of that." As I spoke, my voice deepened and turned sultry on its own.

His fingers tightened around mine. I could tell he thought desperately about pulling away, but I held his gaze.

He looked so cute and off-balance. My breathing quickened, and a flush ran over my body. I realized I very much liked the idea that Chip Farren desired me.

His mouth opened, but words failed him. He shrugged and looked down at the floor.

I reached up, one hand tipping his chin to look into my eyes. "I want you, too."

I released his hands and clasped mine together, trying to still their trembling. I continued to stare, unable to speak.

The energy in the room had gotten way too intense. I glanced away, taking a deep breath until my inner shaking subsided.

Chip looked ready to bolt out the door, and I could hardly blame him.

I walked over to the flower bundle, grabbed the Go-Cup, and filled it with water.

"So, what do I do?" I called over my shoulder. "Cut the bottom of the stems?" It seemed I'd heard something about that.

"You can. The florist said it's supposed to help them take in more water."

I kept my back turned, reaching out and pulling open the drawer. I mechanically located the scissors and attended to the task of arranging the flowers in the "vase." The blue carnations created an attractive arch of beauty over the faded image of the Taco Bell logo.

Finally, I turned to see Chip sitting in the black La-Z-Boy recliner, intently watching me. Enjoying his gaze, I walked over, putting a sway into my hips. I stood next to the chair, hovering over him, and slipped my hands into his.

They trembled in mine.

I pulled, urging him to stand.

He rose, towering over me, but even as our bodies pressed together, his gaze dropped toward the floor. Again.

I reached up, clasping my hand around the back of his neck.

He let me pull him close so I could speak into his ear. "Thanks for the flowers, my dear, dear friend. But if you wanted me, all you had to do was ask."

I pressed my lips against his. A gasping exhale blew into my mouth, and I giggled against his lips. "You're not supposed to hold your breath, love. It's a lot more fun if you just relax and go with it."

This time, his lips met mine, and his arms wrapped around my shoulders. Much better.

We separated gently. "Let's go to my room."

I watched his face change from a dumbfounded stare to an awareness of my meaning. "I've never...tried to be with a woman before. I didn't know. I wasn't sure if...if you wanted–"

"Shhhh. Be sure."

He tried to speak again, but I brushed a finger against his lips. "Later. We've more important things to do now."

I smiled up at him.

His arms enfolded me. Then he lowered his face to mine.

Our lips met in mutual hunger.

My knees went limp, but he held me tight.

With a sudden burst of confidence, he scooped me off my feet, and I floated in his arms.

We continued to kiss while he held me. Passion overcame me, and I slid my tongue forward. He pulled back a moment, then welcomed the kiss.

My entire body flushed in heated response. I broke away to catch my breath.

I giggled. "So my big, strong, handsome Chip. Now that you've got me, what *are* you going to do with me?"

He grinned back a moment then cradled me against his chest, his mouth meeting mine once again.

Before long, a euphoric buzz overcame my senses. I separated from our kiss, our mutual panting filling my ears, and basking in the security of his arms. "Come on, my sweet. Carry me down the hall. My bedroom's at the end."

He paused at the doorway, and I reached out, turning the knob and opening the door.

With infinite gentleness, he lowered me to the bed. I grabbed his hand and held it to my chest, sharing the pounding of my heart.

His lips found mine again, his face pressing me back against the pillow, while his hand brushed a hesitant question against my breast.

I moaned against his mouth, enclosing my hand over his, pressing in urgent firmness.

He needed no further instruction.

The universe turned giddy with shivers and stroking and hot kisses.

Soon, my blouse lay open while his mouth left fluttering butterfly kisses along the nape of my neck. And that's when ecstasy fled before the insistent urging of responsibility.

"Wait...Chip..."

Even while I pressed my hands against his shoulders, the edges of the room blurred in yet another wave of pleasure.

"We need to...cool off a second." Chip's look of confusion snapped into focus six inches from my own.

"I don't understand." His confusion turned to hurt. "Oh, Blue, I'm sorry; I thought this was what you wanted. We don't have to—"

I laughed. I couldn't help it. "Stop, stop, stop. No, silly. That's not it. This *is* what I want. And don't even *think* about backing out *now*, mister. But we need to be smart about it."

I waited for my sentence to penetrate his fog of confusion.

Finally, he shook his head, a vague look of guilt on his face. "I guess I wasn't thinking we'd end up—"

"Well, we're ending up. Now, when I packed to move, I had to hide my box of condoms from Mom. I think I know where they are, but we may have to search through several boxes in my closet to find them."

I underestimated how focused Chip could get when given the proper motivation.

Three minutes later, he placed the small wooden trinket box in my hands.

Shortly after, we picked up where we'd left off.

LATE SATURDAY NIGHT, Chip figured out my body. My world dissolved into blind screaming energy and then limp darkness. I buzzed and floated, basking in the end result of a full day's work, incredible, fun, exhausting work. After my release, spent and deliriously happy, I slept. Comforting arms held me snug for the rest of the night.

I drifted into wakefulness to find his mouth caressing mine. I kissed him back, welcoming and returning his love.

Last night's euphoria lingered in the quiet of the room.

Chip settled on his side next to me. His gaze held mine, sober blue eyes that spoke their utter sincerity.

I opened my mouth to say something, but my voice had fled. I could only smile back, shaking my head and tapping my fingers against my chest in a swooning gesture.

He laughed, and then his face softened. "I love you, Blue."

Like a stab of dread, his declaration penetrated my euphoria. A flush of shame settled over me. I'd wooed and seduced this boy, and he'd fallen for me, head over heels, exactly as I'd planned. Now he waited with a hopeful look for the expected response.

The smile froze on my face. I couldn't make myself say the words. Tiny doubts and questions buzzed in my head. *Can I love him? Do I want to love him?* The time had come to give my heart, and some internal reflex wouldn't let me. *Ah, typical. Shit!*

The moment lingered, and my voice returned to me. "I'm trouble to you, Chip."

He shook his head, gripping my hand and kissing my fingers. "You're wonderful." He lay his head on my shoulder.

Even now, my body responded with a shivering tingle. "You think so now. But you don't know everything about me." I massaged his head.

"No. You are." He reached up and stroked my tangled hair with infinite gentleness. He rolled a blue strand between his fingers, and dangled the end between us. "Don't ever change. No matter what."

My eyes stung, and I pulled him close. *What have I done to us?*

CHAPTER TWENTY

I drifted in nothingness.

"Blue."

From a distance, someone whispered my name.

No, not just someone. And not just any name. "Blue," my love teased again, his voice a gentle tickle across my ear. The word, more accurate than a fingerprint, assured me that Chip lay as close as a whisper in my ear.

I'd settled like a limp rag on the bed. I eased into a slow, numb wakefulness; my mind and body synched to a world of total safety and security. A feeling I'd not had in a long time.

Scratch that. A feeling I'd never had in my life.

Savoring the moment, I took my own sweet time waking up.

I gripped the pillow, pressing it tightly against the side of my face, wanting to hide in its darkness. I could feel the warmth of Chip's body, spooned against me, his mouth hovering close to my ear.

His hand caressed my bare shoulder, causing an answering shiver to travel across my skin.

I sighed in pleasure. "What is it, Chip?"

"How did you get the name Fi-Fi?"

I opened my eyes, becoming fully awake. "It's just a name, Chip."

His chuckle reached me in the darkness. I imagined him shaking his head. "Janet is just a name, Blue. Fi-Fi is a name for a poodle."

I took in a deep breath and turned to face him. I could make out his silhouette in the dim light. He laid propped up on one elbow, just watching me from his side of the double bed.

From the intensity of his gaze, I'd wondered if he'd been watching me for hours. The idea sent shivers of loving warmth through me.

But what if I snored or kept him awake for some other embarrassing reason? God, how do I even ask? The loving warmth vanished, and I shivered against him. My traitorous mind had determined to sabotage all the positives from this moment.

I blinked sleep from my eyes, then reached out and entwined his fingers with mine. "Fi-Fi was a nickname I sort of adopted for myself. It was...originally used as a term of affection by somebody who was very close to me."

"So does that mean you'll want everyone to call you 'Blue' now?"

I giggled. "No, sweet Chip. You can call me that, but no one else." I squeezed his hand. "Just now, when I was waking, I heard you say it, and I knew it was you. I felt very safe and loved."

His arms pulled me close, and his face nuzzled into my neck. I reached up and scratched his soft, matted hair. "When I hear it, I want to know it's you every time."

His breath brushed against my arm. "I can live with that."

He planted light kisses along my shoulder, and then I picked up the discussion. "So this very special man was a sort of mentor to me when I was a child. He was very kind to me. I think he was my father."

I could feel Chip pause in mid-kiss. I waited while he pulled his face back to speak. "I don't understand."

Oh, Chip. Maybe I don't want you to understand.

Yet here I was, telling him. "Well, it's not exactly casual conversation, not even between Mom and me. But I've never met my father. Or maybe it's better to say, we've never been introduced."

"So who was he?"

I shrugged. "Your guess is as good as mine. I've never been told."

From nowhere, a deep well of emotion swirled within me.

Where is this coming from?

I covered my face in my hands, fighting back tears. "I just don't know, and she won't tell me. I've asked several times. And the last time, she screamed at me never to bring it up again."

"That's terrible." No longer whispering, Chip sounded angry.

"I suppose Mom decided to get herself pregnant and have a child. So she did. And that's all she thinks I need to know."

"You don't talk about your mother much."

I fidgeted against him. When Mom came up in conversation, I'd get riled. Only this time someone asked what no one had before, and I struggled to control the shaking in my body.

A tear escaped, slipping down my cheek. How he saw it, I don't know, but his hand brushed across my face.

I sniffled. "Y'know, it's not like any man could ever deal with her, so why she decided to have a child is beyond me. She's an enormously successful businesswoman. She led her law firm to a prosperous town. She can demand prime dollar for her time and professional advice. There's no way she'd let a man get in her way."

Words kept flying out of my mouth, out of my control. "Somehow, she got some man to cooperate. She banged somebody and got them out of the way, and, nine months later, I was born. Me. Fi-Fi, the pet daughter."

He stroked my back. "Don't talk about yourself that way."

As the words poured out of me, heat burned my face. "It's like that Heart song they played on the radio when I was a kid. Pick up a hitchhiker, quick bang in a hotel, and send him on his way. 'All I Want to do is Make Love to You.' Convenient for everyone involved. Everyone except me."

In the dark, I could hear my panting breath. I wiped my eyes and sniffled. So many times in the past, people would ask, and I rattled off bullshit without batting an eye. Now *Chip* asked, and I babbled away like a fool.

I slammed my head into the pillow. "Sorry."

"It's okay, Blue." His hand stroked my back. "It's okay."

I closed my eyes. My breathing calmed, and my tears stopped.

A few moments passed. "Can I know about this man?" Chip whispered.

I reached up and placed my hand over his, trying to control my tone and emotion. "His name is Paul Willis. He was one of the senior partners in Mom's firm. Paul and Mom dated on and off until I was about eight years old."

I took a deep, shaking breath. "Before they broke up for good, he would come over all the time. He was very affectionate and playful with me, but not in a gross stepdad kind of way. And there was one thing we agreed on. He hated my real name."

Chip spoke the dreaded syllables. "Fiona Felicity?"

"Have you ever heard anything so stuck up? When they'd fight, my name would often come up. He'd say she may as well have called me 'Fi-Fi' because it was just as attractive and didn't sound as snotty."

"They had fights about your name, and you're wondering if he's your father?"

"Do you think he is? Really?" I couldn't hide the hopeful tone in my voice.

"Well, based on that alone, I'd say the chances are pretty good."

I turned in the bed to face him, ticking off the facts that had rattled around in my head for years, facts I'd shared with no one. "He was the only man my mother let me go places with. We took special all-day trips, like, to the zoo, or I'd stay at his apartment on weekends when Mom was carrying a big case load. He must've been my father; I'm sure of it."

I stopped, biting my lip, but unable to prevent the next words. "But Mom drove him away, then refused to tell me one way or the other, no matter how often I'd beg her to. It's just one more thing I hate her for."

"Don't say that. You don't really mean that you hate your mother."

"You have *no fucking idea* how much I hate my mother!"

Chip almost jumped out of the bed at my eruption.

Still angry but exhausted, I started crying again, covering my face and wanting to crawl into a hole.

We wallowed in silence for a long time before his voice reached me again. "It's so...beyond my experience."

"Chip...there's more. I ran around with the Broad Ripple college punks since I was thirteen years old. And don't get me wrong. They're great people, most of the time. Except late at night when some of them got drunk. I had to learn how to protect myself, because, sometimes, I didn't get back home as early as I'd planned. Most of my friends were very protective of me. But the others..."

Apparently, Chip decided it was safe to scoot close because his arm gently wrapped around my waist.

"Chip, I hung out with a twenty-year-old wasteoid last year. He was so neat at first. So nice and so attentive. He told me how beautiful I was, how mature I was for my age. I bought all that bullshit. But then one night I came over, he decided it would be a kick to break into one of the bars."

I blinked away tears and could see Chip's eyes widen at my words. There it was. I'd said it out loud straight-up and hadn't even tried to steer the conversation away.

And I kept on talking, telling the secret only Joey and I shared until tonight.

I hid my eyes while I spoke. "Well, anyway, I stayed at the door while he messed with the safe. Jackoff didn't know how to break into it, even though he swore beforehand he could.

"Then the alarm went off, and the cops were right there on top of us. We were one lucky turn down an alleyway from getting caught. I was ready to tell him to take a hike the next day, except I chickened out.

"Joey swore up and down that he was drunk, and that it wouldn't happen again if I gave him another chance. So I stayed. Like a fool, I stuck it out. But guess what my bitch-of-a-mom did?"

Chip's body jolted at my expletive.

"A couple days later, during breakfast, Mom starts reading the newspaper out loud. It's something she does sometimes. You know, when she can't bitch about me, she'll find something we can bitch about together. I guess that's her idea of mother-daughter bonding."

"Doesn't sound like a fun way to spend your mornings," Chip said wryly.

"So, she read the story of the break-in. Mom even commented that it was a good thing I had stayed over at my girlfriend's house. And I'm sitting there, about ready to pop from the guilt, and then the bitch just dropped the topic and moved on to another article."

I could hear the confusion in Chip's words. "Well, that's good, right? That she didn't suspect? Would you have rather she kept on you about it?"

"*No*. Not at the time. For the next several weeks, I went to bed every night, praying she *wouldn't* ask. But then I started thinking about it, and, damn it, she *should* have wondered. What kind of mother doesn't ask her kid questions?" Before he could answer, I rushed on. "The kind who doesn't care."

The tears forced their way out again. "She does what she can to enjoy her career, and as long as I...stay out of trouble...she's happy." *Shut up, shut up!*

I heard his breath draw in to respond, but I kept talking.

"Chip, I'd never done anything like that before, and I'll never do anything like that again. I'm not that kind of person, and I didn't want to be. So after that, I made a point to come home early and steer clear of Joey when he was high." *Why do I keep blabbering my head off?*

"Good for you."

"And my mother doesn't even notice, except to tell everyone how my grades have improved. 'Look, everyone, my pet daughter has a new trick. Come over after work...'"

My eyes stung and the tears flowed. Again. *Damn it! Why am I doing this? Why around him?*

I shrugged him away. "Leave me alone."

He pulled his hand back.

In the smoldering silence, my tears soon stopped. "Chip, if you repeat a word of this..." I stopped in mid-threat, appalled at my own reflex.

I didn't need to see him to know he was hurt. "Oh, shit. I'm sorry. For everything."

"It's okay, Blue. Everything is okay."

His fingers clasped gently around my waist. "I want to cuddle for a bit, if that's okay with you."

I trembled at his touch, needing him to hold me. And I sensed he knew it. By reaching for me, he gave me an out and let me keep my pride. It was so damn lame.

I let him do it.

The shell that had hardened around my heart since that night with Joey loosened and fell away. I turned into his arms and buried my head against his thin chest.

Like a newly hatched chick, I settled into Chip's protective wings.

But a part of me still remained uneasy. Like that chick, I now felt exposed for all the predators to find and attack. And I didn't like that feeling, not one bit.

CHAPTER TWENTY-ONE

Special Agent George Carson of the FBI stormed into the waiting room of the Perionne Municipal Hospital. They'd stuck him with the Perionne bank robbery case that afternoon.

He'd received the assignment and took the three-hour drive from Indy to Perionne, not counting the ten minutes it took to find the miniscule dot labeled Perionne in his road atlas. Between then and now, the perps had slipped away.

The local bumpkin cops had identified the two assailants, but locating the rednecks proved a different matter. The yellow T-bird showed up abandoned at the rest stop, but, from there, the trail went cold.

They'd tightened the screws on Lilly Mills, girlfriend of the psycho who went on the shooting spree. They'd threatened the pregnant waitress with a federal indictment. They painted a detailed picture of her serving a life sentence in a women's prison, never to see her child again. He'd traumatized her and felt like a total asshole in the process. All for nothing. Mills didn't know anything.

And the psycho's mama was no help, though she cooperated easily enough.

He'd run out of leads. Crimley had no family or close friends, at least no one but Gunther, bless his mass-murdering, shooting-spree psychotic head.

Carson's afternoon in Perionne didn't change his dim view of small towns. He longed to wrap this case up and get the hell out of here as fast as he could.

He worked late into the evening before giving up. He checked into a local dive of a hotel, only taking the time to leave the number with Perionne P.D. before collapsing onto the rock-hard mattress.

The phone rang at the ungodly hour of 3:00 a.m., jarring him awake. The calm voice of the dispatcher told him a local patrolman had found one of his perps, who now lay dying in the hospital. He was damned well going to get a few answers before the guy kicked.

CARSON APPROACHED the nurse's desk, his nose burning at the nauseating smell of alcohol and stale vomit. As a Fed, Carson had spent a lot of time in hospital wings identical to this one. It used to upset him, bringing back memories of his dad slowly giving in to the cancer. The sickness and death didn't affect him so much these days. But he still hated the smell.

He opened his mouth to address the nurse but paused as he spotted a fortyish man with a thick shock of salt-and-pepper hair and wearing a white coat approach him from across the hall. The doctor extended his hand. "You must be Agent Carson. I'm Dr. Eric Lee. I received the call from the police station."

Carson nodded back, returning the doctor's firm handshake. "Dr. Lee, I understand Jeff Crimley's your patient. I need to talk to him now."

Dr. Lee grimaced. He motioned Carson to follow him. "I'm sorry, but I have a problem with that. If I wake Crimley up, I'll most likely end up zipping him up into a body bag later tonight. The patient is suffering from hypothermia, as well as severe loss of blood from his stab wounds."

Carson fumed. *Of course, the doctor needs to give me hassles now.*

They approached the door to a private room. A Perionne police guard straightened in his chair, seeming to come to life at the sight of the federal agent.

Carson folded his arms. "Let's start at the top. Is he going to make it or isn't he?"

The doctor shrugged. "I doubt it. We'll do all we can, of course. We just didn't get to him in time."

"Well, then, what are we discussing? If you can't keep him alive, then I need him awake now. He won't do anybody any good once he's dead."

Dr. Lee puffed out his chest. "Listen to me, agent. That man has little enough chance as it is. If we rouse him at this stage, the shock alone could kill him."

George Carson bristled, frustrated to be on the verge of breaking this case and going home, only to have this man fret about the health of one of the criminals. "No, *you* listen, *doctor.* Two people were murdered in cold blood at the Perionne National Bank today. I need to tell their families something. We know who two of these monsters were, but we also know, because of the way they blew out of there so damn fast, that a third person was very likely involved. We've tried patrols, roadblocks, and house-to-house searches. Nothing. If I can identify that third person, I can't let my only opportunity go."

Dr. Lee sighed. "There may only be one person to find. When we brought Jeff Crimley in, he babbled that he'd killed Gunther Stalt in a fight. That's what you wanted to know, right? So the murderer's dead, and the co-conspirator will likely die before the end of the night."

"He said that? Gunther's dead?"

The doctor referred to a note pad. "The admitting physician heard Crimley say Gunther gave him the stab wounds, but he still managed to kill Gunther before it was over."

Carson grunted, not impressed. "I'll still need to speak with Crimley to corroborate that. Then, I'll have to tell Gunther's mother. Damn shame. She's a sweet lady. Even if her son turned out to be a bastard."

Dr. Lee shook his head and frowned. "It puts my patient in jeopardy."

Undeterred, Carson barreled on. "There may still a third man out there."

Dr. Lee squinted and rubbed his temple. "God, I hate this. Don't you have anything else to go on?"

Carson threw up his hands. "I've got nothing, doctor. We found the getaway car this afternoon. Stolen last week. They'd abandoned it at a rest stop. Not a useful print on it. They must've had a second car waiting, but we can't find a good set of tracks."

Carson fished into his jacket and drew out his badge. "Look, we can do this one of two ways. You can wake him up now and save us all a lot of time, or I can make a phone call and have a court order dropped off early this morning. And you'll still have to wake him up."

"I doubt it's quite as easy as you make it out. But, yes, I see you'd ultimately get your way. Sit tight a minute."

JEFF CRIMLEY FLOATED in a haze of pain, gradually rising to consciousness. A weight pressed on his chest, making each breath a great effort. He opened his eyes, his vision blurry, but he could tell he lay in a narrow bed in unfamiliar surroundings. *A hospital?*

The monotonous beeping of his vital signs recorded on some unseen machine reached his ears.

I'm dyin'.

He looked into the face of a serious-looking man in a brown rain-spotted windbreaker.

A cop.

"Crimley? I'm Agent Carson of the FBI. Can you hear me?"

"Yes." Crimley forced the word from his lips. His throat felt raw, and his voice sounded hoarse. *I need to rest.*

"Crimley, do you remember the bank robbery? I need to ask you questions about it."

Crimley nodded. It was easier than trying to speak.

"You were identified as a participant in this robbery, along with Gunther Stalt. Can you verify for me that Gunther was involved?"

Crimley nodded again.

"Where's Gunther now? If you cooperate, we'll make things easier on you."

Even in his condition, Crimley detected an uncomfortable urgency in the man's voice. The agent was trying to play him for a fool. Well, there was no need to hold back about Gunther.

Crimley took a deep, painful breath. "Dead."

"Dead? You mean Gunther's dead? Did you kill him?"

Crimley nodded, struggling to breathe. "I stabbed him. He stabbed me. He died." *God, my chest hurts! Just let this end.*

"Crimley, there was a third person involved, wasn't there? You had a getaway car driver. Isn't that correct?"

The words slowly penetrated Crimley's fogged brain. *Poor Jim. He'd never asked to be a part of this. I forgive you, if it means anything now.*

"Can you tell me who he was?"

He remembered Jim yanking him from the car, abandoning him to die at the side of the road. But he couldn't work up any anger toward the man. *We're the ones who dragged Jim into this mess. Can't ruin it for his family.*

Crimley took a deep breath. "Getaway driver blackmailed. Forget him. No danger." Even as the world darkened around the edges, Crimley drew some satisfaction at seeing the fed's face turn a bright, angry shade of red.

"So there was a getaway driver. Tell me who."

If this is dying, it's not so bad. Just slip off into the black and see what happens next. "I'm dying. Just go away. Leave me to it."

The agent's voice faded into the background. He barely heard the next words.

"Listen, Crimley, we want to help that man as much as we want to help you. But we can't do that if..."

But for Crimley, the world blurred away for the last time, and a heavy darkness settled over him. He closed his eyes and drifted.

AT SEVEN-FORTY THAT MORNING, Jim pulled the blue Buick Regal into his driveway.

He'd driven all night, until the panic settled, and he could finally focus again. More punch-drunk than worried, he pulled into the parking lot of a 7-Eleven and purchased a bottle of Fantastik and a rag.

He scrubbed on the many bloodstains ground into light-gray cloth of the passenger seat. When he finished, the spots left behind resembled old chocolate more than mayhem. He'd burn his jacket later.

Exhausted, he arrived home, not noticing the squad car parked at the curb until he reached his front door.

A chill of terror ran through his body. *All this work, all my worrying, and they already knew. They've been waiting for me to show up.* In an odd way, relief washed over him. *Better to come clean early, pay for my sins, and not look over my shoulder for the rest of my life.*

But how will I explain to Jesse?

He took a deep breath. *No sense fighting. I'll surrender peacefully.* He opened the door. They'd take him away from his family and lock him away in a hole, where nothing and no one could get to him. *Nothing but the sound of Crimley's voice calling out, over and over for eternity. That's one thing they won't take from me.*

He stepped through the back door, which opened directly into the kitchen and breakfast bar. The pleasant aroma of bacon and coffee wafted toward him. Had he ever smelled anything so good, so much like home? Would he again?

Standing in front of the oven, Jesse turned and smiled at him. He could hear the still-whistling tea kettle of boiling water.

"Good morning, honey," Jesse called. He detected the strain under her nonchalance.

"Hi." Jim walked past the bar, where he could see Deputy Fred Lovison seated in the dining room. Jesse must have insisted that the informal breakfast bar wasn't an appropriate place for an officer of the law to eat.

Jim had seen Lovison, with his stocky frame and thinning brown hair, create a dominating presence, mainly when trouble broke out at the Cat's Cradle. This morning, the officer beamed a toothy smile at him. "Mornin', Jim."

"Mornin', Fred. A little early for a social call, isn't it?" His voice sounded surprisingly calm.

"I'm afraid that's true. I'm here on official business. Well, at least I was."

"Oh?" Jim noticed the almost-empty plate in front of the deputy. Lovison picked up the last piece of bacon and took a bite.

Jesse waved the spatula. "Fred drew the tiny straw. He's been going door to door since late last night, trying to find out more about that bank robbery. You remember. The one we saw on TV." She turned her back on the deputy, facing Jim, the look in her eyes penetrating like a pair of pointed daggers.

It was almost too much to take. His wife, who he'd wanted to protect most of all, was lying for him.

"Right. The bank robbery. That sounded...absolutely awful, deputy." He didn't dare say anymore. He'd avoided the news reports on the radio the last few hours.

Deputy Lovison swiped at his mouth with a cloth napkin. "It was. Relax, Jim, your wife already told me you were working around the house all day and watching TV with her, just like you always do."

Jesse stepped toward an overhead cabinet, fishing out a coffee cup. "We watched *Casablanca*. It's one of Jim's favorites."

The deputy chuckled. "I saw it, too. Love old movies. Can't beat that Bogie. And Ingrid Bergman was a dish."

Jesse entered the dining room, the mug in one hand and the kettle in the other.

The deputy grinned at her, then at Jim. "I figured since I have over half the damn town to patrol, I might as well take up Jesse's offer for breakfast. Say, what was wrong with the car?"

Already punch-drunk, Jim jumped as if he'd been slapped. "What's that?"

The deputy waved vaguely in the direction of the driveway. "Jesse told me you were having car problems."

"Oh, yeah. Spark plugs. Replaced 'em this morning with a spare set. Car's driving fine, now." A comment formed in his mind about being a former racecar driver and preparing for those emergencies, but he stopped short of saying it out loud.

How many other lies has Jesse told?

"You didn't see Gunther or Crimley recently?"

Jim shrugged and stared, maybe too long. "Uh...no. No, definitely not. That is, Gunther visited a few days ago. Hadn't heard from him in months, then he showed up at my door. He had a lot to drink, but he just blew off some steam about losing his job."

The deputy stared quizzically at Jim. "I don't suppose he told you anything useful or hinted at what he planned to do?"

"No." Jim shifted from foot to foot while the deputy waited patiently. "Well...he said he needed money because of Lilly. Hinted about a loan, but I ignored the hint. I didn't think he'd do something like rob a bank. Crazy."

Jim stood before the deputy's stern gaze, biting back the urge to scream.

The deputy took a long sip of his coffee. "Say, hear the latest?"

Jim shrugged. "I'm not sure."

"They found Jeff Crimley and took him to the hospital. Someone stabbed the poor bastard nearly to death. He'd been tossed out on the road. He died early this morning."

Jim's mind raced. "That's horrible. Did he say anything...useful?" To his amazement, his voice sounded calm.

"Crimley said he killed Gunther. He also confirmed that someone else drove the getaway car. But Crimley refused to name him. Said it didn't matter, and that we should let it alone. You believe that? Now that's loyalty."

Jim stood on wobbly legs, blindsided by the memory of dumping Crimley on the side of the highway, and humbled that, in the end, Crimley had shown him mercy.

Jesse hollered from the kitchen. "Would you like some coffee, dear? I got a fresh pot ready."

Jim mumbled, "Yes."

The deputy nodded. "You do look mighty tired. Probably got up a lot earlier than you wanted to, eh?"

He nodded and said nothing, still trying to absorb what the deputy had told him. "So now what are you going to do?"

The deputy shook his head. "Keep going door to door like a damn vacuum cleaner salesman. My hunch is this other guy doesn't even live around here. They probably hired some professional. They say Crimley had some pretty shady connections." He took a sip of his coffee. "But, the FBI says 'do it,' so that's what I gotta do. After all, I'm just a bumpkin small town cop, what do I know?"

The sizzling of frying eggs reached Jim's ears from the kitchen.

Jesse called out. "Would you like some breakfast?"

"Okay. That sounds good."

The deputy held the coffee cup up and made an appreciative noise. "Good stuff! I'm sorry I have to bust in on you good people and bother you so early in the morning."

"It's no bother," Jesse said.

"That's right," Jim added. "You've got a thankless job ahead of you. We appreciate all you're doing."

The deputy moved on with casual questions about the neighbors. Jim answered as best he could, his mind still contemplating the tragic news about Crimley.

Finally, the deputy finished his plate and rose. He extended his hand, offered his thanks, and let Jesse lead him to the door.

Jim tottered out of the dining room and into the connecting living room, collapsing onto the leather chair. He listened to Jesse say goodbye, his head still spinning. At the welcome sound of the door closing, he placed his hands over his eyes to hide his relief.

Jesse came into the room, letting the silence linger before she finally spoke. "I don't want to know."

Ashamed, Jim looked down as her bitter, disappointed voice penetrated his soul.

"I just want you to answer about a few points, and we'll never speak of it again."

He nodded.

"Did you kill anyone? Did you shoot anyone? Did you stab Gunther? Crimley? Did you do anything else but drive the car? And I want the truth."

He swallowed down shame. Tears filled his eyes. "I didn't. I swear. I couldn't. I didn't want anything to do with—"

"Shut up!" Her shriek stunned him to silence. She took a deep, shuddering breath, holding back tears. "I just want to know that you didn't hurt or kill anybody. Nobody saw you in the bank. Nobody knows what happened after. And I don't want to know, either. Just tell me you didn't kill anyone."

"I didn't."

Jesse sobbed.

Jim sat, listening to his wife's weeping. Along with his other crimes, he'd broken Jesse's heart.

He clenched his fists and made a vow.

I'll spend the rest of my life making this up to her.

CHAPTER TWENTY-TWO

I knew being Chip's "first" would change our relationship, perhaps taking us somewhere intense and unpredictable.

For him, it was simple. He loved me. He had eyes for no one but me. I told myself it's what I wanted. I hoped I was right.

Chip and I took to texting each other during class. I certainly had enough boring classes where I could send back a few random thoughts, along with some references to our previous weekend, just to make sure he missed me.

Somewhere in one of his mid-week texts, Chip wrote that he needed to meet me in the woods for a "supr secr8" meeting. He carefully described the forested area next to the school where a road ended abruptly, blocked by a large pile of dirt. Beyond that, a recently harvested cornfield spread out over the next several acres.

According to his text, our rendezvous would take place behind the dirt pile after school on Friday. We needed privacy for this "supr secr8" discussion, his text said. I rolled my eyes. Chip and I had not followed up after our first encounter, and I figured this must be at least part of what he had in mind.

Not that I had a problem with that.

I ARRIVED FIRST. The dozen or so trees that made up the "forest" looked invitingly private for snuggling later on, but not private enough for anything *too* intense. Darn it all.

For all my doubts and concerns about my long-term feelings, I jumped up when I saw him approach, his arms filled with a large scrapbook. I abandoned my own backpack and rushed up to him. I needed to show how much I'd missed him since last seeing him, lunch break three hours ago.

He gratefully welcomed my insistent kiss, even while clutching the scrapbook to his chest.

My mind still wrestled with this relationship, but my body had given in days ago.

Chip put his arm over my shoulder and walked me back to the dirt path. "Thanks for coming, Blue. I want to show you something."

I cooed in my best Marilyn imitation, "I haven't come yet, Mr. President, but maybe *after* you show me."

He laughed. "Down, girl. I'm serious."

I rolled my eyes. "Oh, yes, I know. I can always tell when Chip has his serious face on. You get such a stern crinkle between your eyebrows."

He motioned to a patch of ground behind the mound. "Here, let's talk a minute."

I dropped down and folded my legs in front of me.

He deposited his five-pound scrapbook on my lap, (as well as his trademarked stack of computer paper) and talked some craziness about breaking into the Pirates of Perionne boat ride to find hidden treasure.

"I found it!" He pointed at Gunther's picture. "All we have to do is dig it up. Once we find the money, we'll be famous beyond our wildest dreams. We'll be heroes." His eyes lit up with a sort of spooky gleam that scared me.

What is he babbling about? What have I gotten myself into?

My knees started cramping from the heavy book opened up on my lap.

I looked down at the newspaper articles, trying to buy myself time. I'd aced my folklore midterm earlier in the week and thought that made me an official Gunther Stalt expert. But I'd never seen some of these articles.

Chip sat across from me, his knees pulled against his chest, dark hair rumpled. I'd seen it that way before whenever he'd been working on a computer project all night. I was getting to know this look all too well, obsessed programmer tracking down a lost equation. But this time I was only partly right.

I ran my hands through my hair, breathing in the cool October air, wondering what I should say. Nothing came to mind. Chip reached out and put a hand on my shoulder. "Listen, Blue. Nobody knows what happened to Gunther's money. Except me. And with your help, I can get it. Surely you can't tell me that you're not just a teensy bit interested."

I glared at him.

He dropped his hand from my shoulder.

"Chip, I know you're obsessed with this Gunther thing, but, to me, that was just test material; and as far as I'm concerned, I'm done with it." I shrugged. "I really don't care about some hick psychopath robbing the local bank. What bothers me more is how—"

"You're not hearing me!"

The passion of his cry took me aback and silenced me.

Chip scowled. "I know where the money is, Blue. The biggest damn secret in the town, and I know it." He folded his arms across his scrawny chest, appearing as little more than a bunch of folded angles.

I sighed, reaching out and grabbing his wrists. "Chip, get out of the clouds. Listen to me." When I saw him look into my eyes, I continued. "You're talking about breaking and entering. You could get into serious trouble."

That seemed to rouse him. He composed himself, losing a lot of that idiot look. "I know that."

"Then why take the risk?"

"So that we'll know."

That sounded consistent, and yet I still had my doubts. Maybe Chip wasn't interested in the money or even the glory of having solved *the* mystery of the town. But to tell me he wanted the satisfaction of knowing, it didn't sound right to me.

So what's really going on?

Then, he proceeded to expand on his scheme. And the scariest part was I could tell from his voice that he was going through with this, with or without me. Even though he was certain it wouldn't work without my help. *Of course. Let's fuck up two lives, why just one?*

But I had some kind of responsibility to him, as his friend, and as his lover, too, but as his friend first. For now, I had to put aside all the chills, tingles, and the emotional baggage within me caused from last weekend. I had to help him because he'd helped me in so many ways. I couldn't let him do this alone.

I reached out and took his hands in mine. "Okay, start over. Let me hear what you have in mind."

He opened the scrapbook filled with Xeroxes of old news clippings and reports all related to Gunther and the robbery. I shuffled around to get a good look. He leaned close, and I snuggled against him, and that was pretty nice, too.

He settled on a fuzzy blueprint scanned from a computer graphics file. It was the blueprint Phil had haplessly helped Chip recreate from his notes, a blueprint of *The Pirates of Perionne* ride.

I studied it while I talked. "Okay. What have you got?"

Chip sat up straight, forcing me to do the same. I watched, amused, as he glanced past trees and the road that ran beyond it. He looked straight out of a bad gangster movie.

I had to grin. "There's nobody here, Chip."

"I know there was a getaway driver, and I know who he is." He'd lowered his voice to a whisper.

"Oh," I whispered back.

He waited for me to ask, but, certain the name would mean nothing to me, I didn't.

He continued. "Look, Blue. This is going to sound crazy, but a couple of months ago my father came home with one of his old bowling buddies, and I overheard the guy telling my dad all about it."

I shrugged. "So this guy drove the getaway car? I suppose you have something to back this up with."

"You need to take me seriously. We need to be very careful about this. What he told my dad was in confidence. I just happened to be going across the loft to get a book at the time."

I could envision the length of hall in question. It stretched about twelve feet. "And how long did this trip across the loft take?"

Chip's face flushed red. "Well, hell, Blue. He mentioned Gunther at just the moment I was stepping out. What did you think I was going to do?" He turned his face away from me.

"Oh, C'mon, Chip, I was just razzing you. I would have done the same thing, if the conversation had meant anything to me." Which should not have consoled him much, but for some reason it did. "So tell me what you heard."

Chip shrugged. "Well...since it's their bowling night, and the guy's speech was kind of slurred, he must've had a few too many beers that night. My Dad kept trying to shut him up, but...he kept talking on and on like he had to get it out."

"That would fit the mold."

"So then he told my dad the whole story."

And at this point, Chip proceeded to do the same. I listened, trying to keep a skeptical view, but as the tale unfolded, all the facts fell into perfect place.

By the end, I was as convinced as Chip that he'd stumbled onto the biggest secret in the town.

"...Who could blame him for not going back all of these years?" Chip finished. "He's probably just some family man wanting to stay as far away from the situation as possible. And to this day he has to hear the stories and the theories, hoping that no one ever closes in on him."

He reached out and took my hands.

I looked into his blue eyes, alight with fervor. "It doesn't matter who the driver was. I might know, but you don't need to, and no one else does, either. What matters is, we can solve this and return the money. And the poor guy who's been living with this guilt all these years can finally let it go. And no one need ever know who this guy is but me."

I gave his hand a gentle squeeze. "And your dad."

"Right. And my dad. C'mon, Blue. I've been working on it for months. You and I could sneak into the park and dig up the money. With your skills and my brains, we can do this easily."

I stared at him, appalled. The eagerness with which he told the tale, the scary gleam in his eye as he rattled off the details, staggered me. "Tonight? You want to break into Perionne Park tonight after closing?"

"Not exactly. But close enough. I'm more concerned about whether they lock up the pirate building itself than the gate to the park, but you said that you knew something about breaking and entering, so—"

"That's not exactly what I said. I can pick a lock or two, but—" And then the connection hit, like a two-by-four to the back of the head. A nasty piece of the puzzle slipped into place.

Fury erupted from me. "You bastard!"

I jumped to my feet, sending the scrapbook tumbling into the dirt. "You've been working on this for months? *Months!* Let me guess, looking for the perfect little girlfriend accomplice with some lock-picking skills?"

Chip stood next to me, jaw dropped, arms spread apart. He had the decency to look appalled at the accusation. "Blue, no. C'mon, you know that's not true."

I swatted him on the chest, forcing him to step backwards. "What, Chip? What do I know? I know what you're *capable* of when you want to get your way. I know that I'm a pretty damn *convenient* piece to your *pet* project. I also know you did some pretty wonderful favors to get my attention."

I took a step back, lowering my hand. Sure, I could beat up on him, but what would be the point? *How stupid I'd been. And here I'd been feeling sorry for him!*

Chip glared back at me, looking equally hurt. His hand came up to his chest where I'd struck him. "Oh, yeah, right. How clairvoyant of me to know all about your criminal past weeks before you told me about it. And don't forget how I seduced you. Wasn't that just brilliant of me? I came at you like James Bond last weekend. I had you eating out of my hand."

I bit back an acerbic reply. He was right about the last part, and he didn't even know it. Last weekend, he'd left me one moment sighing in bliss and the next twisted in knots.

Exactly how I feel now.

I couldn't strike out at him, so I scraped at the ground with the toe of my boot. "Damn you, Chip!"

I kicked the dirt and stomped a few feet, causing a cloud of dust to rise up around me; I growled in anger to keep from shouting at the top of my lungs. "Well, fuck you, then! I'm ruining your plan, do you hear me? I'm not going along with it."

I stopped, gasping to catch my breath.

Chip sighed, and his shoulders slumped. "I...guess I can't force you to go. I told you because of how I feel about you, and because this is important to me. That's the truth. Somewhere last weekend, you really opened up to me, and I wanted to do the same. I thought you would want to help."

I shook my head. "I can't." I grabbed his arm. "Chip, damn it, listen to me. *You* can't. It's too dangerous."

He gathered up his papers, brushing dust from the scrapbook. "Well, then. I guess you'll just have to wish me luck. You know where you can catch up with me if you change your mind."

I clenched my fists in exasperation. "Chip, use that logical brain you rely on so much. You don't have a chance. I bet you'll get caught straddling the gate, and you'll go to jail. And who knows how bad it can get? You won't be a minor much longer."

Chip hung his head in resignation. "Blue, I have to know. Finding this treasure has been my only goal for years. Except for pleasing you. Hell, it would be worth it just to pull this off and you'd see what I'm capable of. Then you'd see that I'm not as incompetent as you think."

And damn if my heart didn't melt, even as I bit back a laugh. "Will you *stop* it!"

He remained hunched over, holding the scrapbook in his lap.

I stepped up to him and sat down, reaching out to touch his face. He wouldn't look at me at first, and then he did.

His eyes were wet.

And my heart broke all over again.

I pulled his notebooks from him, easing them to the ground. Then, I wrapped my arms around him.

His arms tightened around me.

I held him close. "Just stop. You're not going in there alone, damn it. If you're going to do your damnedest to fall, then I have to try to catch you."

He snuffled against my chest. "What do you mean?"

"It means, shut up and kiss me."

And he did.

I DON'T REMEMBER MUCH about the walk home, except the world glowed with brightness. I skipped and hummed a tune to release my cheer to the world. "When you're a Jet, you're a Jet to the end..."

I skipped past Sylvia's house, hopping onto the stepping stones and up to my porch. I risked a glance across the yard.

What I saw froze me in place.

A *FOR SALE* sign in Sylvia's yard that had never been there before today.

And yet, from the weather spots, the area of dead grass surrounding the sign, and the rust on the framework, the sign had clearly been in the yard for months.

I walked to the front of the house, taking in the familiar porch with the rocking chair, but the chair sat unused, covered in layers of matted webs across the seat and down the sides. And while it bore a striking resemblance to the off-white cloth Sylvia had been knitting, these were clearly spider-webs, several of them still inhabited. No living body had rested in the chair last week, probably not even last year.

But where's Sylvia? On reflex, I looked at the front door with the two small windows inset toward the top, like a pair of eyes. Windows I remembered a couple of days ago. Now, twin boards ran across both in an X-shape.

My gaze traveled across the front of the house, seeing for the first time the boards across the windows, set firm with nails turning brown from months of exposure to the elements.

Boards and nails I had not seen yesterday.

"Sad, isn't it?"

I jumped at the sound of the unfamiliar voice. I turned to see a woman dressed in a sharp gray business-suit, similar to the sort my mother might wear.

She held out her hand.

I extended mine automatically, letting her place a business card into my palm. I glanced at the text identifying her as, *Hariette Sanders, Certified Real Estate Agent.* The spiffy card included a full-color logo and photograph.

She stood beside me, brushed a rebellious lock of short brown hair from her eyes, and sighed. "I don't know what I'm going to do. But neither did the seven agents hired before me, so I guess I shouldn't feel bad."

My head still reeled, but I found my voice. "How long has the house been on the market?"

"Oh...the owner died over five years ago. I've been stuck with the listing for six months. Neat hair, by the way."

Five years ago? "Thanks. When you say 'the owner', you mean Sylvia?"

The real estate agent laughed pleasantly. "Oh, yes. Sylvia. *That* Sylvia. Sylvia Stalt, Gunther's mom, bless her pointy little head. They found her body on the porch, still in the rocking chair."

Hariette crossed her arms, warding off a chill. "Sylvia willed the house to Lilly Mills, Gunther's old girlfriend."

I nodded. Like a lifelong local, I knew exactly who she meant.

The agent shook her head. "Lilly split town after the robbery. She's lived in Madison, Wisconsin ever since. Raised her daughter there. Anyway, I guess Sylvia figured giving Lilly the property was the least she could do, given how Gunther treated her. Ms. Mills hired the first agent, and ordered him to sell the property any way he could. But stories had already circulated about the house being haunted. And now, I can't give the house away."

"But that's not possible. I just..." I stopped, knowing I'd sound insane if I finished the thought. Instead, I said the one thing I cared about the least. "Why is the rocking chair still on the porch?"

Hariette shook her head. "We've all dragged that piece of junk to the curb for the trash pick-up, but, every time we'd return, it was right back there on the porch, cobwebs and all. Maybe some kids playing pranks. I finally decided to leave it there. I'm not about to get my suit dirty, again."

My focus returned. I couldn't accept the obvious conclusion of my experiences. "So what do *you* think? That someone's playing a trick, or the house is haunted?"

Hariette shrugged, clearly not interested in giving the matter much thought. "Haunted or not, I was a fool to accept this challenge, and I'm stuck with it until my listing agreement runs out. One month left to go."

I stepped toward my house, biting back what I wanted to scream. *Who did I talk to? What did it mean? Am I losing my mind?* "Well, good luck."

The agent nodded, still standing in front of her cursed property. "Thanks. If you know any crazy friends who want to buy a haunted house, give me a call. I'll make them a great deal."

I approached the sanctuary of my own home, inserted my key, and opened the door.

Shaking off the chill, I walked across the living room and dropped my backpack on the couch. Someone was playing tricks, some sick old hag having fun at my expense. I could rationalize some prankster removing the sign. I could even accept that I'd been so awed by the creepy old lady, I'd never noticed the boarded-up windows. *Doesn't matter, I'll get my revenge later. I have more immediate concerns.*

Ghosts weren't real. And a good thing, too. Because tonight, I had enough to worry about dealing with the real world.

CHAPTER TWENTY-THREE

I burst into my bedroom, my mind already five steps ahead, focused on what I needed to bring for later tonight. I grabbed two bobby pins off my dresser and stuck them into my hair.

Pack light, Chip had said to pack light. He'd take care of the tools. I pulled open the closet door and placed my hands on The Box, still hidden away behind my shoes and winter boots.

I hadn't opened The Box since that day Sylvia, or whoever she was, made me return the switchblade. Somehow, I couldn't get rid of the items inside, no matter how much I told myself I would never need them again.

I flipped up the lid, fished past the top layer of buttons, and grabbed at the sharp metal pins. I found the three or four most useful ones from the dozen Joey had filed for me.

My fingers brushed across the carved wooden handle with the tell-tale metal switch, and a tingle ran up my arm. I scooped up the knife. It lay across my open palm, from my wrist to the second joint of my middle finger.

I closed my hand over the weapon. The silver blade *snicked* into place, doubling the length of the weapon. Light reflected on silver, and I could stare back at my own widened eyes in the edge of the blade.

Shocked eyes. Weak eyes. The look of someone who'd gone to the edge and walked away.

At the time Joey gave the illegal knife to me as a misguided birthday present, he showed me how to kill with it, all theoretical information. I'd never been in that dire of a situation. He also showed me how *not* to kill with it. Most times, the simple appearance of the blade and a couple threats got me out of almost all nasty situations in 'Ripple.

I heard the front door open and shut.

Without further thought, I retracted the blade into the sheath and slid the weapon into my pocket.

I could hear determined footsteps cross the living room and enter the hall.

I closed the box as casually as I could and placed it back into its hiding spot.

I heard the door open behind me as my hand closed around a flashlight.

I stood and turned. "Hi, Mom."

No salutations. She stood, hands folded across her chest, leaning against the doorframe. She jumped right in. "Fiona, did you have a boy over at the house while I was away?"

Oops. "Uh, just a friend, Mom. He picked me up, and we went to a movie."

Her eyes glared disappointment and fury. "You're lying to me. Your friend was Eugene Farren, and he didn't leave here all night."

"Excuse me?" I stared into her angered face. "You...spied on me?"

Undeterred, she continued with the riot act. "What could you have *possibly* been thinking? His father is a very important contact with our firm."

I still couldn't get past the first point. "*Now* you spy on me? *Now?* What did you do, pay one of our fine neighbors to watch the house for you?"

She sighed and dropped her hands to her hips. "Fiona, does it matter how I found out? If word gets out to Eugene's father, it could be a problem for the both of us. I can't believe you would jeopardize my position like this."

The train of thought only now began to sink in. "Wait...you're angry...over *who* I slept with?"

Mom's nostrils flared, and I could see her teeth grind. "I don't pretend I know how to control you. But I thought you'd be more discreet. I thought somebody should keep an eye on the house since you're never home these days. Instead, I find out that when I'm gone you never leave the bedroom."

"Well, I figured one of us should be having fun."

She opened her mouth to say more, but nothing came out. Her face contorted into a grimace I'd never seen before, and it scared me.

Then, without another word, she turned on her heel and left, slamming the door behind her.

I heard her storming through the house. I stood in the middle of my room, not daring to move. Then, she started shouting, loud enough that she knew I could hear, about how I didn't respect her and didn't know how hard she worked for me. The usual tirade.

I waited impatiently until the ranting stopped, and an uneasy quiet settled over the house.

I knew the time had come to split. I placed the flashlight into my hip pack, zipped it, and strapped the pack on.

I threw the door open and cut across the living room.

"Just one second, young lady!"

I froze in place, my hand on the doorknob.

"Look."

Like a fugitive caught by the cops, I turned, slow and easy, and relaxed my arms.

She sat on the white couch. From where I stood, with her face in profile, I could see the age lines around her eyes and mouth in clear contrast to her smooth white skin. "I suppose I should take some of the blame. I kept you on a pretty loose leash in Broad Ripple. I never could get you to behave."

I cringed at her unintentional references to my "pet daughter" analogy.

She blinked tears from her eyes. "But you're in a community now, Fiona. Everything you do has consequences in ways that they never did in Broad Ripple. I didn't try to 'spy' on you, much as it might please you to think so. Your little antics came my way quite by accident. The same way they always do."

I flinched and looked down at the rug. *She knew.*

I heard her ironic chuckle. "Oh, yes, *all* of your antics. Even the Broad Ripple break-in."

The lie started by reflex. "I don't know what—"

"Of course, you do." I heard her deep sigh, and I wanted to disappear. "Dammit, Fiona, do you really think I'm that stupid? Do you think my daughter could attempt a felony that made the newspapers, and I wouldn't figure it out?"

I glanced up, shocked.

She leaned forward on the couch. The hard, disappointed look on her face overwhelmed me with guilt and forced me to look away again. "I didn't think it was worth mentioning at the time for two reasons, one of which was how badly you botched the job, and I knew the fear of God must have hit you in a way that I never could. Anything else was redundant."

I looked down at my feet. I couldn't believe she knew, that...she'd always known.

She paused, apparently to collect her thoughts, and then took another deep breath. "It was obvious, Fiona. The way you looked away whenever it was brought up, the stiffness in your shoulders; everything you did reflected your guilt." She spoke as if giving a public testimony. "You couldn't possibly hide that from me."

My anger finally overrode my guilt, and I looked her in the face. "But I don't understand. Why didn't you say anything? Not one word the entire time."

Mom shrugged her shoulders. "Because it wouldn't have done any good. And because you've since done more to punish yourself than any punishment I could come up with."

She knew, and she noticed. But she never said a word.

Mom brushed her hands across her face as if to wipe the new wrinkles away. "Fiona, I can't pretend that I understand you. When I was going to school, I didn't behave the way you do. You can be a real pain in the ass, but I also know, deep down, you're not a bad kid."

My breath caught in my throat at the half-compliment. Back-handed as it was, those words were the closest to praise than I'd heard since...well, since I couldn't remember.

She must have noticed. "It's true. And I know it. I could never afford to spend the time with you that children require. It just wasn't possible. And when you did something wrong, sometimes it was easier to just look past it."

She started blinking rapidly and rubbed at one eye with a palm as if trying to work out a lash. "But I also think I ignored you when you did good things, and I'm sorry about that. I just wish you didn't hate me so. But I guess most teenagers feel the same way, and sooner or later, you'll get over that, too."

Her shoulders slumped and her body seemed to more-or-less mold itself into the couch. "Somewhere down the line, you grew up, and I missed it all. When I heard what you had been doing this weekend...I thought about how much you'd slipped away from my life. If you were here to start dinner and disappear so I could rest, I was happy. But at some point, I lost touch."

Her body shook with a final sigh of defeat. "And when you turned against me, I didn't want to know you anymore."

"I never turned against you," I lied, feeling guilty because I had done exactly that.

"Oh, Fiona, of course, you did. And I reacted badly, of course. I don't know you. I've never even tried to understand you, and I don't even remember when that started happening."

I took a tentative step toward the couch where she sat, her face looking more defeated than I'd ever seen in my life. "Mom...all these years, you've been just a peripheral part of my life. I stay out of your way and I make my own space. Hell, you *taught* me how to do that. And now, all of a sudden you're concerned."

My hands balled into fists. "But you're not concerned because of me. You're more concerned about your *business* and how my latest actions might affect it." I approached the couch, gaining new strength. "But it's not about me at all. So don't pretend for one minute that it is."

She sighed, staring straight ahead with a look of resignation. After a long time, she finally spoke. "You're right." Her voice came to me in a whisper. I had to strain to hear her. "It's absolutely pathetic, but you're right."

I shook my head and matched her quiet tone. "Doesn't matter now. It's all different. As soon as we moved, it all became different."

"But...Fiona, maybe I was upset for the wrong reasons, but this afternoon I came to a decision. I want to get back in touch with my daughter. I know that we...what I mean is...just because we fight all the time, I never stopped caring about you." She swallowed. "Or loving you."

"Mom..." I couldn't recall the last time she'd said that.

I sat down next to her on the couch. She reached out to me, squeezing my limp hand and sniffling in a motherly fashion.

I'd never seen her cry. Not ever. I didn't know what to say or do.

Tears continued to run freely down her face. "Look at you. You've become a woman on me. And I've missed it."

"I've been here, Mom."

"But...you look like you're getting ready to go out, even now. Can you stay?" I heard the *please* she couldn't bring herself to say out loud.

Dammit. Now *my* eyes were stung from fresh tears. *Why is this happening tonight? It's not fair that I have to choose.*

I shook my head. "No. What I mean is, I have something I have to do tonight." I couldn't look at her. I focused on the glass coffee table in front of us.

"Will you be with Eugene?"

"Yes. Chip. He's taking me to Perionne Park." Well, that much was true.

"Oh."

We wallowed in an awkward silence. From the corner of my eye, I could see her wiping tears. "Is he...a nice boy?"

I smiled, and my composure broke. I swallowed back my own tears. "Yes. Oh, yes. Very nice. You'll like him."

"Oh, my. I've heard that tone of voice before. I sounded just like you, a long time ago." She leaned forward, trying to see my face. "Fiona, you're in love!"

I opened my mouth to state a denial, then paused. "I don't know."

I looked into her eyes and flinched, seeing genuine concern reflected back. "You sound like me, a long time ago." Then, after a moment, she added, "Be very careful."

What was she talking about? "I sound like you?"

She nodded, but didn't elaborate. A thoughtful expression covered her face. I could see, for the first time, individual gray strands standing out in her dark hair. "Listen, I'm blowing off work tomorrow to take it easy. What do you say we..." She shrugged. "...we find out what there is to do around here?"

I took a breath and prepared to tell her I couldn't. "I'd like to; I don't know."

She nodded, keeping her face emotionless, but I could read her disappointment. "Okay, well, you think about it." With that, she rose and stepped toward the kitchen.

I called out to her retreating back. "Mom?"

She stopped in mid-reach of her briefcase, which she'd earlier placed in the recliner. "Yes?"

I paused, gathering my courage, wondering if this was a good time. Then decided to plunge ahead. "What happened between you and my father?"

A pained look crossed her face, and she reached a hand up to cover her mouth. "I never told you?" Her voice trembled.

I pushed forward. "No. You refused to tell me. I always thought Paul was my father. Was he?"

Mom lifted the briefcase and placed it on the ground, seating herself. She stared into space and didn't answer for many seconds. At first, I didn't think she would. "I'm sorry, Fiona. I really messed up."

I gripped the arm of the couch, my hand digging into the arm. *Finally, I'd know.* "Will you tell me what happened?"

Mom nodded and then drew a deep, shuddering breath. "It's always been painful for me to talk about. I didn't realize that...you still remembered him." She seemed to drift off, and then return, speaking from a distant place. "You still remember your father. I think you were, what, maybe, five years old the last time you saw him?"

I pressed the question I really wanted to know. "Why did he go away, Mom? Why did he leave me? Why did he leave *us?*"

She looked away. "He was a senior partner in the firm when we started dating." Her voice took on a high, drifting quality at the memory. "Paul was a wonderful man, and, for a long time, we were *so* happy together. I would have done anything for him."

Her voice hardened with bitterness. "Then I became pregnant.

And..." She shrugged, as if words failed her. "He...decided fatherhood wasn't something he really wanted."

I shook my head, not wanting to hear what she said. "But he seemed so ... he always tried really hard...to make me happy." *I had it all wrong.*

"Oh, yes. He was a great weekend dad, wasn't he? But that's all he really wanted." She shrugged. "I kept hoping some day, given enough time, he'd want to build something permanent for all three of us. But he never..." Her shoulders slumped, and she let the thought trail away. "And I got tired of waiting."

She raised her arms, then slapped them on her lap. "And then he received a job offer from New York. He's been contributing to your trust fund like clockwork, but otherwise I've never seen him. It hurts too much."

She stood, looking down at me with a sad, sober expression. "And he's never wanted to see me, either. Even at the end, if he'd offered to marry me or take us in, I would have gone. But he never offered."

She dropped down next to me on the couch. "And I didn't want you to know that your father didn't want us. And for that, I'm sorry, because you deserved better."

The world lost focus. The painful truth that my father had chosen to leave us was more than I could take. I wept, overwhelmed, aching to my soul. Unimportant tears spilled down my cheeks.

Loving arms embraced me. "Fiona, honey, I'm so sorry."

"God...I'm sorry, Mom, I didn't know..." I couldn't go on.

Like a small child, I cried against my mother's bosom. Her soft voice shushed me to a numb calmness.

I've hated her for so long...for the wrong reasons. How can I make that up?

I sniffled and took a deep breath. I reached out and gripped her arm. "I'll be here tomorrow."

"Good."

I sat up, wiping my face clean.

Her face showed visible disappointment. "But now you have to go."

"Yes. I really do. It's vitally important, or I wouldn't." On a weird impulse, I leaned over and kissed my mother's cheek. "There's something I have to do. But I'll be here tomorrow. I promise."

CHAPTER TWENTY-FOUR

As the sun dipped down below the horizon, I approached the two-story brick home. The looming presence seemed to swallow me.

I reached out and knocked on the thick door made of solid redwood.

The door opened. The light from the room behind him placed me in the darkness of Mr. Farren's overwhelming shadow.

He looked down at me and grinned, folding his beefy arms across his solid lumberjack's chest, an image strengthened by the now-familiar red-striped button-down shirt and blue jeans. I couldn't shake an odd fear that he'd reach down and pat me on the head.

Did he know Chip and I were sleeping together? If he did, did he care?

"Fi-Fi. How are you?" His bearded face reflected only friendly concern. "Chip tells me you two are going to the park. Probably need a break from cracking the books, I'm sure."

Sounds pretty clueless to me, or is he being sarcastic?

I shifted my weight from foot to foot. "Yeah, Mr. Farren. I guess the park's not going to be open much longer." *Duh. No kidding, Mr. Obvious.*

But if Mr. Farren found the comment lame, he kept it to himself. "Oh, I imagine that come the first really cold weather in the next week or so, they'll decide to call it quits." He nodded vigorously, looking ready to grab his coat and join us.

Instead, he stepped aside, and I shuffled past into the small wood-paneled foyer leading to the carpeted living room. "Is Chip upstairs?"

"Yep. I imagine he'll be right down, but you can go up if you want."

"Thanks." I ascended the stairs toward the loft, my hiking boots making a loud clomping noise on the wood.

Halfway up, Mr. Farren called out. "Say, Fi-Fi, how's your mom doing? I stop in to see her sometimes, she might have told you. She looks like she has a pretty full plate."

I turned, pivoting on the step. *Have any nice chats about your son and me?*

Out loud, I said, "She's always been that way, Mr. Farren. I guess I'm used to it." *Is this still bullshit conversation, or is he fishing for something?*

Nope, I'm not paranoid.

For once, Mr. Farren had to look up at me. "I would imagine you've had to be pretty independent."

Oh, God, I just want to go upstairs. Why does he keep talking to me?

I crouched down, sitting on the stair, resigned to an extended conversation. "I get along by myself pretty well."

He nodded. "I reckon you do. But a girl your age could find herself in all kinds of trouble, left on your own." He put his hand on the railing. "It's good to be with people. That's why I stayed around after my wife died. There's always someone looking out for you, no matter what happens. Know what I mean?"

A chill ran along my back, but I gave him my best innocent grin.

"I guess so. I'm just not used to it." I stuck my thumb up toward the loft. "I'm going to go upstairs now."

"Okay, sure."

I retreated up the wooden steps, feeling his gaze on my back. The thudding of my footsteps matched the pounding of my heart.

CHIP SAT AT HIS DESK, staring intently into the blue-lit screen. I wasn't sure he'd heard me enter until he said, without turning, "Find some room on the bed, Blue."

I stepped over to the cluttered wreck he called a bed. I moved aside a copy of *Ruby on Rails for Dummies*. I plopped down after I made enough room to wedge my butt between all his books.

After a couple minutes, I started to feel a bit like the discarded paperback, set aside until Chip was ready for me. My dear friend had tunnel-vision of the brain.

His fingers flew over the keyboard, scanning the screen for information and typing in several lines of some sort of programming code.

A few keystrokes later, he closed the window and shut down the computer with a push of a button. "That's enough for one day. Did you bring the stuff?"

I tapped my messenger bag. "Right here."

"Okay." He grinned at me then reached out and grabbed my outstretched hands. "I'm glad you're here."

I smiled back at him. "Me, too."

He led me to the door, grabbing his tan jacket off the bed. "Let's go."

We walked through the park. I curled an arm around Chip's arm, snuggling against him. In my opposite hand, I held a sugar cone, two scoops; one chocolate, the other mint chocolate chip. *Next best thing to heaven.*

The full moon glowed bright overhead, beaming white. Appropriate for mid-October, I guess.

We'd spent the last couple hours shuffling from ride to ride. Midnight approached; the crowd had thinned down to only a few of us teenagers.

As we walked along the wooded path, I glimpsed several couples hiding away in the bushes, developing a sudden and keen interest in botany, no doubt. I debated pulling Chip into the fauna to categorize a few leaves together.

The temperature had dropped rapidly. The chill failed to penetrate the warm and fuzzy energy coursing through me at the moment.

I guess Mom's right, I'm beginning to fall for this little computer geek. So be it.

I let Chip lead me along the darkened path.

He motioned toward wooden roller coaster support beams just off the path to the right. The track arched overhead. "If we cut through under the *Whirlwind*, we'll save some walking time."

I let him lead. He diverted from the main walkway into wet grass. Crisscross shadows lay across the ground where we stepped. We entered near-total darkness.

A churning rumble built up above. High-pitched screams passed overhead. Out of my peripheral vision, I spied the shadowy figures of another couple studying the track foundations, undoubtedly for a future architecture project.

As we walked arm in arm, moonbeams broken up by the track overhead created a flickering across Chip's face. I couldn't ignore the eerie, erotic sensation that drove me to act.

I stepped forward, turned in front of him, and placed a hand against his chest. The train passed overhead, causing a rumbling through the wooden planks that vibrated down my spine.

"Kiss me."

He smiled, leaning over me. The warmth of his breath traveled across my face.

I sighed and hugged him. "You drive me crazy, Chip."

A second train passed overhead, the noise building into a rumbling crescendo; a dark shadow fell over us. Playful screams overcame all sound.

A charging body slammed into us, and Chip sprawled. The blunt force caught me full in the back.

Off balance, I tumbled into a wooden support rail, hitting it with my shoulder.

Still stunned, I kicked blindly at the moss, trying to find my bearings.

A bulky pair of hands gripped my jacket at the shoulders and lifted me off the ground.

My legs kicked into the air. I locked my hands around a pair of beefy wrists, but couldn't stop myself from once again being slammed into the wooden support.

Pain shot up my back, and my vision cleared into sharp, painful focus.

I blinked, staring into the snarling face of a furious Clinty Buckner.

"Surprise, bitch!"

I kicked and twisted to no avail. His arms pulled me forward and pushed back. My back smashed into the wood.

The world exploded in pain. My legs would not respond.

Stupid, to get caught like this. Now Clinty would kick the shit out of me.

He grabbed me up, getting close to my face, showing his over-sized teeth. "I knew if I followed you, I'd get you. Now we square up for the other day. You're gonna be beggin' me. C'mon, beg!"

Fuck him. No matter what I do, he'll cream me.

I drew a deep breath of desperately needed air and snarled back. "Please...you fat shit...don't breathe on me again." I kicked my legs back against the supports, but I couldn't budge.

His eyes bugged in fury.

Someone tackled us.

Clinty staggered, releasing my jacket.

I fell back against the support.

Clinty stumbled past me.

Chip grabbed Clinty's arm.

Clinty grunted and flung his beefy hand into an arch that sent Chip sprawling.

I stared, watching, horrified, as Chip spun off and tripped over another support.

Reflex took over.

I growled, drawing my knife out of my pocket. My thumb flicked the trigger, and I charged forward.

I slashed the blade across his huge chest, cutting a thin slice through clothes and skin from his huge shoulder to prominent belly.

Clinty screamed, falling backwards.

He collapsed to his knees, his hands clasping his chest.

I stood over him, panting for air. As I watched blood trickle through his T-shirt and jacket, satisfaction welled up within me.

The overhead rumble built up around us again, drowning out all sound and light.

When I could see Clinty again, he lay sprawled on his knees, grabbing his stomach as if to keep his innards from leaking onto the grass.

His eyes darted to me. His lower lip trembled. "Oh, God, you cut me. I'm gonna die. You bitch, you cut me—"

I advanced on him, holding the blade out in front of me and trying not to wince from pain. I swiped the point toward his face. "Shut up! If I wanted to kill you, you wouldn't be talking now."

He squealed like the fat pig he resembled and scuttled away from me, his arms rising in front of him to protect himself.

The rumble built up again, and, when the cloak of darkness fell over us, I jumped around his back, leaned over, and grabbed a handful of greasy hair. I placed the point of the blade beneath his chin and pushed hard enough for him to feel it. Then, I urged him forward, forcing him onto his hands and knees.

He reached up.

I pressed the knife into the flesh under his chin. "Don't. Or you die now."

He yelped in shock and pain and then let out a pathetic sob.

I relished his helplessness.

I straddled his prone body, putting my face behind his, whispering into his ear like a lover. "You...cowardly fuck!"

"Don't kill me."

"Oh, Clinty," I whispered. "You're already begging. How disappointing. How boring." I drew the blade up as if to slash across his throat.

He screamed, his body shaking from the blow I never delivered.

And I enjoyed watching it. I enjoyed *causing* it. The arrogant bastard needed a solid dose of terror, and I aimed to deliver in spades. "Oh, but I could kill you, Clinty. Slit your throat before you could raise a hand to stop me. So fast, I wouldn't even get blood on my hands."

"*Please* don't."

"'Please don't,'" I whined a high, mocking imitation. "Don't tremble so much. It's annoying me."

But Clinty had nothing left. No threats, no pride, no bravado. He lay beneath me, begging, overwhelmed from pure terror, pleading for his life. "I'm sorry. Please, *please* don't kill me. I'll do anything you say."

I pressed the knife. "Shut up! Listen to me. You're not going to die from that scratch I gave you. I didn't even begin to cut through all that lard, but yeah, you're bleeding like a stuck pig. Big surprise."

I continued to keep one hand entwined in his hair, the other still pressing the point to his neck. "Do you understand now, who you're fucking with? But I'm giving you this one last chance. You come near me, or Chip, or Phil, or any of their friends, I'll kill you. I won't bother kicking your ass again."

My own hand, holding the knife, started to shake from the strain. I tightened my grip. I heard him wince in response. "I'll find you, and I'll cut your heart out. This is your only warning."

His head shifted in the start of a nod, unable to complete the motion from the knife pressed under his chin. He groaned something similar to a yes.

The coaster roared overhead again. I tightened my grip as he blacked out of my sight for a second.

He didn't even think about moving.

Light poured down on me again. "Now, I'm going to pull away. When I've reached Chip, you will drag your fat ass off the ground, and be careful not to dribble any blood on your way home. Otherwise I'll have to tell everybody what happened tonight. Lucky for you, I'd rather nobody knew about this."

Air blew out his nose in shaking spurts. "Okay. That's cool. You bet!"

I pulled the knife away from his neck, and, mustering my pride and strength, managed to rise to my feet and stand over him.

I walked in unsteady, stumbling steps to where Chip sat, his back against the support. In his eyes, I saw utter shock at my performance.

I watched Clinty totter to his feet.

He looked down at the slashed ruin of his T-shirt, still stupidly unaware that his injury was a simple surface wound.

His eyes met mine, reflecting sheer terror.

I crouched down next to Chip, keeping the blade out in plain view. "Get out of here."

He turned and scrambled away.

The rumbling of the coaster overhead blocked out the moonlight.

By the time the joyful screaming ended, he'd vanished, leaving in his stead a few drops of blood reflecting in the grass.

The shakes hit. My arms and legs trembled out of control.

The knife fell to the ground.

Gentle arms encircled and cradled me.

I clung to Chip, and he held me tight.

I cried into his chest, punctuating my sobs with curses. Finally, the flow stopped.

"Chip...you really came through this time. He was ready to pound me into the emergency room."

"*I* came through?" Chip's shaking voice betrayed his shock and terror. "I'd be surprised if Clinty ever shows his face in the school again after that. Jesus, Blue. Where did that *come* from?"

A bitter laugh escaped through my tears. "Oh, Chip." I whispered the same words I'd used moments earlier. "Do you understand now who you're fucking with?" I felt his body stiffen.

I looked up at the moonlight reflecting off a wooden beam. "I told you I was trouble for you. Some of what you saw, part of that's the real me. The part I had to bring out in 'Ripple, just to clear a path to an exit. And afterwards, I told myself it's just an act, but I know I'm *this* close to something dangerous and awful."

Chip held me tight. "Maybe a little dangerous. But never awful."

I laughed and wiped my face.

Chip shuffled in the grass. "We need to go. They're going to close down soon."

Loud shrieks cut through the air, and the train passed overhead. I shivered and leaned against him. "I know. Just hold me. Just for a minute."

CHAPTER TWENTY-FIVE

With only a few minutes until closing, the line to the Pirates of Perionne ride no longer existed. Holding hands, Chip and I walked down the stairs, our feet clomping on the wood. We descended to the circular platform. A single bored attendant leisurely leaned on a long wooden stick marked with a red line at roughly four and a half feet high. The platform continued its endless slow rotation.

The stocky, college-aged attendant reached up, tipping his hat to reveal thick blond hair, now pressed tight around his head from too many hours of wearing the required cap. "Good evening, Sir. Milady."

His slap-happy charm made me smile.

I took a step toward the boat, but he moved forward in front of me, thumping the stick down and making a show of eyeballing the red line on the marker.

"I don't know if you're tall enough. It's going to be close."

I folded my arms. "How'd you like the stick shoved up to the red hash mark?"

Chip put a hand on my shoulder. "Blue..."

"Chuck!" An unfamiliar voice called out. "Are you flirting with the ladies again?" I peered into the darkness to see the silhouette of a second attendant, exceptionally tall and thin, with strands of dark hair peeking out from under his cap. He walked with practiced diligence along the wheel-shaped dock, using a squeegee with an extra-long handle to wipe out the boats as they emerged from the ride.

He looked over at me and tipped his own cap. "I've heard about her. She can probably do exactly what she says."

Chuck called back. "Just keep wiping the boats, Bob. Don't forget who wears the striped pants around here."

Bob grumbled. "I'm just sayin'. If she does it, I'm not pulling it back out for you."

Chuck grinned and stepped aside. "After you, Milady." He removed his hat, waving me forward.

Chip shook his head, pulling me behind him. "Must've been a long day." We walked along the dock, and he quickly outpaced me.

Bob removed his hat and waved it in the direction of the semi-dry boat. "This way, Sir. Milady." He bent over in a corny bow. "Your chariot awaits."

Chip took my hand, but I resisted, my wicked mind already foreseeing the possibilities. "You first."

Chip stepped into the boat and straddled the still-damp seat. I stepped in, but instead of settling down in front of him, I fell backwards, dropping into his lap.

He grunted *oof*, and his arms encircled around me in a tight squeeze.

Bob raised his hat and shook it above his head. "Just a friendly reminder. It's a three-minute ride." With a wink, he stepped across the dock and away from us, approaching the next couple.

My positioning on Chip's lap proved to be a happy accident. With a casual glance over his shoulder, I could confirm what we'd figured and hoped, based on what Chip had observed from past visits. The attendant had escorted the next couple to the closest ride from the entryway, leaving three empty boats between us.

Our little capsule drifted against the double-doors, which split aside. We floated through into the noisy wonderland of cackling puppets, organ music, and "Yo-Ho-Hos."

As if to ward me off, Chip pushed the flats of his hands against my lower ribs. "C'mon, Blue. We should get ready."

But my body ached from pent-up excitement. I twisted in his lap and pressed against him. "You heard the man. We have three minutes." I planted a hard, rough kiss against his mouth.

Given his agitation and nervousness, he still responded. Sort of.

As our boat drifted through the room, I sensed, more than saw, the large pirate ship.

Like palpable electricity, tension filled my body.

I separated from his unresponsive lips, and instead leaned forward into a hug, my mouth brushing against his ear. "It's going to be okay," I whispered.

Who am I trying to convince?

Breathless, I turned to confirm that the pirates were still fighting off the natives on the island and the other pirate still chased the wench on the ship.

The boat turned in its track, lining up with the double doors to the final room.

I pushed myself forward to my own seat. "Are you ready?"

"Yes."

I gripped his hand, squeezing his fingers in mine.

"Anything going on behind us?"

I craned my neck backward. "The next couple hasn't even entered this room."

The doors split open.

The boat emerged to begin a slow semi-circle around the small islet.

The large pirate with the eye patch swung his machete at us. "Get your own gold, Matey! This be all mine!"

Chip released his hand from mine. "Now!"

Chip bolted from the boat first, landing onto the sand and darting for the cardboard palm tree mockup with catlike agility.

I jumped after him.

My foot skidded off the vinyl siding, and I toppled into the sand. "Damn!"

I rolled across the ground, fighting down panic. My body slid to a stop at the edge of the pedestal, and I jumped to my feet. With one fluid motion, I stepped onto the wooden plank, gripped the sides of the plastic pot, and side-jumped into the gullet of the oversized cauldron.

Crouching down, I could hear the thump of double-doors being driven apart. I had no way of knowing if I'd been seen. I held my breath and waited.

The pirate called out its eternal warning. "Git your own gold, Matey! This be all mine!"

Sound muted by the ancient plastic surrounding me, I strained to hear beyond the warped music tape and the gurgling water.

I released my held breath, adjusting to a squatting position, and waited for what seemed an eternity.

The unpleasant odor of mold tickled my nose. I stifled a sneeze.

If someone saw us, how long would it take before they shut the ride down and conducted a search? When would we know?

"Git your own gold, Matey! This be all mine!"

A high feminine shriek pierced the air, making me cringe. A hysterical giggle followed the shriek.

I rubbed my itching eyes, which made my nose complain further.

God, how am I going to survive?

"Git your own gold Matey! This be all mine!"

Frustrated, I banged my head against the back of the pot, and then quickly hunched down against my knees.

What if someone heard that?

How could anyone hear me? It's way too noisy in this room.

But why take the chance?

Great; now I'm arguing with myself.

Hey, stupid. You slipped and fell. How could you let that happen? This little adventure could have ended in disaster before it started. And it would have been your fault. And you harped all over Chip because you didn't think he could handle it.

"Git your own gold Matey! This be all mine!"

Ha, ha, Gunther. You're a funny guy, hiding the money in this room. Wouldn't you love to know your irony is appreciated over twenty-five years later?

How long has it been? Chip said the park could remain open for another half hour or so, depending on the crowd.

"Git your own gold—"

"Hey, fuck you, one-eye!" A deep, loud voice called out. "I got your pot of gold right here!"

I shoved a hand into my mouth, biting down to keep a loud laugh from escaping.

Is that guy passing a bottle with his buddies, or trying to impress a date? Ooooh, you're so cool, man. Now, bend over and moon it.

"Git your own gold, Matey! This be all mine!"

I wiped cold moisture from my forehead. "Screw you, Gunther. It's ours, now."

I HUDDLED in the confines of the plastic cauldron, biting down on my chattering teeth and waiting for the shakes to pass. Instead, they increased. The sides of the container seemed to fold over me, and I found myself holding back a scream.

I closed my eyes. *I can do this, I can do this, I can do this...*

When I thought I couldn't take another second, just when I knew

I'd pop out of the cauldron like a demented life-size jack-in-the-box terrifying whichever boat riders happened to be traveling through the room at that moment, the pirate drone stopped. The loud, constant organ music also cut off. I sat engulfed in dark and silence. Only the pounding of my heart, thumping loud and fast in my own head, interrupted the otherwise total quiet of my surroundings.

I closed my eyes, hunkering down against my aching legs, but it made no difference against the sickening vertigo that insisted the room was spinning.

I panted deep breaths, a harsh hissing sound that echoed loudly off the confines of my prison walls.

My pounding heart, my gasps for breath, and a trickle of water in the distance overloaded my senses.

I forced myself to count slowly to ten; forced my hands to reach with purpose above my head. No mad jack-in-the-box antics at this point.

In my plastic-shelled confines, the rustle of denim struck me as obscenely loud.

I gripped the edge of the pot, pulling myself up. My legs stretched gratefully, the knots of pain easing.

My back, where I had taken the beating beneath the roller coaster, throbbed.

I looked over the lip of the cauldron; a blast of cool air fluttered against my face. I drew in blessed fresh air in deep, grateful gulps.

Instantly, the pounding in my head quieted and the sickening motion settled.

With intentional calm, I reached down into my messenger bag, identified the telltale thin rod via the Braille method, raised the flashlight to point in front of me, and flipped the switch.

My thin beam of light beam cut through the darkness.

I looked down, illuminating the wooden porch-like platform beneath the pot in my spot of light. Shiny plastic coins lay sprinkled on the ground around me. The platform itself was barely wide enough to hold the plastic bowl. The planks of the platform were widely spaced, showing large gaps in the pedestal. Its only purpose seemed to be to provide stability for the cauldron on the otherwise sandy island. The wood, upon careful inspection, showed varying grades and conditions, indicating several repairs through the years.

Additional twin beams lit up the night. I turned to see Chip depositing two pen-sized flashlights onto the ground. He held out his hands.

Grateful for the help, I put the penlight between my teeth. I gripped one of his hands and reached down with the other to support myself on the cauldron. With one easy hop, I cleared the edge and landed in the sand.

I took a moment to assess my surroundings. The three penlights did little to illuminate the islet. The engulfing darkness pressed in all around us.

I stared down at the wooden platform beneath the cauldron. Two people could lift and set the platform aside with ease.

I ran my hands over my face, trying to shake a surreal, dreamlike essence to my vision.

Somewhere in the room beyond the light, I heard a continuous gurgle of water, an annoying white noise further deadening my senses.

Growing annoyed, I directed my beam to the double set of doors leading to the outside. Through these doors, the boats took their exit back to reality.

I called out into the darkness. "Well. Now what?" My voice echoed several times through the domed chamber.

Chip jumped, startled. "Let's keep it down, okay?" He opened his knapsack and produced a hammer and a military-styled shovel with collapsible handle. "Umm, the thieves came through the door and onto this island, burying the money right underneath this pot."

"Chip, are you *sure* about this? If we spend the night digging up this island and we don't find anything, I'm going to stick the shovel in a *very* uncomfortable spot."

Chip looked down at the platform and shrugged. "I'm sure about this. As sure as I am about anything."

I wiped my hands across my face again, but the surreal buzzing only intensified. I'd never experienced such a level of claustrophobia before. I didn't think it affected me, but the light kept seeming to dim out and darkness kept overtaking the room. The huge, cavernous walls wanted to close in and bury me forever. "I'm sorry; I'm hot, and I'm pissed, and my back hurts. I was almost caught due to my own stupidity, and we haven't even started digging yet. And you're the only one here to take it out on."

Chip nodded. "It'll be okay, Blue." He stood on one side of the cauldron, bracing his hands along the outwardly curved lip. "Help me. It's not as light as it looks."

I gripped the other side.

Together, we lifted the cauldron to reveal the wood beneath.

"So we move the platform and dig under it? And we'll find the bag with the money in it?"

"Should be."

I smiled. "And we make the front page of the morning paper, Special Souvenir Edition? And then I don't have to hear another word about Gunther, ever again?"

Chip grinned back at me. "No fair peeking at the last page."

I extended an arm. "Okay. Hand me the hammer. And if you have any more flashlights, turn them on. It's too damn dark in here."

Chip handed me the oversized hammer with a clawed end. Gripping the handle, a surge of energy coursed through me, clearing away the surreal buzzing. Excitement filled me; excitement over finding this treasure, excitement over fulfilling Chip's long-awaited hopes.

Chip snapped on two additional flashlights. The darkness receded further, and my sense of reality returned.

The platform, though well-settled into the ground beyond the thin layer of sand, popped up with ease after I pried it with the hammer.

Together, we made short work of moving the platform, and soon he and I were standing on the flattened bare earth.

Chip grabbed a second shovel, snapped it open, and held it out to me.

With our area now exposed and well-lit, Chip raised the shovel and turned in my direction. "Ready?"

"Ready. But first..." I leaned over and kissed him quickly. "I'm sorry I got so pissed."

Chip smiled, his blue eyes glittering in the light-beams. "You're fine. Your spunk is helping me to get through this."

As if on cue, we raised our shovels together and brought them down, breaking the ground in two separate places.

CHAPTER TWENTY-SIX

I drove the clawed hammer into hardened clay dirt, the *chunk* of breaking soil creating an answering weak echo throughout the domed chamber.

Splattering sweat stung my eyes and forced me to stop.

I stepped aside, pressing the hammer into the ground and leaning on the handle, wiping my sleeve across my face. My breath came in heavy gasps, and my palms stung from developing blisters. *I'll never make a living as a manual laborer.*

During the last couple hours, we'd dug down about a foot and a half, sticking to the twelve-foot circumference, large enough for two people to stand side-by-side and dig. We deposited the growing mound of dirt beyond the circle.

I'd long pushed aside all fears of getting caught, instead focusing on the exhausted ache of simple hard work.

The light, already too dim, flickered between near darkness and back again. I looked over to spy one of Chip's flashlights pulsing in irregular repetition. Losing the light would create a handicap we really didn't need.

Outside, the harsh whistling noise of a windstorm rattled the flimsy building, adding an intense vibrating backdrop to our work and making my skin crawl.

I wondered at the ferociousness of the windstorm. Although such storms were not unusual for October in Indiana, the evening had been calm, outright pleasant, up 'til now.

Getting annoyed at our decided lack of discovery, I straightened, bringing the hammer up and over my shoulder. "Are you *sure* they buried it underneath the cauldron?"

Chip paused, glaring at me, his own shovel raised at his shoulder. "Yes, I'm sure."

I bit back my own annoyance. "Because that's what your father's bowling buddy told him? He was that specific in detail?"

Chip stood straight, letting the shovel jab into the soil. "Yes. That's what he said."

I nodded, still chewing over the facts. "Well, then. Are you sure that this pedestal hasn't been moved since then? It's been over twenty years, right? Maybe they shifted the display from one side of the island to the other."

"I...don't think so." But he couldn't hide a look of shock that told me he hadn't considered the possibility.

I raised my hammer and pounded it into the dirt. "Great."

"Well, I can't think of everything, Blue." A whine entered his voice that danced on my last nerve. "This is an old ride. It hasn't changed since it went up, at least as far back as I can remember. But I can't swear the cauldron has been here in this exact spot since before we were born."

That didn't appease my building frustration. "I don't want you to swear about anything, I just want to find something."

I slammed the hammer deep into the sand. The clawed metal impacted something. A crackling noise echoed through the chamber.

I snagged my penlight from the ground and pointed the beam toward the newly turned dirt. "Oh, shit."

Chip rushed forward. "What!"

The light reflected off small broken pieces of dull white stones.

I squatted on my haunches and picked one up. I brushed my thumb along the texture, and knew with certainty I held a small bit of bone, maybe a knuckle bone.

Chip pointed, indicating all around me. "Look. Here's more. It looks like..." His voice trailed off.

I gripped the rough digit lengthwise, holding it under the light. "Gunther?"

Chip nodded. "Has to be. They buried him here. Buried him next to his stash. This confirms it."

With a morbid fascination, I held my hand up next to the knuckle bone. The bone extended a half inch beyond my own knuckle.

The strange, buzzing nausea overtook me again. "This just seems so...wrong."

Chip stood, walked across the dug-out dirt back to his own spot, and brought his shovel down.

I passed the penlight beam across the ground. At the same time, I kept shaking my head, trying to clear it of the buzzing energy.

Exposed bone sprinkles scattered along newly exposed soil, and, at the edge, a large protrusion poked out of the dirt. Gingerly, I extended my foot, tapping away the powder and exposing a larger white bone, stuck into the ground at an angle.

An upper arm, perhaps. I couldn't be sure.

A sudden creaking noise made me jump. The billowing wind had strained the double doors.

I shifted the penlight beam to view the shaking doors, surprised at the intensity of the rippling effect across the water. The waves traveled across the surface and washed up on the islet.

A shivering dread, like insects crawling below the surface of my skin, drove me to my feet. "Christ. We could find all of him. I'm not digging anymore." I pulled myself out of the hole and stepped up to beach level.

Again, Chip paused in his work. "What? Why not? They might have buried the money underneath him."

I stared down into the hole, battling a sudden onset of nausea. "Chip, it's a fucking grave site, and you want to know why I'm upset?"

Chip raised his shovel. "It's just a pile of bones. It can't hurt you. Look. There's no rot, there's no bugs. It's clean. It's been clean for years."

I fought back rising bile. "That's not the point."

Chip brought his shovel down.

A skewed rustling noise cut through the air, releasing a cloud of dirt that puffed around him, forcing him to step backward.

My nausea forgotten for the moment, I peered down into the hole, spying a cloth-like gray-leather pillow in the dirt. I pointed the penlight at it. "Oh, shit, Chip, that's it."

I dropped down to my hands and knees in front of the exposed cloth.

Chip joined me a moment later. His fingers clawed at the dirt. "Hold on." He broke away clay soil, exposing a large piece of gray cloth with black stenciled letters, much of it illegible, but _ionne_ and _ank_ stood out against the material.

Chip gripped the cloth and yanked, exposing a metal handle pulled loose from the dirt in a cloud. He gathered up a sizeable bank bag still securely clasped shut.

I watched Chip's face light up in euphoric relief. "Oh, God. This is it. We have it. We did it."

I laughed with delight. "Damned right we did. Never had a doubt."

He grinned. "Oh, you never had a doubt, huh?"

Seeing the look on Chip's face left me giddy with a joyous surge of happiness. "'Course not." I'd deny any statements to the contrary.

Chip fumbled with the snaps and drew the handles apart, kicking loose another cloud of dirt.

I coughed, the sound echoing through the room and joining the noise of the creaking double doors.

He peered into the open bag and then reached his hand in.

My eyes locked on the opening, anticipation filling my being like a palpable ache.

He withdrew a wad of bills, extending them to me. I took a few of them, gripping a hodgepodge of cash a couple inches thick.

I ruffled the bills. They puffed dust, and the green ink had faded to virtual nonexistence. But they still had the distinctive odor of United States currency.

My head reeled. The bag practically *bulged.*

Chip said, "You realize, you're about to become a very *famous* outsider to the town of Perionne. And probably an outsider no more."

I rubbed my itching nose. "You mean, they'll be telling stories in American Folklore fifty years from now about how the poodle with blue hair dug up the money?"

Chip laughed. "Something like that." Distracted, he turned his gaze back to the ground. "Hey, what's this?"

He aimed one of the penlights toward the ground and kicked at a small object, dislodging the item from the dirt.

I crawled around to get a better look.

Chip held a small object of reflective metal. A gray, rusty-metal handle that piqued my curiosity.

Is that what I think it is?

Even as Chip held it under the light, I reached a hand out and snatched it from him. "Hey!" I held it up to my own eager gaze. "A pocket knife." The thickened handle held at least eight various blades and contraptions.

I rubbed my hand along the handle, scraping away crusted brown corrosion, then dug my fingers into the thumb groove of the blade and pulled. It resisted.

Undaunted, I tried a second time, yanking loose a rusty, crusted blade twice the size of my palm. "An *excellent* pocket knife."

I stared, transfixed. Even after being buried all these years, I could make out intricate ornamental designs carved into the hardened wood. *With a little cleaning and some TLC, I could restore this to like-new condition.*

As I brushed crust from the blade, a realization hit me. A chill traveled across my fingertips.

"You said Crimley stabbed Gunther?"

Chip nodded. "That's what I heard."

I peered at the blade. "From your dad's bowling buddy. Well. Well, well." Somehow holding the murder weapon did not spook me the way picking through Gunther's bones did.

I looked away with an effort. "I guess I found me one hell of a souvenir."

Chip reached out. "It looks pretty crapped up, Blue. Maybe you'd better just put it in the bag."

I folded my hand around the handle and pressed it to my shoulder. "No. I want it." My tone came out whinier than I'd intended. I looked over at him, wondering at my own petulance. "I can have it, can't I?" I tried to keep my voice normal. "You keep the money and turn it over, but I want to keep this."

Chip shrugged, dropping his arm. "Sure, you can have it. Now, we've got to get this dirt back in place and get out of here."

I nodded and stood, placing the pocketknife in my jacket pocket so I wouldn't get it confused with my switchblade.

I glanced at the mounds of dirt and the huge hole, sighing. My nausea had passed for the moment, but I still dreaded the task of shoveling all that dirt back in.

CHAPTER TWENTY-SEVEN

Once we started, the shoveling took only a few minutes. Without much trouble, we adjusted the platform back to its original spot and slid the pot over it and into place.

Chip waited on his side of the cauldron as I brushed dirt from my jeans. "We need to make sure we spread the coins out like they were."

I walked over and stood across from him. "I know."

In unison, we lifted the cauldron and side-stepped together over to the platform, centering it, then setting it down.

Chip grinned at me. "Y'know, it could have been a lot worse. At least you uncovered his real hand. You might have dug up his prosthetic hook. Think about what kind of a souvenir *that* would have been."

The thought of a curved, rusted, metal hook protruding out of the soil sent a shudder through me, bringing on another bout of nausea. I leaned over the lipped opening on the cauldron, trying to keep the contents of my stomach where it belonged. "Ugh! What's wrong with me?"

Chip's hand fell onto my shoulder. "Are you okay?"

I nodded, indicating for him not to worry. *Just nerves.* Instead, I smiled.

Our light flickered and one of the questionable flashlights suddenly died. The smile froze on my face.

It was the third one to go out in the last hour, but the first one that made a major difference. Now, we were back to the original two penlights, and the details in the chamber were much harder to see.

I looked around for a way out. I could barely see the door frame at the back of the room. "Wait a second." I rushed over to the door and reached out to turn the knob. *Surely it can't be that easy.*

I'd guessed right; it couldn't be that easy.

I tried to twist the knob, only to meet solid resistance. What's more, the keyhole faced to the outside. I had nothing to pick. "Shit. I guess we have to go with our original plan."

I had disliked the original plan. And had hoped somehow the chamber door would have a fire lock designed to allow people to exit at will. *Of course not.* Chip's casual words from several weeks ago echoed in my head. *Perionne hasn't had a safety commissioner in over five years.*

I stared across the islet into blackness. I heard the trickling water but could no longer make out the double doors.

Kneeling down, I grabbed one of the penlights and then walked along the man-made beach of gritty packaged sand.

I gave Chip's backpack one last regretful glance. "I don't suppose you brought a pair of waders with you?"

"Sorry. They'd never fit."

"Didn't think so."

I looked down at my shoes until I saw water's edge, where the moat began.

Squinting off into the distance, I could barely see the double doors, though I had no trouble hearing them strain against the windstorm.

Chip called out. "Be careful. There's a guardrail that runs underwater the entire length to guide the boats."

I nodded, stripping off my shoes and socks and handing them to Chip. Then I rolled my blue jeans up to my knees.

I stood on the shoreline, taking a deep breath and coaxing my courage.

My toes stuck into water, cold enough to make me draw in a breath. Trying to ignore that, I told myself this was the only way out. I took my first step into the moat, my bare foot sliding on the slick, algae-covered surface.

My toes pressed against a slimy metal bar, and my balance shifted forward.

My foot slipped off the metal and sank into mud. "EEEE-yyyyuck!"

I caught myself, though my foot sank mid-shin into mud and slime. I drug my other foot off the shore and into the water, and then brushed against a small vertical bar, some sort of support holding the track in place. Again, my balance shifted and I waved my arms to keep on my feet.

Chip rushed forward, his shoes already off.

I waved him back. "Nope. I'm all right."

He stood on the shore, watching me, shifting his weight from foot to foot, his arms folded.

With deliberate slowness, I inched toward the double doors, the chill water sloshing around my calves. I tried to ignore the chattering of my teeth, and the part-tingling, part numbing sensations in my feet and legs. Step by step, the waterline slowly rose, eventually covering my blue jeans until I stood in water up to my waist.

It seemed to take forever before I stood in front of the double doors.

I reached out, pressing my palm flat against the left door. I could feel the vibration of the blowing windstorm through my hand. I pushed.

The door opened a few inches then stuck.

I pressed harder. The door wouldn't give.

A flash of anger made me see red. "What...the...*hell?*"

I heard cautious splashing approach from behind me. "What is it?" Chip called.

I stepped forward, aiming the penlight beam through the small gap between the doors. "I'm not sure." I could just make out something threaded across the opening, hip-height.

Linked metal.

"Shit!" I slapped my hand against the wood, sending a tremendous boom echoing around the chamber. "It's chained."

"What?"

"The door! They wrapped a chain around the handles from the outside. I can't get to it."

Chip stood at my side, watching me with a worried expression. "You have to be able to get to it."

I sighed. "What do you expect me to do? Detach my arms and stick them through?"

"Well, how far does it open?" A hint of mild annoyance entered Chip's voice.

I shoved against the left side with both palms. The gap opened about eight inches and then caught.

Wind billowed into my face. Buffeting turbulence made both my arms vibrate from the strain. After a few seconds, I eased the pressure, and the gap closed. "That far."

He bent his head toward the gap. "Hmmm. Well, maybe we can slip under it." With that, he pressed the one side open as far as it would go, then wiggled into the gap, head-first.

As he forced his head through the opening, I grew anxious. The wood dug at his ears, and I winced. But to his credit, he shoved forward.

Only after he'd locked his head in the gap between the doors did it become apparent that his shoulders were too wide to fit through the opening. "There's no way I can do it."

I braced the door so he could pull his head back. "Here, get out of there."

I placed one hand on each of the doors and pushed against them with all my might. I estimated a total clearance of about fourteen inches, if someone forced the doors open and held them for me. "Okay...I think I can make it, but I need your help."

I linked my hands together, stirrup-style, and held them down at thigh level, demonstrating. "Do that."

Chip looked at me, then at the door, then back.

"You think you can make it over?"

I nodded. "Gotta be safer than trying to swim under. And I'll have a much easier time than you."

Chip shook his head and linked his fingers. "Famous last words."

I pinched the penlight between my teeth. "You ready?"

He bent his knees, waiting. "Okay."

Once more, I pressed against the doors, shoving them as far apart as possible. The wind created a resistance.

I braced my legs, steeling my courage.

I stepped up with my right leg, grimacing at the stiffness from my bruises, and pressed my bare foot into Chip's hands.

I jumped; he lifted.

I sailed up into the air.

Chip propelled me four feet off the ground. Gravity reasserted itself. I was above the chain, but still on the wrong side of the opening. Reflex took over, and I kicked out with my left foot, slipping it between the doors.

My foot came down onto the chain.

My own weight forced the doors together on my leg.

I flailed with my hands, grabbing the sides of the door to catch my balance, but the gap closed over my foot.

The door shifted and widened.

I realized Chip had diverted his attention to holding the doors open. I grunted approval and wrapped my fingers around the edges of the doors.

I shoved forward; my head squeezed through the opening. I willed my body to come through after it.

No luck.

After a little push and pull, I wedged my shoulder through the gap.

Brisk, chilly October wind buffeted my face, stinging my eyes. The doors tightened, like a clap, against my chest and back.

The wood pressed tight, digging into my sternum. I clawed my nails against the wood but couldn't push myself forward.

I pulled. I pulled again, to no avail.

Sweat dripped from my brow and into my face. I ached with the need to draw a deep breath.

I reached up, taking the penlight from my mouth then grunted, "shit!" Somehow, the profanity made me feel a little better.

Chip's voice reached me from within the chamber. "Blue, are you okay?"

I spat. "Fuck you."

"What was that?"

I drew a shallow breath, since it was all I could manage, ticking off in my head a mental count to three.

I pressed against the outside of the door with my arm, willing my other shoulder to come through behind me.

The door scraped against my right breast and shoulder blade. Flaring waves of hot pain burned over my chest. I kicked and pulled, trying to ignore it, shutting my eyes to the wind.

I yanked one last time, and then pushed with all my strength. My grunt turned into a growl.

My shoulder popped through the opening, with a momentum that pitched me out over the water into a backward plunge.

I flailed my arms and legs, shrieking the whole way down, making a tremendous thrashing splash into the muddy pit.

I gasped on impact. A fresh, unexpected burst of pain shot through my upper thigh. I doubled over, trying to cry out, but could only gurgle water.

I crawled up on all fours, spitting rancid water and blistering obscenities.

I struggled to my feet, knowing that if there was anyone, *anybody*, in the park, they had to have heard me.

Chip called out from behind the doors. "Blue?"

I took a first step forward, opening my mouth to reply, but stumbled over something metal and screeched.

"Blue? Are you okay?"

I cleared the distance in a single hop before my strength gave out. I collapsed against the double doors, realizing in a detached way that I'd closed the gap on Chip and shut him in. My feet, previously numb from the extreme cold, now hummed with the fresh agony.

"Blue, it's awfully dark in here. There's only one flashlight."

Panting, I braced myself against the double doors. I snarled between chattering teeth. "Chip...darling, sweetheart...will you shut the *fuck up* a minute?!"

My legs gave out, and I leaned against the door, panting heavily and listening to the sweet, blessed silence.

I brought my hand up to cover my mouth and sobbed, shaking from pain and cold. Gradually the worst of the throbbing faded, and I gulped back my tears.

I wiped my hands over my face and back over my now-slicked hair. Twenty pounds of denim hung heavily over my shoulders. I knew standing in the water would cause my bleak situation to grow even worse but struggled to clear my mind and force my abused body to move. I brought the penlight up to examine the chain.

At what point did they attach this? I recalled being in the cauldron, music blaring, water gurgling; the attendants could have attached it at any time prior to turning off the soundtrack tape, and chances are, we would not have heard it from inside.

The chain wrapped around the handles of the double doors and hung loose, a fairly standard padlock holding it in place. Standard chain, standard lock. This was not high security stuff. But then, why should it be?

The distance from shore to shore stretched across about twenty feet. Finding a good-size piece of sturdy board to straddle the moat would be a simple enough task.

From out of nowhere, a blast of cold blanketed my body.

Then, just as fast, the wind stopped.

I clamped my chattering teeth shut. Now after midnight, the temperature had probably plummeted to around forty degrees. As far as I was concerned, it was fifteen.

I wondered a moment why Chip hadn't called out from behind the doors. Then I remembered I'd frightened the hell out of him.

I reached out, gingerly tapping my knuckles against the wooden door. "Chip...darling...I'm sorry I lost it like that." My voice trembled as I forced words between my shaking lips. "I'm going to attempt to pick the padlock. I don't want you to be concerned, but, if this doesn't go smoothly, you're going to have to talk me into not leaving you here until morning."

"You wouldn't!"

"Can't talk now." I put the flashlight in my mouth.

"Blue, that's not very damn funny!"

I reached up, pulling the two bobby pins from my hair, and got to work.

A strong wind buffeted me, making my hands shake and my teeth vibrate all the more. I had to bite down on the light.

A whisper traveled on the wind. *Bluuuuuuue...*

I almost dropped the pins.

Chip called out. "Blue, it's dark. Hurry up."

I locked the first pin into place.

Return the money, Blue. You can't keep it.

That wasn't Chip. And it came from *this* side of the door.

I grabbed the penlight from my mouth and pivoted, flashing the beam over the surrounding trees and bushes.

"Who's there?" I called.

A taunting burst of wind cut through me to the bone.

I won't let you keep it...

I strained to listen but could only hear wind in the hollows of the trees.

But I'd heard words.

No, I didn't hear words, I'm creeping myself out.

Shaking my head, I bent back to my work.

This time, I heard laughter, an evil cackle that caused my hands to tremble.

I paused, fighting down nausea and panic.

Get your own, Matey! This is mine.

I shook my head. *Now I'm hearing the pirate.* I took a breath and twisted the wires.

The lock snapped open.

I pulled at the chain. No sooner had I untangled it from the handles than the doors swung open, pushed from the inside.

I stepped back. "Chip!"

He stepped forward, the backpack slung over one shoulder and holding the moneybag in his free hand. His arms wrapped around me into a hug I could barely feel through the freezing denim. "Are you all right?" His face changed to a look of alarm. "You're freezing to death."

I let him guide me out of the water and onto dry land. "I'm sorry. I'm so sorry. Everything got so out of control. And I spooked myself."

He dropped the bags, and, to my surprise, produced an oversized towel from the backpack.

I stepped into his clasping embrace, letting him enfold and cocoon me in the billowy cotton softness.

I shivered and babbled nonsense apologies, burying my face in his chest.

"Come on," he said. "We need to get you home and into some dry clothes."

I nodded against his chest. "Yes...home."

Everything will be fine then.

CHAPTER TWENTY-EIGHT

Chip returned into the drink and reattached the lock. Throughout the entire affair, he'd stayed dry from the waist up. I just sat in the grass and pulled the towel tight.

The chills aside, scaling the fence and getting out of the park proved far easier than getting out of the ride. It wasn't as if they surrounded the park with barbed wire. We scaled a tall metal fence made of small vertical and horizontal squares. The biggest trick involved pulling ourselves over the top without getting injured on the speared points of the fence poles.

Once on the other side, no longer concerned with secrecy, we cut through a couple of yards to save time. Even wrapped in the towel, the cold drove me to move at a fast pace.

Several blocks from home, a sudden gust of wind kicked up, blowing over us. The gust penetrated my soaked clothes with a cutting-ice impact of burning intensity.

I froze in my tracks; my breath escaped out of my lungs.

In the distance, I heard a wicked cackle.

Chip's arm fell across my trembling shoulders. The shadow of a warm rush coursed through my chilled body, and I gazed at him in thankful relief. He returned my look with one of intense concern.

In his other hand, he hefted the moneybag. "We did it, Blue. All we have to do now is get somewhere safe and call the police. Then this will all be over."

I nodded, leaning against him. We stumbled together along the sidewalk, surrounded by the elegant single- and two-story houses of suburban Perionne, heading toward my house, the closest by half the distance.

Chip wanted to secure the treasure and turn it in as soon as possible. Waking Mom at one in the morning had its consequences, and I wondered if our newfound closeness could stand the disruption. But the unbearable cold forced the issue, and so we headed toward my house without any need for discussion.

I huddled against his inadequate warmth. Ominous, thick trees loomed in every yard, draping us in shadow. I kept ducking under bent branches, which seemed to reach out for us from the front lawns.

Dead leaves crunched under our feet. Reaching branches hid the moonlight, and coal-black darkness surrounded us. A sudden gust created a mini tornado of brownish leaf bits.

I bit back a squeal, and paused to cover my face, blocking the onslaught.

Then I heard the voice up ahead. *"Bring back the money, Blue. Tell him to bring it back. It belongs to me."* The voice erupted into a sinister laugh.

I called out. "Dammit, who are you?"

Chip turned to look at me, puzzled. "What?"

I gripped Chip's arm. The wind died down.

I could hear my anxious, panting breath in the stillness. I looked at Chip, growing alarmed. "I heard a voice." Thin clouds of vapor rose with my words. "I heard someone. In the park earlier, and just now up ahead. I think we're being followed."

"How could we be followed? Nobody knew what we were doing. It must be the wind."

Chip's bland response only served to set me on edge. I stared at him, frustrated. "I heard a voice. It wanted me to talk you into taking the money back." I stared at him, frustrated.

I heard a rustling in the trees up ahead.

Chip looked away. "Take the money back? No way. Besides, nobody knows about the money."

"Oh, but that's not true, Chip. And you know it." The voice spoke loud, deep, and clear directly in front of us.

A bulky figure stepped out from the bushes several yards ahead of us, standing tall and confident on the sidewalk, blocking our path. He wore a rumpled, dirty denim jacket and blue jeans. Though he stood some distance ahead and the trees continued to obscure the moonlight, I could see, with shocking clarity, the patch of thin, graying hair atop his head, and the details of the savage expression on his middle-aged face. He looked vaguely familiar, but I was certain I hadn't met him before.

Chip dug his nails into my arm, and a moan of terror escaped his lips. "Oh, Christ." His face paled with fright.

"Hey there, little boy. You know me?" The stranger stepped forward, hands in his pockets, walking with a slow, comfortable stride.

Chip took a step backward, but I stood my ground, watching in startled amazement. "Chip, come on. He won't hurt us."

Chip nodded, eyes wide. "Yes, he will."

But I'd had enough.

I took a step forward, letting the towel drop behind me. "Hey!" I wondered if the tough-gal bravado that freaked out Clinty would work on this loser. "Back off, shithead. You may have a score to settle with my friend, but now's not the time." I took another step toward him. "Maybe you saw something, maybe you didn't, but there's nothing you can do about it."

I risked a quick look behind me.

Chip stood erect, the moneybag clasped in a two-arm embrace against his chest. "Blue...it's Gunther."

"Gunther?" Unimpressed, I squinted in the dark at the scowling stranger. "Oh, yes, I see the resemblance now."

I sized up the would-be con artist. "So you're the guy wandering around pretending to be a dead man, scaring the hell out of everyone."

I glanced back at Chip. His eyes stared, riveted forward.

"Take it back, Chip. Take the money back now and bury it, and we'll forget everything."

I reached into my hip pocket and withdrew my switchblade. "All right, you sick fuck." I walked toward him, bringing the blade forward and ready. "You've got him seriously spooked now, and I don't like it. You back off, or you're going to regret it."

"How's the old man, Chip? Think he'd like a visit from me? I'll bet that'd be quite a treat."

From behind me, I heard a sickening groan.

I switched the blade to my left hand, then back to my right. "Hang in there, Chip." I closed the distance fast.

The stranger glared at me for the first time. A cruel smirk crossed his features.

I met his look with a threatening one of my own. "Last chance. Back off."

He shrugged, obviously unconcerned, and continued to approach.

The arrogance of this impostor set me off. I'd almost lost control but had enough sense to palm the knife, pointing the blade toward the ground, keeping it handy but out-of-the-way for now. Crouching low, I intended to tackle him at the knees and knock him out of the way.

The wind caught me, propelling me forward, and my body tumbled against him. I braced for an impact that never occurred. Instead, I fell through him, flailing my arms in a vain attempt to avoid spilling into the yard.

I landed hard on the grass, my accumulated bruises crying out fresh pain.

Sprawled on the ground, my mind reeled, unable to accept what had just happened.

I rolled over and scrambled to my feet, the pain from the fall registering, but distantly.

I jumped through him. Jesus, I jumped and passed right through him!

I just tried to tackle a ghost.

I stumbled back to the sidewalk in a daze.

I heard voices up the street.

"You can't have it!"

"It's mine, you little punk. It was never yours to take."

I heard a shuffling and a yelp.

Still reeling, I took a few shaky steps. "Chip?"

Then one thought overrode all my disbelief. *Chip's in trouble.*

And just like that, I assimilated the situation and broke into a run toward the struggling figures.

Ahead, too far ahead, Chip struggled as Gunther pressed him back and across another front yard. They each had one hand grasping the moneybag. Gunther's other hand squeezed Chip's throat.

With two houses between us, I pumped my legs with all my might.

Gunther pushed Chip against a large tree.

"Chip!"

I knew I'd be too late.

They twisted, and Chip fell and sprawled across the ground. Gunther's arm swung up. His hook glinted in the moonlight.

Closing in, I watched in helpless horror as the hook slashed down.

Chip's scream tore through the air.

I propelled myself, slamming full into a solid body that grunted and toppled.

I drew myself up between Gunther and Chip.

The ghost and I regained our feet at the same time.

He glared at me and then reached out for the moneybag that lay between us.

His hand passed through the satchel, and he howled in frustration.

I waited, not daring to attack again. Apparently, the ghost couldn't control his solidity.

I kept my eyes on Gunther. "Chip!"

"My leg's cut. Be careful, Blue."

A sudden burst of wind caused a blast of cold that rocked me.

The apparition grimaced, fixing me with a withering glare. *"You can't touch me, you know."*

I snarled back. "You seemed solid enough a second ago." I shifted the knife, pointing the business end at him. "I'll bet you have to make yourself solid to do anything to me, and then we'll see."

He vanished. One moment he stood in front of me; the next he faded away.

I ignored the mental hiccup. I'd always prided myself on adapting to new situations, but this took the cake.

"You're a very foolish child, Blue." I turned my head in the direction of the voice, across the street.

Gunther watched me, arms folded across his chest. Smirking, he raised the index finger on his good hand, wiggling it back and forth like a well-meaning father chastising an infant.

"This runs much deeper than you know, Blue. I will not let you turn the money over. I can't. Now, last chance, bring it back, or you'll pay in blood."

I turned to Chip. "It's your call."

Chip had pulled himself into a sitting position by the tree. I could see blood leaking across his jeans from what might have been a nasty gash.

Chip looked at me, but his voice rose toward the apparition across the street. "I can't. I won't. I've been through too much to take it back now."

"Brave words from the little man. Fine. Let what happens next be on your head."

With that, he vanished into the blowing wind.

I stared after him into the misty dark.

I turned back to Chip. He struggled to stand, a crumpled figure, looking like a long, angled bug. I grabbed his precious moneybag and walked over to him.

I extended my hand to help him up, but for the first time, I doubted my resolve. "What have you gotten us into?"

His tear-stained face looked up at me, but he didn't take my hand. "Please, Blue. Help me. It will be all right. I just need...to get this to the police. That's all."

Then I remembered. "Wait a second." One-handed, I unzipped my messenger bag and pulled out my cell phone. As I unfolded it, I noted with a growing dread the absence of backlighting or any other response.

I gave the phone a quick shake, hearing the telltale swishing of trapped water. "Shit."

I looked at Chip hopefully, but he shrugged and shook his head. "I didn't bring mine. It had a low charge."

I bit back a nasty response. "Well, that's...great."

I sighed, folding the useless device up and dropping it back into the hip-pack.

I reached down, and his hand grasped mine thankfully. I looked into his eyes as he rose up beside me. "Did you know...that this..."

The shocked look on his face spoke his sincerity. "What? God, no, Blue. How could I know? The very idea of a...spirit...it's beyond me."

I nodded. "That makes two of us, but the idea better get within our realm of understanding real damn quick. He can jump us again at any time, and I'm not sure there's much we can do about it."

"I know...but he pulled away. "I feel as if—"

"As if he's gathering strength." Even now, one of my feet tapped on the sidewalk from pent-up nervous anxiety. I stopped it with an effort. "The wind, the streets, there's a wild energy through here, like out-of-control electricity. We don't know how much time we have. So let's get going."

Chip stumbled forward and clasped my arm to keep from falling. "Ow! Dammit."

"Hold still." I bent over. The gash ran deeper than surface, but I didn't think he'd cut a vein, either. The bleeding had already slowed.

I sighed. "You'll live. C'mon, put your hand on my shoulder."

We took a couple quick steps, practicing. It proved slow going, about a quarter speed of our walk.

"Let's go. The sooner we get to my house, the better. If you want the cops, Mom will ring every alarm in the neighborhood if she has to, and do it in about three seconds."

"But—"

"Chip, don't argue with me!"

He opened his mouth and then snapped it shut, nodding instead.

"Good boy. Let's go."

While we still have time.

CHAPTER TWENTY-NINE

About twenty minutes later, we stood on the porch of my house, cloaked in total darkness. Even the moon had vanished behind the clouds. I helped Chip up onto the porch and then fished through my still-damp hip pack for the keys.

I found the key-ring, then hunted for the keyhole.

"Forget the keys, Blue." Chip said, extending a finger toward the doorbell.

"Chip, wait, it's after mid—"

I heard the faint sound of the chime ringing and laughed off a burst of nervous energy. "Nice one, Chip. That's going to make a great first impression."

We waited. I bit down against my chattering teeth. In just a few seconds the door would open, and...

"I don't see any lights coming on, Blue."

My head reeled. *He's right.*

Fresh panic sent my fingers grasping, and I dropped the keys. They tumbled into the dark and rattled across the cement.

"Hurry, Blue." He pounded on the window. "Mrs. Shaefer, open up!"

I bent down, feeling around frantically until I wrapped my hands around the icy ring.

I popped the key into the lock and pushed the door open. "Come on."

I snapped on the light. "Mom?"

I ran across the living room to the hall. "Mom! Answer me!"

In my terror, I forgot how a doorknob worked. I clawed at the closed door, then reached down and flung the door open. "Mom, wake up!" I flipped the switch.

The room lit up in bright white.

Mom lay on the bed, staring wide-eyed at the ceiling.

A flood of relief washed over me. "Mom, I need help. We—"

Then I saw the red puddle soaking through the sheets where she lay.

"Mom!" The room tilted, and my legs stopped working. I collapsed on the hardwood floor.

I crawled, pulling myself up and onto the bed. My vision blurred, spotting to red, the color of the sheets. "Mom! Mom, no."

My hands reached out, shaking her. She didn't move.

I fought back the terror. There was still a chance. I pressed a finger to her neck, probing and searching for a pulse I couldn't find.

And like that, it hit me. *My mom's dead.*

"No. Oh, *no!*"

I shook her. She was still warm, and red continued to leak, darkening the white of the sheet.

I saw the nightstand drawer pulled open. Her hand lay unmoving by her head; her fingers still curled around the tiny gun she thought would save her life from the intruder.

I slipped down the bed to my knees. Turning away, I could see the opposite wall, where three bullets had left holes in the marbled white surface. I needed to leave.

I tried to stand, but my legs wouldn't obey the command.

Then I saw a word scrawled across the white wall. In blood.

Mom's blood.

RETURN.

Reality faded along with my eyesight. Red and white phased to black.

Mom's not dead. Mom can't be dead.

Crimson drops pooled a couple feet from where I lay in a crumpled heap.

But Mom's body isn't on the bed. It can't be. Mom's not dead.

A sickening queasiness rushed through me, doubling me over as I coughed in spasms.

Distantly, I noticed Chip standing in the doorway.

Chip is here. He can fix her. He can fix everything. He'll notice what I missed, and everything will be all right. That's what he always says; everything will be all right, Blue...

Then I heard his cries, his yells of denial, and I knew he couldn't fix her.

Mom is dead. Mommmyyyy!

My face touched the cool wood of the floor. I could find no comfort here.

The puddle inched toward me, but blessed blackness overcame me first.

I OPENED my eyes and couldn't figure out why I was lying horizontally across the big leather recliner in my living room, wrapped in a blanket my numb body couldn't feel.

I shook myself, fighting back from the void of shock by sheer willpower.

Focus on the now. There's too much to do.

I heard Chip's voice, but he wasn't talking to me, probably on the phone. I drifted into shock like a zombie.

Mom's dead. And I did it.

The room spun, and I closed my eyes against a shudder.

Reality seeped into me. *No, Gunther did this. But I have to do something to stop him from hurting anyone else.*

In a minute. I continued to lay in black numbness, listening to Chip talking rapidly in almost incoherent phrases, pouring out the story.

There wasn't supposed to be a ghost! Maybe we'd be caught at the park and get arrested, but...I'd thought it through very carefully...had everything under control.

This wasn't supposed to happen.

Chip's words penetrated to my consciousness. "Okay. We won't move. We'll wait for the police. Be careful, Dad."

I never had a dad. Now I don't have a mom anymore, either. The fact sank in. *I don't have a mom anymore because of Chip.*

I closed my eyes against sudden nausea. I waited for it to subside and then brushed aside the blanket. Pulling myself up onto shaking legs, I stood on my own two feet. The stiff, damp denim chafed my thighs.

I need to stay focused and finish this. I owe her that much.

Nausea gave way to a burning anger.

I heard the receiver of the phone land against its cradle. Chip limped into the room from the kitchen, a white rag tied around his leg.

At the sight of me, Chip's face softened to anxious concern. He took a step toward me. "Blue, you'd better take it easy. You're still in shock and—"

My rage burst out. "Bastard!" I advanced on him.

He froze in midstep, perplexed.

"Did you see my mother? Did you see what you did?"

"Blue, I swear, I didn't know."

"You had to know. He told you. We'd pay in blood, he said. Son of a bitch! And now she's dead because of you."

I saw the moneybag, propped on the kitchen table where he must have set it. I brushed past him. *I have to get that bag, and he's not going to stop me.*

He pivoted to watch me, but did nothing. "The police are on their way, Blue. Everything will be okay in just a minute." His calm, measured voice spoke its hypnotic reason but didn't calm my anger.

Grabbing the moneybag, I snarled his words back at him. "Everything will be okay? My mother's dead and everything will be okay?"

I swung the bag in an arch with all my might, smashing it into his chest. "My mother died over this!"

Weakened by his wounded leg, Chip toppled backward without uttering a noise.

The lack of reaction fed my fury. I pounced, grabbing him by his jacket and forcing him into a sitting position against the wall. "A bag of old money, you son of a bitch!"

Hurt filled his shocked eyes, but his arms hung, unresisting, at his sides.

I screamed at him. "Damn you and your treasure hunt!"

"Blue, I'm sorry, I didn't—"

"Stop apologizing, you coward." I threw myself at him, yanking him forward by his jacket. "You think the cops can fix this? You think the police can shoot the big bad ghost?" I threw him against the wall with all my might, forcing a groan from him.

Still, he didn't fight back. *Fine with me.*

I stood, looking down at his crumpled, pathetic form. "Useless. Coward. I'm taking the money back. Now."

"Blue, you can't do that. He's beyond all control. We need to give the money to the cops." His words came out faster. "We can expose Gunther. That's what he fears most. If you reveal his secret, his legend dies. The threat to his legacy is what's feeding his power now. You can't fight him anymore."

I rattled the moneybag at him. "You don't get to call the shots anymore. Gunther's out there, getting stronger by the minute. And if this is what he really wants, then I'll find a way to use it to stop him. Or die trying."

I strode toward the front door. Chip's voice followed me, rising in pitch as I walked away from him. "He won't let you live no matter what you do."

Chip's pleading voice rose. "Blue, he'll kill you. Don't go!"

I ran out the door and into the cold night, following a distant laughter traveling on the wind from the direction of the amusement park.

CHAPTER THIRTY

I ran through the sleeping neighborhood, my boots pounding an uneven rhythm on the sidewalk. Damp denim hung over my aching shoulders, and, before long, I gasped deep breaths of frigid night air.

The wind blasted, causing dry, crumbling leaves to billow up around me. I stopped to shield my face from cutting bits. The gust penetrated my jeans and pushed against the moneybag. My hand ached from the ongoing struggle to maintain my hold on the satchel.

A sudden, vicious blast knocked me off the sidewalk, and I toppled onto someone's lawn. As I fell, I heard a distant cackling.

I hid my face until the sound passed. Sprawled on the grass, I looked up at the brick house in front of me and its immediate neighbor. I spied the narrow alley between the homes, and beyond the yards, an open field of wild grass against the horizon.

Cutting through the field would lop six blocks off the road route, plus lessen the wind.

I hopped to my feet, sprinting across the yard and between the houses.

The gust blasted again. I threw myself against the brick wall. Again, I could hear a stifled chuckle.

I yelled into the air. "Having fun, you bastard?" Gunther may have had some sort of supernatural power over the weather, but that didn't matter much between the houses. I took advantage of the respite to collect my wits.

His voice reached me, more a frustrated howling of the wind than spoken words. *"You'll pay in blood, Blue."*

"I've got the money!" I yelled. "I'm bringing it back. What more do you want?"

"You'll return the money, regardless of any deal I might offer. I know you will. You'll try to save the day and protect everyone. Better hurry, Blue. I'm getting bored. I might kill another one of your friends. How about that nice Mary Rowan or your buddy, Phil?"

"Bullshit." I called into the air. "I have what you want. No one else does. Stay with me, and we'll finish this."

I raced out the alleyway and across the unfenced backyard, heading for the field beyond. I expected constant blowing harassment, but, to my surprise, the supernatural wind stopped pursuing me. *Maybe Gunther's finally tired of that game. Small blessing.*

I swung the moneybag low into the wall of tall grass, using it as a makeshift shield to bend the blades over while I pressed forward. The dried grass rose to my chest, crackling and falling as I plowed through them.

The air erupted in evil laughter. *"I'll just go kill Phil now. It won't take but a minute. Hey, 'Kill Phil,' that's funny. I like that. Don't you, Blue?"*

"No! No more killing." I turned in a slow circle, watching the horizon for his distinct form. "I'll ditch the money in the deepest lake around here. A place you can't get to."

"So certain of yourself? I'm a god in this town, far more powerful than any bully or mugger you've fought in your miserable, pathetic existence. Not Clinty or your teachers or the Broad Ripple police. For years, my power has continued

to grow. But only while the money stays lost, and the mystery remains. And you're trying to end that."

I mumbled under my breath. "Yeah, I get it." *I may be a slow learner, but I'll find out how to play his game.*

A figure stood just beyond the clearing, atop a small mound leading to a backyard. The denim-jacketed apparition grinned at me.

I stopped a couple feet away from him and stared, perplexed.

Rather than the glowing spirit I'd seen earlier, this figure looked solid, real. *"I feed off the paranoia of this town. You know something about paranoia, don't you, Blue? And now I grow stronger by the minute. The more you struggle, the stronger I become."* His head bent back as his cackle traveled on the wind.

I knew better than to jump at him. "What do you want? If you want me to hide the money somewhere else, tell me. Tell me what you want, and I'll do it."

"Poor little fool. You really were just a pawn in Chip's schemes, weren't you? Still, you know far too much. I can't possibly let you live. So if you really wish to appease me, lie down and take out your switchblade."

He stepped aside and waved his hook toward the grass. *"Once you've done that, drive the knife through your own belly and across your chest. Then we can both rest peacefully after I hide the money myself. Maybe."*

I reeled at his casual request for me to kill myself. Though I had no intention of honoring it, I reached into my jacket pocket, trying to control my shaking hands.

My hand brushed against the rusted pocketknife I'd found at the grave site. I drew the knife out of my pocket. My hand tingled, and I flicked copper-colored rust from my fingertips. *No, I don't want that one.* I withdrew my hand, reached into my jeans pocket, and drew out my switchblade.

I held the moneybag out toward him. "So...if I...offer myself, you'll leave the rest of my friends alone?"

He reached for the bag. *"You have my word."*

I pulled it away from him. "Go fuck yourself. What good is your word?"

He growled, jumping forward, and his hand gripped the moneybag.

When I felt the tug, I swiped downward, slashing the switchblade against the tendons behind his knuckles.

He howled in fury and pain, falling back.

I lunged, swiping at his arm.

I swept my arm through empty air. He'd gone ghostly, but that didn't matter. I was merely feigning. I didn't expect to connect, and, when he lunged at me, I dodged out of his reach easily.

He howled and cradled his wounded hand. Blood splattered onto crackling grass.

At the sight of the blood, a snarling grin formed on my lips. "You're the one who's paying in blood, Gunther. You need to touch me to hurt me. And I bite back." I moved around him and continued across the lawn. "You killed my mother, and that little scratch doesn't begin to make up for it."

He winced. *"You bitch."* Unable to cover the bleeding hand with his hook, he cradled it awkwardly under the opposite arm. Blood continued to flow from the cut.

"That's just the wind talking, Gunther. And the wind can't really hurt me."

He grimaced at me. *"Let's see how badly you can hurt, Blue. I know what you fear."* He turned ethereal and faded away, a final cackle still vibrating over the air.

Shit. The air calmed, no longer howling. Gunther had vanished. But had I weakened him first?

From that scratch? It didn't seem likely. I turned and bolted across the grass. The sooner I could get to the park, the sooner this madness would end.

I ran to the next yard and rounded the corner to reach another alleyway. I crossed over two more streets and emerged, facing the west-side fence of the park.

I darted across the street, and, without slowing, hurled myself at the fifteen-foot fence. The metal rocked as I kicked into footholds and reached with one hand to pull myself up. For one crazy moment, I thought of pitching the moneybag up and over.

No. Stupid idea.

I crab-walked up the side and then threw the moneybag over the top, holding onto the handle with one hand, and the fence with the other. I kicked my leg up but not quite over.

I paused, hanging on the metal, trying to catch my breath. What I'd scaled so easily without the bulk of the money bag now proved a major challenge.

I tried to throw my weight over to the other side, but I shifted awkwardly and, *oh, hell!*, all my weight came down on my crotch, and I hung, straddling the fence.

I tipped drunkenly, kicking and grimacing as the metal sharpness dug into my thigh.

I screamed between my teeth and forced my leg to move up and over. The denim tore, along with a few inches of skin. I twisted and fell. Somehow, I managed to hold on with one arm, the other still gripping the bag. Weight, mass, and gravity conspired to drop me toward the earth.

My fingers ignored my mental command to hang on, releasing their grip. I'd stopped my fall, but I dropped the final six feet or so.

The moneybag hit the cement and my forearms hit the moneybag. Pain shot through my arms and into my shoulders. I slumped, unable to go any farther.

"Christ." With all I'd been through tonight, I knew I'd show horrible black and blue marks in the morning...assuming I survived that long.

As if on cue, the wind billowed up around me. *"You're too late, Blue,"* the directionless voice called.

I looked up the deserted pathway, seeing only the slightest stirring of the leaves. "What? What do you mean? If you killed anyone, I'll..." I stopped, unable to finish. *What can I do? I can't hurt him. I just have to see this through.*

The wind blew a pile of leaves, which rustled over a nearby park bench. *"Killed? Oh, no. At least, not yet."*

A large tower-shaped building lit up against the not-too-distant skyline. He'd powered up one of the rides.

I limped along the pathway toward the structure, my arms still singing their chorus of pain. Other injuries added their accompaniment.

After only two trips, my directional sense of the park layout remained rudimentary, but I didn't think I was walking toward the Pirates of Perionne moat. "What are you up to, Gunther?"

"Just making some plans, Blue. Oh, I see you noticed the lights, hmm? Another evil laugh. I guess I can't fool you for long."

"Shut up and tell me what you're doing."

"Just keep walking, bitch."

I realized where the path would take me, and I strode with growing confidence. Being one of the park's most popular rides, the turnbuckle started several hundred yards from the structure.

I stared at the sign over the wooden archway above me announcing the Whirlwind roller coaster. I could see the brightly lit entrance ahead, and, in the distance between the trees, the wooden supports of the ride itself.

"What are you doing?"

"Get over here. Chip's heroic old man called the cops. They'll be here soon. I need this lit building to guide them in the wrong direction. Now move your ass, girl."

I maneuvered through the metal brackets forming the line blockades. A couple of times a turnbuckle refused to budge, and I jumped over the bar with growing impatience. My cut thigh and other bruises screamed in pain each time.

I approached the wooden stairway, leading to the upper boarding level.

Gunther stood on the attendant's platform, arms folded with a grin on his face. Between us, one of the roller coasters crouched on the track like a sleeping dragon.

I stepped up onto the illuminated wooden-planked platform, my footsteps echoing hollowly. "What now, Gunther?"

He held a finger out for silence. *"Quiet."* A dramatic grin of grotesque glee cracked his face.

"I thought you said we didn't have a lot—"

Then I heard the sound of shoes on wood, climbing stairs, on Gunther's side of the coaster tracks. Behind him, I saw the silhouette of an awkward figure limping on a spiraling stairway, climbing upward.

Chip shuffled into the light, and I bit back a gasp. His eyes lit up when he saw me. But then he took in his surroundings, realizing he shared the small platform with the ghost and that the track and coaster separated me from them. "What's going on?"

I resisted the urge to leap over the coaster and run to him. Gunther stood between us. He could strike long before I could maneuver my way around the coaster and get to Chip's side.

A mad chortle escaped Gunther's lips. *"I thought we should have a little reunion."*

Chip's gaze darted around, like a lion trapped in a cage, trying to escape.

Then his eyes focused on me. "Blue, I'm sorry. He told me he had you. He was going to kill you if I didn't come."

"And you took long enough with that bum leg, Chip!"

I ignored the ghost, speaking directly to Chip. "He didn't 'have' anyone. The bastard kept blocking my path and delaying me." I glared at the grinning apparition. "I see why now. But get out of here, Chip. Now. I'll take care of this."

Chip shook his head. "No. You're the one who should run

away." He directed his next statement to the ghost. "You don't need to involve her anymore. It's me you want. You've hurt her enough."

"I'm not leaving," I said. I knew Chip wouldn't stand a chance alone against Gunther. "However this goes down, I'm not leaving you here."

Gunther cut off my protests. *"How romantic. Each of you trying to make the ultimate sacrifice to save the other, trying to bargain with me, when you have nothing to bargain with."*

Gripping the switchblade in my hand, I held the point out, centering on the apparition like an accusation. "I've got a deal for you, Gunther!" I spat out. "You hurt him, I swear I'll kill you and make sure this time you stay dead and in Hell."

Gunther's gaze met mine, and to my surprise, he looked away. *"I believe you. But, now, I think I'll hold on to my bargaining chip."* He assaulted my ears with more abrasive cackling. *"Bargaining chip, that's pretty good."*

"Enough," I said, waving the knife. "We want the same thing. You don't need to hurt him. Either of us."

"Perhaps not. Still, I think I'll keep him close."

Gunther stretched out his arms, in all ways resembling a zombie in a bad monster movie, stomping toward Chip and blocking the stairwell.

My vision flared, and I lost all sense and cool. All I knew at that moment was that I had to get over to Chip. Now. "No. You can't have him."

Dropping the bag, I dropped down into one the cars and bounced out the other side. Swiping with the switchblade, I crossed the distance and forced myself between them.

I stabbed at the hook. Metal clanged against metal, and Gunther's body jerked sideways.

I crouched, ready to attack, knife poised and ready. "You never learn, do you?" I taunted.

Gunther took a step back, so I came forward. He swung with his hook, making an obvious slash at my face.

Overconfident, I countered with the knife.

With unexpected speed, his hand thrust forward, and vise-like fingers gripped my neck, cutting off my air.

I gagged, dropping the knife and reaching up with both arms to loosen his grip.

Too fast, the world blackened around me. I pulled at his thumb with all my remaining strength, but it gave only slightly. In a fuzzy haze, I could see him draw me close, grinning.

My feet flopped against the floorboards in spasms. *I need air!*

I heard Chip's voice and felt, rather than saw, a figure charge into us. The taut fingers slackened.

My vision cleared, only to see Gunther slam the back of his hook across the side of Chip's head and feel the fingers tighten around my throat again.

Chip flew back, sprawling across the deck.

I tried to push away a final time, but my legs refused to work. I reached up and dug my fingernails into his too-solid flesh. *No air, and the world is fading away.*

Blackness enveloped me, and my body slumped. I no longer cared about my own imminent death.

"I have a special death just for you, Blue."

Dimly, I felt Gunther picking me up and throwing me. I only distantly realized that I collided with wood and metal and bounced against a shallow wall.

Nothing made sense. I flung my arms and legs around randomly, and kept hitting the walls of a wooden compartment, low and contained.

Gasping precious air, my body surged with a renewed strength and panic. I struggled into a sitting position, blinking through spotted blackness.

He let me live, for the moment. If he gives me a few more seconds to clear my head, he'll regret it.

Chip's panic-stricken voice reached me. "Blue! Get up!"

I shook my head, trying to clear away the black spots. Reaching out, my fingers gripped a flat, flush surface above me. *A seat. He's thrown me into a coaster car.*

I grabbed the seat and pulled myself up on shaky legs. The seat shifted into blurry focus. Looking up, I saw Chip crawling across the platform toward me, arms outstretched. But I didn't see Gunther.

A squeal of metal broke the quiet, and the coaster surged forward.

The floor fell out from under me. I toppled sideways, tumbling across the tops of two cars.

I pitched into the hollow of the car behind me, my feet raised and flailing through the air, unable to find purchase. As the car shifted around its first curve, I grabbed and twisted, trying to right myself.

The car chugged over the tracks and into the darkness. No lights cut through the chilling black, only the sound of a high-pitched cackle.

The wind blasted a fierce torrent.

I grabbed the seat and forced my feet down where they belonged. Grabbing the front of the car for balance, I dragged myself to the edge. I braced my legs under me, pulling myself into a half-stand, preparing to hurl myself off.

The coaster shifted into a sharp upward tilt, beginning its ascent for the big drop. Again, I tumbled across the cars, falling against wood, plastic and wind. I reached out, gripped the seat, and held on with all of my strength to right myself. The car tipped into a sharper angle, and my back wedged against the seat.

Chug...Chug...Chug...

The car slanted to a near vertical position, continuing its ascent.

In a wild panic, I clawed the side of the car, pulling myself forward and staring out into the night.

Chug...Chug...Chug...

I saw the tops of the trees, and then I didn't. I'd missed the moment between safe-to-jump and no longer safe.

Chug...Chug...Chug...

The wind blew, rustling the trees below me. *Dear God.*

I couldn't see the tracks.

And then I realized nothing held me in!

Chug...Chug...Chug...

Terror overtook me, and I froze, unable to act.

The car would drop and I would die. I called out in the blackness. "Mom! I don't want to die."

Chug...Chug...Chug...

The straps! I lunged to the front and the left. *A strap has to be here somewhere.* My nails brushed a small metal hook. *Fuck!*

Chug...Chug...Chug...

I clawed at the opposite side, and my knuckles brushed the loose fabric.

Chug...chu-...

The car slowed,...leveling,...preparing to plunge.

I gripped and pulled. Any second, the car would speed off and fling me to oblivion. Not enough time, in total blackness, to hook myself in.

I twisted my forearm... once, twice, three times; I wrapped the strap around my arm. I pulled it taught with my other hand, folding my fingers into a fist.

Best I can do.

My legs locked, preparing to somehow absorb the shock of what came next.

Chug...

I could see an unobstructed view of the entire Perionne landscape surrounding me, a few yellow dots in all directions, surrounded in the distance by oppressive blackness. The half-moon showed wicked orange teeth, laughing down on me.

The wind blew in my face. "Okay!" I snarled through my clenched teeth. "Take your shot!"

The train toppled into the abyss, and the world screamed at me. My arms jerked back. Wind tore at my face. My legs gave way, and my body bashed against the back of the seat.

The car pulled up from the drop, and then cut into an immediate right turn.

My body slammed against the side of the car, slapping my ribs into the wood. The car jerked, and I hurled across the side, pummeling my shoulder. New pain shot through my body as brutal winds ripped at my face and hair.

The train tore into another ascent. All I could do was hold on, with no control, as the strap whip-lashed my body, slamming me against the support.

My hands locked like steel around the strap. I could no longer feel my fingers, only burning agony through my arms. Still, I held on as the car twisted and spun madly.

My legs locked against the seat, and the blackness became palatable, a living thing. I secured myself, somewhat.

The car vibrated into a mad, tumbling descent, the large corkscrew, I recalled from a distant memory. The ride would end any moment.

I have to let go, or he'll find me before I'm ready.

Even as the thought penetrated, my arm moved on its own, untwisting itself from the strap.

The wind blasted me up, yanking me from the security of the floorboards. My ears rang with the screeching wail of slamming brakes cutting through roaring wind.

The car shook. The wind lessened.

I released the strap, flying off into space, over the side and into the trees below.

For a moment, the wind embraced me. The car slipped away, and pain overcame my senses.

I fell into a waiting blackness.

CHAPTER THIRTY-ONE

I couldn't move. I wanted to stay in my daze, drifting above a haze of pain.

A familiar, comforting voice called to me.

"Fiona! Fiona, get up!"

"Mom?" No mistake. I could hear her voice, calling to me. She hadn't died after all.

"Fiona, I love you. Listen to me, baby. You need to get up and finish this."

"Mom." I tried to lift my hand, but it seemed too much of an effort, and the darkness claimed me again.

I AWOKE to pain throbbing through my body.

Blurriness gave way to clear vision. I blinked, realizing my face was pressed into the grass. A leaf came into sharp focus, and a loamy scent filled my nostrils. Slowly, I reached up and curled my fingers around it; the brown-veined papery texture crumpled in my fingers. I rolled over onto my swollen shoulder, winced, and shifted. Faint moonlight threaded through the tree branches overhead.

"Mom?"

No response. Had I just imagined her speaking to me? But I remembered the urgency in her message and made an effort to sit up.

Movement was agony. With careful, gingerly motions, I straightened to my feet and peered up through the wooden supports.

I'd fallen some distance from the tracks, but only a few yards from the boarding platform. I'd probably rolled through the woods. I saw the broken bush that had apparently halted my momentum.

Standing in the dark, I assessed my options. *Gunther might think I'm dead. He might not think to look for me this far out.*

I had to kill him, if that was still possible. No more banter, no more bargaining. He'd killed Mom, thought he'd killed me, and would kill Chip as soon as Chip had done his bidding.

Creeping through the woods, staying out of the light, I approached the platform from below. *How long was I out?*

I approached the rear stairway and heard arguing above me. I stepped quietly onto the first wooden stair, trying to control my shaking body. Part of me wanted to bolt forward and another part of me almost collapsed where I stood.

Gunther's command reached my ears. *"Come on, boy! Take the bag. The old man should be along soon enough, and you can bury it together. Come on, boy! Pick it up. What's the matter?"*

"Go fuck yourself."

"Oooohhh! All of a sudden, you're growing a pair, eh, boy? It's too late to help your sweetie. She's dead. You failed her. Take it like a man."

With determined stealth, I tiptoed up the planked stairway. I could see right through Gunther, whose back was to me, to view Chip on his knees in front of the moneybag.

"And now you want to torture my father, like you tortured Blue. Because of what you think he did."

"Oh, what happened to Blue is nothing. Your father betrayed me, boy. And he'll watch his son die before I deal with him. But if you cooperate, you, at

least, might earn a quick death. Think about it, boy, it's the only reward you'll get for trying to be the big hero, sticking your nose where it didn't belong."

Chip knelt by the moneybag, eyes closed, as if contemplating the options he didn't appear to have. All he had to do was look up and he would have seen me through the apparition. But try as I might to will it, he never did.

I reached for my pocket and then stopped, cursing at the memory. My switchblade had fallen from my grasp earlier, and I had no idea where. My hand traveled on its own to my jacket pocket. I had stashed the ancient pocketknife there.

I withdrew the rusted tool, staring at the crusted handle. Would this dilapidated relic still work after being buried in soil for twenty-five years? It didn't seem likely.

My thumbnail found the notch, and I wiggled the blade free. In spite of its appearance, the blade still felt firm between my fingers. As I wrapped my hand over the ornamental handle, my fingers tingled with anticipation, as if the knife wanted to jump from my hands.

"Pick up the bag, boy."

"Kiss my ass, Gunther."

I could see the resolution on Chip's face, the acceptance of his fate, better to be dead than live with this torture any longer.

No, Chip! Hang in there.

And he wouldn't look up.

Gunther raised his hook. *"Oh, the hell with you. Let that be your epitaph."*

Chip vanished from my sight, blocked by a more substantial Gunther.

I let out a war cry and leapt, knowing I'd be too late.

The hook swung in a clean arc down into Chip's unmoving shoulder.

I slammed into Gunther's muscled back and thrust the blade between us, sinking it into solid flesh.

He jerked, the momentum carrying us sideways. As we tumbled over, I could see his eyes bulge with surprise.

"Fucker!" I screamed. "Die for the last time!" I clawed my fingers into his jacket, holding onto him with a death grip. The force of my charge drove us across the platform, spinning off the edge and into the darkness.

I kicked away from him in mid-fall, landing on soft, wet ground and rolling with the impact. My whole body screamed in pain; I could no longer distinguish one injury from another.

Ignoring that, I came up on my knees, stealing a quick glance at the rusted blade, which now dribbled fresh blood.

Across the field I could see Gunther, who now looked quite solid and hurt, struggling to his feet. I bolted into the woods and the darkness, toward the wooden coaster support beams. I crunched leaves beneath my feet with no regard to stealth, making sure he knew his prey was escaping.

Under cover of darkness, I doubled back, squatting behind a beam.

Gunther swiped his hand across his belly where I had made the fresh wound. Even from this distance, I could see he wobbled on his feet.

"Come on, Gunther!" I yelled. "I'm not done playing with you yet!"

I darted beneath the coaster, hearing an enraged howl closing the distance behind me. I slowed, rebounding off several of the wooden supports, grabbing others and taking quarter turns. Blindly, I darted beneath the supports, making as much noise as I could, intentionally smacking the beams with my hands.

As I hoped, Gunther gave chase. Expecting me to flee the area in a direct and sensible path, Gunther darted after me as fast as he could run. At the same time, he tried to hone in on the audio cues I'd deliberately made. I heard him stumble around, screaming and tripping. When he'd get close, I'd call out and run away again.

Gunther howled, finally choosing to stand in place for the moment. *"Where are you, bitch?"*

I darted away, certain I could goad him further while I thought out my next move.

I doubled back, circling his noisy traipsing. "You're sounding pretty solid, there, Gunther," I taunted. I turned again and retreated, trying to avoid the supports. I wasn't always successful, but the adrenaline spiked me through the pain of impact. *If I survive this, I won't be able to walk for a week.*

I crouched behind another beam. I couldn't see him, but I could hear him stumbling toward me.

I gasped for air, but knew I had to keep enraging him, taunting him, so he couldn't think straight. "How do you like all your power, Gunther? Getting all your flesh back? Stubbing your toe? Banging your head? I'll bet you just love it."

I crawled low in the grass, angling closer to him. I rose to my feet, then ran toward the noise of his stumbling. I dodged the first beam and slid around the second just as he came into view.

He turned at the sound. *"You mockin' me now, girl?"*

"I'm about to kill you!" I turned and ran back the way I'd come, weaving by the supports I'd just passed, waiting by another.

Gunther screamed, charging after me. His foot caught on a support, and he pitched forward with an indignant cry.

I advanced on him, pocket knife in my hand. "This knife killed you once already, Gunther. I suspect you're now meaty enough that it can kill you again."

He leapt at me, swiping the air with his arm. Prepared, I jumped backward. The hook swept uselessly through empty space. I stumbled back, stopping when I felt solid brace of the support beam against my back.

Gunther recovered from his first swing and drew back again.

I dropped sideways.

The hook swept across where I had stood a moment ago and

caught with a *thunk* into the wooden beam.

As he grabbed for me, I backpedaled away from his arm. He pulled back short, turning and looking perplexed at the prosthetic limb which would not come unstuck.

Again, I summoned my war cry, charging, the blade held high. I slammed into him, burying the knife deep into the flesh of his exposed belly.

Gunther staggered backward. His mouth hung open in befuddlement. He gurgled and attempted to yank out his hooked arm, but it remained wedged in the wood.

"This knife has already killed you, Gunther."

He made a grab for my throat.

I caught his hand, twisting.

Gunther leaned over me, trying to gain leverage. The stench of sweat and vomit assaulted my nose.

I yanked my knife loose from his chest and slashed across the back of his wrist. His howl of pain cut through the air.

"This knife is...part of your grave...part of...the spell."

He could only return a blank stare, moaning. "No." His body slackened against me, and I shoved him away.

He dropped to his knees, one arm slack at his side, the other pulled upward over his head, still caught in the wooden beam.

At the sight of him, hanging and vulnerable, I saw red and attacked like a wild animal.

I raised the blade and slammed it down into his face.

The hook tore free, and Gunther toppled backward into the grass.

I thrust the knife down, poking a divot into his face, no longer concerned about targeting, just driven by a desire to cut and slice. "Die!"

He groaned a last time and lay unmoving beneath me.

Gripping the knife with both hands, I pounded the weapon over and over into the limp body.

"You killed...my mother...you fucker!" I accented each pause with a thrust. "Killed her...for...useless money."

Blood erupted from various puncture wounds, smearing my shirt and jeans. I straddled the puckered carcass and raised the knife again. "Kill you! Kill you! Kill you!" The knife punctuated each word.

Gasping for breath, I soaked in the blood of my enemy. "Kill you," I whispered. An insane giggle escaped my lips.

I pulled the knife free, gripping it in my hand. Literally dizzy with victory, the world spun away, and I collapsed, closing my eyes and basking in the justified murder.

When I opened them a moment later, I saw no body. I lay on the cold, wet ground, no blood.

My clothes, while torn and soaked, were soaked with dew and rain; no blood, except a few fresh spots from my own various cuts. The knife, while slick from the sweat of my hands, showed no sight of blood.

I pulled at my own hair and screamed. I stared at the support beam, which showed a freshly sliced chunk of wood, the only evidence a struggle had taken place.

I stumbled toward the bright white luminescence of the coaster entrance, tottering from support to support, always focused on the light. I could barely feel the mechanical motion of my own limbs. I moved by sheer will to where I knew Chip lay, bleeding and dying.

My body kept moving on its own. I knew Gunther might appear again, and he could go for Chip at any moment. I gripped the iron rail and pulled myself up the planked stairs, dragging myself up to the platform.

I could see Chip lying where he had fallen, his eyes closed, blood seeping from his shoulder.

Fear squeezed my heart. *Is he dead?* I approached him with heavy steps.

He turned his head slightly and saw me. "Blue," he mumbled.

The knife fell from my fingers, and I crumpled forward onto the platform.

The knife bounced loudly across the planks and came to a stop.

I dragged myself over to where he lay. "Chip!"

I reached out, taking his wrist in my hands. I could feel a pulse. "Chip, don't you die on me."

Blood pooled beneath him. He groaned. He stared upward, past me. "Blue."

I grabbed his jacket, shaking him. "Chip, I made it better. I told you I would."

"You got him?"

"Think so. Don't know. He's gone for now."

"Blue, if I die—"

"Shut up! Don't die. You can't. If you die, I have nothing left." Tears spilled from my eyes, splattering his cheek. I swallowed back the horrible, aching sorrow fighting to erupt from me, the pain of what I'd lost and what I still could lose.

His voice penetrated my turmoil. "I'm tired, Blue."

Through my tears I felt his wrist. His pulse beat weakly beneath my fingers.

I folded myself over him, pulling him into an embrace. "Go to sleep, honey. You can sleep."

I heard the thumping of footsteps; someone approached from the stairwell behind me. A figure rose onto the platform. A large figure. I braced.

"Fi-Fi. It's me." Chip's father rushed into the light. "Oh, my God!" Shock registered on his features as he recognized his son laid out prone on the platform.

Mr. Farren ran forward and dropped before Chip, checking for vital signs. "He's alive. An ambulance is coming."

As I cradled Chip in my arms, I felt Mr. Farren's gaze on me. He finally broke the awkward silence. "Gunther?"

I nodded. His hands reached up, covering his eyes, and his intimidating stature seemed to crumple. "He appeared to me a few minutes ago. Told me to come here. That was after your mother—"

I cut him off. I didn't want to hear the words spoken. "We dug it up."

I saw his gaze fall upon the moneybag. "Oh, my God." He stood and retrieved the bag. He pondered the rusted knife for a moment and grabbed that, too.

I bent to listen to Chip's breathing, making sure he still lived. "We need to take it back." My mind reeled at the thought of going back into the ride. Blackness already threatened to close in. I would not hold out.

"Yes. Yes." Mr. Farren nodded.

"They go in the Pir—"

"I know where they go," Mr. Farren snapped. "Fi-Fi, listen to me. I can return this later. I need to remove everything and get it into my car before the police arrive. This bag...and this knife...is that all you found?"

"Uh..." The darkness at the edge of the lamps had closed in around me. "I...don't know. Too hard to think."

"I can't return it while the cops are combing the area for the killer, but maybe once they're gone..."

The distant shriek of sirens cut through the silence.

Mr. Farren crouched in front of me. "Fi-Fi."

Try as I might, I found it difficult to focus on his voice.

"Fi-Fi! Lie back, honey. You're going into shock. I have everything, and I'll hide it tonight. Don't worry. Don't worry, Fi-Fi. Everything will be okay."

Where have I heard that before? My body slumped into blackness.

I came to and found myself strapped onto a bed. I could feel the vibration of a moving ambulance. "Chip!"

An unfamiliar voice spoke. "He's still with us, Miss Shaefer. Chip is fine. Everything will be okay."

Chip's fine. The phrase echoed in my head. But I knew everything wasn't okay.

"Mom?..." But no one answered before I slept.

CHAPTER THIRTY-TWO

Sunlight hit against the back of my eyelids. I blinked, shut my eyes, and tried to roll away from the brightness. A thick cotton dressing taped against my back inhibited my movement. A variety of throbs and aches made themselves known, some of which I couldn't remember noticing during my ordeal.

Warm sheets lay against my bare neck, and the softness of a hospital gown wrapped around me. I twitched my nose at the odor of rubbing alcohol and soap.

I sensed movement in the room and opened my eyes to focus on a small window with a patterned red curtain pulled over it. The curtain failed to keep the bright sunshine from disturbing my sleep.

Odd. I lay in a small private room, not a partitioned hospital space.

Beneath my gown, the tightness of bandages over various areas of my bruised and battered body annoyed me. There were more than I could detect or count easily. The itchy irritation of a bandage on my inner thigh distracted me. Another wrapping pulled tight against my head.

"Oh. You're awake." I turned to see a nurse at the doorway,

dressed in the usual permanent-press pajama uniform with a pattern I couldn't quite bring into focus, her dust-colored brown hair pulled back with a clip. "How are you feeling?" I heard genuine concern in the question.

I tried to take a deep breath, only to wince from the pain in my ribs. "What time is it?"

The nurse raised her wrist, her dark-brown eyes giving her watch a quick, business-like glance. "It's one-thirty in the afternoon." She flashed me an understanding, friendly smile. "You're going to be okay. I mean, for what you've gone through. You cracked three ribs, but everything will mend quickly. The rest looks bad, feels worse, but it all adds up to a bunch of scrapes and bruises."

I bit back a reply about how the loss of my mother added up to a lot more than a bunch of bumps and bruises. "Where's Chip?"

"Recovering from surgery."

"When can I see him? I have to see him."

"I'll fetch the doctor." With that, she left.

I waited, trying to find a comfortable spot on the pillow and fighting the tendency of my eyes to drift shut.

I scanned the room to stay awake, noticing my clothes folded neatly on a chair.

The curtains blurred out of focus and I drifted.

"Fiona?"

I snapped awake, taken aback by a remarkably pretty blonde woman standing next to my bed. Dark blue eyes met mine, framed by a soft, concerned face. "I'm Dr. Deidre Churchill. How are you feeling?"

She's my doctor? I didn't think my reaction came from sexism; she just didn't strike me as a surgeon or emergency room M.D.

I rubbed a hand across an itchy eye. "Tired. But I need to know about Chip."

Dr. Churchill nodded. "But first, the M.D. wants to check you out, and the police want to ask you some questions."

I shook my head, wondering if the blurriness had confined itself to my eyes. "I thought the nurse said you were my doctor."

She laughed, not unpleasantly, and reached out, giving my hand a tender squeeze. "I'm your psychologist. I came in to coordinate with the social worker. I know about...your situation."

I looked down at the covers. "About my mother?"

"Yes," she said in a soft voice. "Your story is all over the news. I'm so sorry, but you should know."

My mind tried to disconnect, wanting to drown in sorrow, but I clung to her hypnotic, reassuring voice.

"What happened last night was horrible and tragic and unfair." Her hands tightened over mine.

A pit of sorrow threatened to swallow me up.

"But we're going to get through it together. I promise."

My mental dam broke. Tears spilled down my face, and I cried out, wailing and sobbing. She wrapped her arms around me and pulled me close. I buried my face in her bosom, and this kind, merciful stranger held me tight, making little reassuring noises.

I called out, "Mom!" The pain welled up from deep inside, agony I'd bottled up for so many hours, ripped from me.

Minutes later, I lay, head against her shoulder, limp and exhausted from my emotional explosion.

Not raising my head from Dr. Churchill's comforting embrace, I grabbed a tissue and blew my nose.

I needed a second tissue, so I swiped another one.

Gunther killed my mother.

I blew my nose again. This time, I could breathe.

He'd made the choice and acted upon it. And nothing could have stopped him.

Nothing.

~

WHEN I WOKE up from a sound sleep, I saw a man peeking at me through a crack in the door.

"May I come in," he asked in a soft voice.

I nodded.

Chiseled pecs bulged under the short sleeves of his shirt. My gaze traced the evenly tanned arm to the notepad held at eye level. Blond waves of hair topped the adorable package.

"Hello, Fiona, I'm Lieutenant Grady. Do you remember what happened to you?" He waited, his eyes cast downward, refusing to meet my gaze.

I pondered the question. In my current state, I could say anything. *What did they think happened?* I started with the obvious. "My mother...she's dead."

"Yes." The voice reached me like a disinterested recording. "That's right. You remember your mother's death? At your home?"

"I...chased...someone."

"Yes." The voice took on a texture of life as the lieutenant's interest piqued. "This is very important, Fiona. Did you recognize the person you chased?"

"I...No. I have no idea who it was. He...wore a mask." I shrugged, unsure of where to take my ad lib story. Instead, I answered his questions, pretending dizziness or a memory lapse when an obvious answer escaped me. I kept my story as simple as I could and let the detective fill in the blanks. Boiled down, my story amounted to this:

My date with Chip was ending, and I decided Mom should meet my new boyfriend. So I brought him home, only to walk in on a masked burglar-turned-murderer. I ran after him while Chip called the cops. Then Chip followed after me.

I chased the burglar into Perionne Park, where he tried to lose me underneath the roller coaster, but I followed him up and onto the platform. We fought, and, somehow during the struggle, the roller coaster activated. The guy overpowered me, but Chip found us and jumped into the fray. The murderer stabbed Chip, but the sirens scared the murderer away where he...just...ran off.

Lieutenant Grady shuffled in the chair, looking up for the first time, focusing a pair of dark, indifferent eyes upon me that diminished his "hottie" potential.

He dropped his notebook and pen into a breast pocket. "Listen, not that this is anything new, but there're all sorts of stories in the papers about Gunther the ghost. Reporters love to throw the paranormal angle out whenever anything strange happens. So I'm asking, just so I can say I did. Did this have anything to do with the ghost?"

I bit my lip, not daring to speak until I regained my composure. Across the room, my "court-appointed social worker" watched me, and her stoic face didn't help me fight the panic welling up within me.

Finally, I shrugged. "What do you want me to say? My Mom died last night, and you want to know if a *ghost* did it?"

The lieutenant's face turned beet red. "Right. I'm sorry. Just forget I asked." He rose. "For what it's worth, I'm sorry this happened. We'll do what we can." He left without another word.

A LOUD KNOCKING STARTLED me awake.

"It's Nurse Thompson, dear." The door swung open, and she stepped though, a Cheshire cat grin on her face. "Oh. I didn't realize you'd fallen back to sleep. I have a surprise for you. I thought it would cheer up your room a bit." With that, she wheeled in a three-shelved instrument cart.

My mouth dropped at the sight of billowing color. I smiled at the Mylar *Get Well Soon* balloons and the potted plants, the vases of roses, and cone-paper wrapped carnations. I could see various index cards with miscellaneous names, most of which I didn't recognize. I spotted a Mylar balloon dangling a card with Phil and Mary's names.

Overwhelmed, a wave of dizziness flooded over me, and I leaned back against the pillow. Try as I might, I couldn't find my voice.

The nurse rushed to my side, placing her hand on my shoulder. "Are you okay, dear? I can get the doctor..."

Even as my body trembled, I shook my head. I choked back a sniffle and wiped fresh tears from my cheeks. *It's happening, again.*

Suddenly, the nurse wrapped her arms around my shoulders and rocked me gently. Her voice penetrated my numb brain. "There, there, dear. You poor dear. Don't worry. You're going to be fine. We'll take care of you. This town takes care of its own."

CHAPTER THIRTY-THREE

I spent the long, tedious hours of the afternoon half-dozing off in the confines of my hospital room, channel surfing through the courtroom TV and talk shows. I'd asked Nurse Thompson for a book, but, after a few pages, I couldn't even follow the inane melodrama of Danielle Steele. So I resigned myself to catching up on my *People* magazines and reading the latest on Paris Hilton and the twenty-five worst-dressed women at the Emmys.

Shortly after five, someone knocked on my door.

I looked up, surprised to see the Ben Gerrold, Mom's partner, standing in the doorway, a stern expression distorting his elderly features.

All business, Gerrold gave my limp hand a brisk shake and seated himself without greeting me or asking how I was coping. He flipped open a laptop, setting it across his neatly tailored slacks, and brusquely explained my rights and options with the comforting sincerity of a Komodo dragon irritated by a persistent fly.

As guardian of my estate according to the final wishes of my mom, he'd arranged the private hospital room, and had pre-signed the release papers allowing me to leave tomorrow. He'd see that I continued to live in a comfortable home if I didn't want to stay in the house where my mother had died.

"Fiona?"

I'd zoned out of the conversation, instead choosing to stare at the overhead vent holes in the paneled ceiling. "Sorry, what?"

With infinite patience, Gerrold repeated, "I said, 'I trust this is satisfactory?'"

"Oh, yes, sounds great." I reached for the plastic carafe of ice water and poured myself a glass. I could only hope the jarring cold on my teeth would keep me awake.

The elderly lawyer picked up where he'd left off, hitting each bullet point in his plethora of information while staring at his computer screen, glazed gray eyes fixated on the facts in front of his face.

He'd see to all of my comforts and provide a generous allowance for my personal use over the next several months until I turned eighteen. He'd arrange for college assistance and make sure any interruptions to my education as a result of this tragedy would be minimal. I should also take note of...

I awoke with a start.

Gerrold must have seen me jump. Though his body hadn't moved from his sitting position, his eyes flickered in my direction, and he paused in his narrative.

I reached up and stretched, and his eyes shifted back to the screen. Whether he continued from where he left off, or he'd backed up a few sentences is something I'll never know. "Seeing as you're so close to the age of independence, I want to assure you that foster care won't be an issue, as long as you and I can work out an arrangement on which we can both agree."

Foster care! I shuddered at the thought, relieved not to have to go there. I guess I had to thank Ben Gerrold for that.

Then it hit me. I'd known Ben Gerrold as my mother's partner my entire life, and yet I knew almost nothing about him on a personal level. He existed in one mode. And he knew nothing about me, except whatever horror stories my mother brought to the office. And now, here the man sat, shackled with the fearsome responsibility of my upbringing. I actually felt sorry for him and reached out to pat his hand.

He stopped in mid-recitation, turning and looking at me for the first time, a shocked expression on his face. He removed his glasses, wiping a hand over the single tear spilling down his cheek.

I repeated the words Dr. Churchill had spoken to me hours earlier. "It's okay. We're going to get through this."

He put his face in his hands, fighting back a sniffle. "I'm sorry. It's such a damn awful thing." He shook his head and folded the computer on his lap. "I suppose this can all wait 'til later." He took a deep, shaky breath. "Your mother was an outstanding, brilliant partner. And she was a good woman. She certainly didn't deserve to be taken from us like this. I'll miss her terribly."

He looked at me and shrugged. "I owe it to her to see to it that you're well taken care of. But...I never had any children. I don't know what to do."

I smiled at his awkwardness. "Relax, Mr. Gerrold, I won't be asking to move in. I don't even know what my options are at this point, but in a few days we can talk about it more."

An uneasy expression crossed his face. "You should get more rest." He stood, shifting uncomfortably. "If there's anything I can do, please let me know." As if on impulse, he reached out and rumpled my hair. Just as suddenly, he pulled his hand back, walking out without another word.

I SAT up when someone knocked on my door. "Come in."

My eyes focused to see the now-familiar, bulky profile of Mr.

Farren standing in front of the curtain. "Fi-Fi?" He noticed my open eyes and offered a bashful grin. "How are you?

I shrugged. "I'm fine. Is Chip awake? I want to see him."

Mr. Farren shook his head. "No, not yet. And they won't let you see him until he's out of intensive care."

I grinned. "We'll figure something out."

He held two paper cups of steaming liquid pinched between his beefy fingers, and extended one my direction. "Here."

My stomach churned at the thought of coffee, but, when I lowered the cup, my nose detected the distinct aroma of chicken broth. *The milk of human kindness.*

Mr. Farren lowered his bulk into a wooden chair near the edge of my bed.

I sucked the first few sips greedily, burning my tongue but savoring the yummy salted liquid. I held the cup in my fingers, enjoying the warmth, focusing on the spinning herbs in the broth. "Mr. Farren, you were there, weren't you? That night, with Gunther?"

Mr. Farren wiggled in his chair, creating a squeal of complaining metal. "You didn't know?"

We exchanged shocked looks, and I shook my head. "No. I didn't. But I don't know how I didn't. Chip told a lame story about you and a bowling buddy." I chuckled. It felt good to laugh. "What a stupid story. If a bowler had lips that loose every time he had too much beer, the whole town would have dug up the ride by now." I wiped at my eyes. "And I bought it."

Jim Farren sighed deeply. "Don't blame Chip for wanting to keep it a secret. He fooled me, too. What you two did, I had no idea he had planned it, but I suppose, like you, I should have seen it coming."

I hesitated, wondering whether to ask the question utmost on my mind, and then decided if he'd share this much, he'd share the rest. "Did you...kill Gunther?"

Mr. Farren's eyes widened in genuine shock. "What? No." He drew in a deep breath. "I did a few things I'm ashamed of. But I never killed anyone." And with that, Mister Farren, *Jim* Farren, told me how, many years ago, Gunther blackmailed him to drive the getaway car, of his terrible, cowardly betrayal of Crimley, and of his loyal wife, who took a terrible secret to her grave.

As he finished his tale, I stared into my cup and let the story fester between us for a few moments. "And how did Chip know?"

Mr. Farren chuckled. "He guessed, the intuitive bastard. He got a confession from me before I figured out he only knew half as much as I thought he did. I had no reason to deny it, not to my own boy. What difference did it make?"

I answered the question, realizing the truth as I spoke it. "You were involved in this...great wrong, these killings and the robbery. And nobody knew how to make it right. Chip didn't want the money, or fame, or anything else." My eyes watered at the realization. "He wanted to make it right. Right for you and for him, so you wouldn't have to live with the shame anymore."

Mr. Farren shrugged. "I guess he did. We had one conversation about it years ago, and haven't spoken of it since. Until Gunther showed up at my house last night."

"What happened?"

"He said he was going to kill you and my son unless I met him at the park. That was after Chip's phone call. I called the police immediately. But it was...almost too late."

"And now?"

Mr. Farren shook his head and pinched his index finger to his thumb, dragging it across in a "zipper" motion. "The money's gone, where nobody can find it. I made sure of that. I couldn't return it to the park. The police were everywhere, all night. And there I stood with the biggest find of the town in the trunk of my car, if anyone bothered to look. Soon as the police stopped questioning me, I drove off, and I got rid of it."

He folded his arms, as if challenging me to change his mind. "The secret is my burden and mine alone, just as it was many years ago. And it's staying that way. That should keep Gunther more than satisfied." He let out a deep sigh.

My hand shook at the revelation, and I almost spilled the soup. "Such insanity. Gunther cares so much about his own infamy that he returned from death to preserve it. Without the mystery, without the legend, people would have forgotten about him years ago. And that's why he can't allow anyone to return the money."

I stared down onto my soup cup. I could feel tears welling up. "But my mother...I know she cared about me, but...I also know...she won't come back. She never will."

Two stubby fingers pinched the lip of the cup and took it from me while I reached blindly for my tearing face. "I'll never see her again."

I sobbed into my hands while Mr. Farren remained silent.

A loud knocking jarred me from my sorrow.

Mr. Farren stood.

A nurse stuck her head through the door, a pleasant smile on her face. "Mr. Farren? Your son is awake and asking for you. In fact, he's asking for both of you."

"Me, too?" I asked.

She nodded, still grinning.

Chip lay stretched out on the bed, monitors hooked to his shoulders. A tight bandage covered his exposed midsection.

Mr. Farren looked at me from a bedside chair.

As I approached, Chip turned his head with great effort.

"Blue," he whispered, and managed a feeble smile.

I smiled at the sight of him. Joy and relief flooded me.

He reached a hand out, and I entwined his fingers in mine. "I guess...you're not pissed at me?"

Just a few hours ago, I never thought I'd touch him again. I gently squeezed his hand. "No. I'm not. Don't you worry. You just get better so we can get into trouble again."

"No. I'm done with getting in trouble."

Mr. Farren stood. "I'll be back." He gave Chip a meaningful glare. "Don't you screw up again." He stepped out.

It didn't seem proper, cutting in before father and son could speak. But selfishness kept me silent. Talking to Chip now was the most important thing in the world to me.

Chip struggled to take a breath, forcing the words out. "Blue...I'm sorry. That can't even begin to cover it. I can't believe you're even here."

"I love you." The words dropped from my mouth before I could stop them.

He opened his mouth to speak.

I reached out and placed a finger over his lips. "Hush."

I tried to squeeze his hand again, but, to my astonishment, I couldn't press his fingers very hard. I hadn't realized until that moment what a beating I'd taken, and how much strength I'd lost. "You were trying to do a good thing. I know that now. But...don't ever hide anything from me again."

Chip drew a shaky breath. "I don't have any more secrets, but I'll keep it in mind."

I drew his hand to my lips and kissed his fingers. "You just get better. I promise I'll be here when you get back."

"Then where will you go?"

I took a thoughtful moment. "I'm not sure. Mom's partner came by. I have a college trust fund, and I'll get an allowance until I turn eighteen. I'm so close to being an 'adult,' I won't have to go to a foster home. But I don't want to go near that house again."

Chip squeezed my hand. "Don't blame you, Blue. I'm so sorry."

I took a shaky breath. "It's not your fault. Really, it isn't. I know that now."

I heard the sound of a clearing throat. Mr. Farren stood in the doorframe, leaning into the room.

I took the hint. "I'll go for now." A sob welled up from deep within, and I shivered. "Don't ever leave me again."

"I won't," he whispered.

NURSE THOMPSON WHEELED me out into the late afternoon sunshine. The hospital surrounded a private outdoor retreat, by a paved path running around and through a tiny courtyard that broke a small garden into sections.

The garden bordered a shallow pond equipped with a fountain creating a subtle gurgling. A half-dozen fish swam in lazy tranquility.

The cool air cleared my head, stimulating senses left docile from monotonous hours of napping in my room. The world snapped into sharp focus.

She pushed me toward the pond then set the brake on my wheelchair. "I thought you might like a few minutes outside before heading back." She parked me beside the gurgling water. The noise lulled me into a peaceful state.

I nodded.

A calming breeze caressed my skin, and a familiar, lulling peace encompassed me.

Mom?

Maybe, maybe not. But if there's one thing I'd learned, *anything* was possible.

I stared into the reflective surface and bent my head, whispering words. "Mom, I know you can hear me if you want. I hope you hear me now."

I drew a deep, shaking breath. "What a mess. I have so many things I wish I could do over, but mostly I wish you could have met Chip, or known what was happening. Or why it was so important I leave when you wanted to talk. I never wanted to abandon you. I left so many things unsaid, and then you died."

I wiped at new tears I thought had been cried out. "And yet you found me, even after your death. I know that you visited me that night, after I fell. I hope you'll always watch over me, because I think, for the first time, I can be the daughter who'll make you proud.

"There's no way I can ever forgive myself for not really knowing you. But for what it's worth, and even though it took me a long time, I realize all you went through for my sake, and what it ended up costing you."

I paused, straining to listen, but only a distant rattling of blowing leaves answered my words. "Just a few nights ago, I told Chip that I hated you. But that's not true. I love you, Mom." I turned away from the melancholy face staring back at me.

I had no more room in my life for sadness or anger. To dwell on the negative meant wasting precious time with the people I love. For the first time in my life, no matter what I chose to do, I could find happiness. I could stay in town with Chip or leave. I could go to New York and look up my father, or escape to Indianapolis as I'd planned when we moved to Perionne.

I had choices ahead. And when I was ready, I would make them.

But not today.

Today, I'd concentrate on loving my mother.

Behind me, the rustling leaves carried a delicate voice. *"I love you too, Fiona."*

The End

About the Author

R.J. Sullivan's novel *Haunting Blue* (2010) is an edgy paranormal thriller and the first book of the adventures of punk girl Fiona "Blue" Shaefer and her boyfriend Chip Farren. *Haunting Obsession (2012)* and *Virtual Blue* (2013) continue the paranormal thriller series. R.J.'s short stories have been featured in such acclaimed collections as *Dark Faith Invocations* by Apex Books and *Vampires Don't Sparkle*. These stories were compiled in R.J.'s 2015 collection *Darkness with a Chance of Whimsy*. Revised editions of these titles were released by Dark-Whimsy Books in 2020.

Commanding the Red Lotus (2016) collects three space opera tales in the tradition of Andre Norton and Gene Roddenberry. New titles to the series are forthcoming from Hydra Publications.

rjsullivanfiction.com

The Original Paranormal Thrills by R.J. Sullivan...

. . . Revised Editions by 

RJSullivanFiction.com

Also Available in Audiobook

Narrated by
Danielle Muething

DanielleMuething.wixsite.com/mysite/about

Haunting Obsession
Elegant Paper Dolls

*Maxine and Loretta
gorgeous glossy color book
4" figures, 10 costume changes!
$5! Sexy and Cheap!*

*Order exclusively from
RJSullivanFiction.com or
at personal appearances.*

*Renderings by Nell Williams,
NellWilliams.com*

This book is part of an author-cooperative urban fantasy universe. Characters created by E. Chris Garrison (including Skye MacLeod and the Transit King) and R.J. Sullivan (including "Blue" Shaefer and Rebecca Burton) interact in a shared world. For example, Chris's Transit King appears in R.J.'s Haunting Obsession, while R.J.'s Rebecca Burton lends a hand in Chris's Mean Spirit. So if you love what you just read and want the entire story, here's a handy guide and timeline to:

The Skye-Blue-niverse

Haunting Blue by R.J. Sullivan *
Four 'Til Late by E. Chris Garrison**
Haunting Obsession by R.J. Sullivan
Sinking Down by E. Chris Garrison**
Blue Spirit by E. Chris Garrison
Me and the Devil by E. Chris Garrison**
Virtual Blue by R.J. Sullivan*
Restless Spirit by E. Chris Garrison
Mean Spirit by E. Chris Garrison

*Also part of The Collected Adventures of Blue Shaefer by R.J. Sullivan
**Part of the Road Ghosts Omnibus by E. Chris Garrison

Enter the Skye-Blue-niverse at:

**https://sillyhatbooks.com/
and
https://rjsullivanfiction.com/**